In your PUCKING DREAMS

Cover Design: Sheridan Anne
Editing: Fox Proof Edits
Formatting: Sheridan Anne
Beta: Holly Swain-Harvey & Kat Uluave

DISCLAIMER

In Your Pucking Dreams was previously published as Jaxon - Kings of Denver (Book 2) 2018-2022

The content of In Your Pucking Dreams remains the same with new edits and tightening up of each chapter. The story within has not changed. Simply received a facelift plus new interior formatting, title, and cover.

PROLOGUE

CASSIE

THREE YEARS EARLIER

Jaxon climbs through my window, the smell of his perfect cologne filling my room with the soft night breeze. I cringe, not wanting him to see my face. The man knows me better than I know myself. He would sense something's wrong. He just knows . . . he's always known.

Closing my eyes, I pretend to be asleep, listening as he undresses. I hear him lose his shirt, dumping it on the couch before I hear his belt buckle clank heavily to the ground. The sound of his zipper follows before he steps out of his jeans.

He pulls the blanket back, allowing the cool air to brush my skin before sliding in behind me. His strong arms curl around me, pulling me into the safety of his body, right where I've always belonged. He's just gotten back from hockey training and most likely had to sit in a cold car on the way home after his parents refused to fix his heating. I'm sure one of my brothers could do it for him if only he stopped being so stubborn and just asked.

"Love you," Jaxon murmurs as he presses a soft kiss to my neck and nuzzles in.

I don't dare say it back for fear of breaking.

My body betrays me as I snuggle deeper into his hold, and I stay there all night. I'm wrapped in his loving arms, listening to the soft, rhythmic sound of his heart, knowing that what I'm about to do is going to tear him to shreds. That knowledge on its own is nearly enough to kill me, and I hate myself for what I'm about to put him through.

It's a little after four in the morning, and I haven't slept a wink. My eyes are red and raw from the constant flow of tears I've spilled throughout the night. Discreetly lifting his arm, I slide out from under him, being as quiet as possible to not wake him. I go to the bathroom and get dressed before quietly pulling my pre-packed suitcase out from under my bed, holding back the violent sobs threatening to tear free from my chest.

Why does this have to be so hard?

Walking over to him and glancing down at the man who holds my heart, I gently press a kiss to his temple, breaking my own damn heart in the process. "I'm sorry," I whisper into the night, fearing I might wake him as I hastily wipe my face. "I love you so damn much."

The knowledge that this will be the last time I'll ever whisper those precious words to him tears me apart, and I let out one last shaky breath before tearing my gaze away from his sleeping body. Taking the handle of my suitcase, I walk out the door before I convince myself to stay. Within moments, I'm out of the home I grew up in and rushing down the long driveway, sobbing so fiercely that breathing is damn near impossible.

This is the right thing to do.

I repeat my mantra over and over again. I need to get away and discover myself. Be happy and confident in my own skin. I'll come back and visit my family every chance I get, but I have to do this for me. It's gonna be fine. It has to be fine. They'll understand.

This is the right thing to do.

Opening the big metal gates, I find my Uber ready and waiting to help me start my new life. The driver gets out and cringes as he takes me in, but chooses not to mention the tears streaming down my face. He takes my suitcase and loads it in the back before opening the door for me.

"Rough night?" he asks.

With a sigh, I let out a shaky breath and pull myself together as I look back at the home that once held my whole world. "Something like that," I tell him, struggling to get the words past the lump in my throat. And with that, I slide into the backseat, hoping to God I'm doing the right thing.

An hour later, I stand at the gate with my boarding pass in my shaking hand. "Miss," the lady at the gate says, trying to get my attention for the third time. I turn my head, and seeing my tear-stained cheeks, she gives me a pitying smile. "This is the last call for this flight. If you're not ready, there's another one leaving at nine. Just visit the help desk and they can transfer your ticket."

Shit. It'll be too late by then. It's now or never.

"No," I say with a shake of my head as I hand her my pass, plastering a fake smile across my face. "I'm ready. I'm coming."

With a tight smile, she takes my boarding pass and scans it before handing it back, unknowingly changing my entire life with that one action.

A few hours later, I touch down in New York. After a mad scramble through the airport and a nerve-racking taxi ride through the breathtaking city, I find my way to the apartment I've rented for the next few weeks as I wait for the semester to begin.

I spend the day unpacking and sourcing some groceries, terrified of turning on my phone and finding countless messages from him. I can just picture him now, wondering where the hell I am, if I'm okay, and terrified that he's done something to deserve this.

By nightfall, I make my way around the apartment and shut off all the lights. I turn my phone on for a brief moment and do my best to ignore the slew of messages that instantly fill my inbox.

I send off a text to Mom to let her know I'm safe before opening a new message to *him*. A million thoughts go through my mind of what I should say, but nothing seems enough. I know he'll never forgive me for leaving him like that, with no goodbye or a chance to fight for me. But had he known my plans, he would have tried to stop me, and I undoubtedly would have stayed. So I type the one thing that also says the million other things that I can't.

Cassie - I'm sorry. Forgive me.

I hit send and immediately turn my phone off before lying down in my big empty bed, in this strange apartment, feeling more alone than ever before.

Big, fat tears begin pooling in my eyes as my heart aches, wishing those arms that have held me every night for the past few years were here with me now.

What have I done?

CHAPTER 1

CASSIE

Pulling my yellow VW Beetle into a parking space outside the senior girls' dormitory, I let out a shaky breath. I can't believe I allowed my dimwit brothers to talk me into this. I turn off the ignition and step out of my car, making sure to grab my handbag and room assignment papers.

A massive, black Dodge RAM pulls up beside me, filled to the brim with my belongings, and all three of my moronic brothers jump out to meet me on the sidewalk. Each graces me with their own version of an encouraging smile. Though honestly, it makes them all look constipated.

"Do I really have to do this?" I whine to Sean, Logan, and Carter, feeling as though I'm about to crumble.

"Sure do, kid," they say in unison, some ridiculous triplet telepathic voodoo shit.

"Fine," I huff, taking off down the pathway toward what will be my home for the next year as an intense nervousness builds within me. "We may as well get this shit over with."

"That's the spirit, little sis," Logan grins, jogging up the pathway to catch up to me while throwing his heavy arm over my shoulder.

"Ugh," I groan, shrugging out from under him. "Get off me, you manwhore. Who knows where your hands have been."

Logan pulls me in closer, tucks my head into the crook of his armpit, and makes sure I get a nose full of manly BO while using his other hand to give me a noogie. I shout for help while I reach around him and latch onto his man titties, giving a devastating nipple cripple as he squeals like a pig in mud.

"Will you two quit it?" Sean scolds, wheeling my suitcase behind him, not bothering to look up at our display. "You're acting like a couple of delinquent kids."

Logan lets out a huff. "She started it," he grumbles under his breath and reluctantly lets me go so he can rub his man titties back to health.

Knowing I've won this round, a triumphant grin tears across my face, but I don't get the chance to brag before Carter pushes his way between us and jolts my body to the side. "I can't wait to get a look in here," he grins, rubbing his palms together like a major creeper.

Rolling my eyes, I fix him with a hard stare. "I told you. You're not screwing any of the girls I meet here."

"Sorry, kid, but if a ten comes my way, you can guarantee I'll be getting up in there," he says, reaching for the door and ushering us all in.

I push in front of the boys and turn, bringing them to a halt as I give Carter a hard stare. "Promise me you'll keep your dick in your pants."

He begins to shrug off my warning when I pull out the puppy dog eyes, knowing he'll cave like a little bitch. "Fine," he mutters, making this my second triumph of the day.

Getting bored, Sean glances around at us all. "Can we get this show on the road? I promised Sara I'd be there to meet the wedding planner."

"Okay, okay, no need to get your panties in a twist," I grin as I turn on my heel and face down the place I'm dreading to call my new home. Taking a breath, I make my way down the hallway with my brothers on my heels. I scan the doors and give polite smiles to the passing girls until I come across lucky door number 12.

A wave of uneasiness crashes through me and, knowing it's now or never, I push open the door and immediately regret it. "Oh, shit," I screech, coming face to face with my new roommate, who's currently stark naked, bent over at the hips, and being screwed within an inch of her life. Her boyfriend pounds into her from behind as I desperately try to back out of the room, but I run into the solid wall of muscle as my brothers try to squeeze in at the same time.

"Shit, shit, shit," I shriek, not surprised by the massive grins that appear on Logan and Carter's identical faces.

Carter laughs, looking like a kid who just woke up on Christmas morning. "Fuck, yeah."

I try my hardest to shove my brothers out of the room, but they all seem way too intrigued with the show. "Would you guys get moving?" I hiss.

"Oh, no need, honey. Stay, we're almost done." The breathy southern drawl comes from behind me, shocking me into stillness. "I'm Bronny. You must be my new roomie, Cassandra? Or do you prefer Cass? Cassie?" I turn purely out of the politeness my parents drilled into me, only to find her hand outstretched waiting for a handshake.

Oh, hell no. Is this chick for real? I can't help but gape at her as she smiles up at me, tits swaying from left to right and the sound of her man's balls slapping against her ass while he groans and picks up the pace.

I hear Logan and Carter's snickers behind me, and good God, I've never wanted to throttle them more.

Carter steps around me and reaches for her hand with his manwhore smile wide on his face. "Hey, Bronny, I'm Carter. It's really great meeting you," he says as she beams up at him. "This is my little sister, Cassie," he says, turning toward me, loving every moment of how incredibly awkward this is for me. But why wouldn't he? My brothers live to torment me.

"Um, hi," I say, pressing my lips into a tight smile and lifting my hand in an awkward wave. "Lovely to meet y—" I start to say when Bronny's outstretched hand disappears between her legs and begins violently rubbing her clit. My face falls and I stare in horror. "Okay.

Nope, I'm out."

Whipping around, I try to flee when Logan catches me around the waist and turns me to face the show again, wrapping his steel arm around me and effectively caging me in. "Stay. Be polite. Watch the show," he says with clear enjoyment.

Carter leans back, shoving his shoulder against the drywall. "So, you're an exhibitionist?" he asks, truly intrigued by her line of work, more than ready to see this through right to the end.

"Oh, yeah," she replies with a pant, pushing back against her partner who grunts and groans as his fingers tighten on her hips, making it startlingly obvious that the show is about to reach its climax. "It's just so freeing. The idea of having people watch me and enjoy my pleasure is simply thrilling, don't you think? Such a rush. Were you wanting to join?"

Oh, hell no.

I give Logan one last shove and fix the three of them with a hard stare. They know that this time, I'm damn serious. Their fun is over. Carter gives Bronny a polite smile and respectfully shakes his head. "Unfortunately, I'm here with family, so you know, maybe next time. But have fun and come hard," he encourages with a fist bump before stepping out of my way and allowing me to haul ass past him.

Once we're all out, Carter closes the door behind us, the three assholes instantly bursting into howling fits of laughter.

Shaking my head, I glance up at Sean as he quickly recovers. "Can you believe that shit?" I ask, as he turns on his heel and takes off. "Hey," I call after him. "Where the hell are you going?"

"Administrative office," he calls over his shoulder, the serious one of the three. "There's no way you're staying in that room. There's probably DNA from one corner to the next." He disappears through the doors, leaving me with the two idiots who are still laughing. Only now Carter's bent over, imitating the way her tits were swinging while Logan stands behind him, thrusting toward him and clapping his hands to mimic the way Bronny's man's balls slapped against her ass.

Trying to remind myself how deeply I love my brothers, I let out a heavy breath and count to five before I accidentally castrate one of them.

"Come on," I say as I head for the external doors, damn near ready to drag them by their ears like Mom used to when they were kids. "There must be a notice board or something with roommate adverts around here somewhere. After seeing that, I think I'd prefer to rent a place."

We walk around campus for ten minutes before finally finding what we're looking for, and just as I had hoped, there are a few ads pinned to the board. Pulling them off, I hand a few to my brothers and get started making calls.

Ten minutes later, Sean catches up to us with a grim face. "Sorry, kid. There are no other dorm rooms available," he says, "But apparently there's an online forum where students can post about this shit. The chick at administration didn't seem overly helpful though."

With my hopes and determination starting to crumble, I hand the rest of the ads to Sean and pull out my phone to search for options.

I'm sitting in the gutter between our cars when Carter finally pipes up, holding the ad between his fingers and pumping it into the air. "There's a place just down the road. Two bedrooms and cheap rent, but it's really small. Apparently, the girl's brother demands that she has a female roommate."

"Woah. The girl's brother?" Logan asks, suddenly on edge.

Carter snorts. "My thoughts exactly. He's an athlete and lives with his team, so hopefully it shouldn't be a problem."

"Ahhh." Logan grins fondly. "Those were the good old days," he says, clearly remembering the time he had on this very campus, living with his hockey teammates.

Wanting to get this show on the road, Sean nods toward the cars. "Alright, let's check it out."

The boys jump straight into action when I throw myself to my feet. "Wait," I call, watching as they freeze and spin to face me. "How much is cheap rent?"

"Don't worry about the rent," Carter says. "We'll cover it, just like we did in New York."

Letting out a frustrated sigh, I take a step toward them, lowering my voice so the people passing by don't overhear our family financials. "I know, but I want to pay."

"Sorry, kid," Sean cuts in, shaking his head. "You know Dad's rules. Just because he isn't around to enforce them, doesn't mean they don't apply."

"But—"

"No buts," Logan cuts in. "That's the way it's always been and the way it's going to keep going."

"Fine," I sulk, cutting my losses. I know a losing battle when I see one. It's not the worst hill to die on, though.

Climbing back into our cars, we get on the road, and a few minutes later, we're pulling up to a small, cottage-style home. "Well, this is going to be different than New York," Carter murmurs as we make our way to the front door.

"Got that right," I mutter under my breath, feeling those same nerves starting to build again.

Sean reaches out and knocks on the door, and a moment later, the door pulls open to reveal a guy just as big as my brothers. The boys stare him down like some kind of threat while the guy does exactly the same. "I thought a chick lived here?" Logan grunts, not liking what he's seeing.

"What's it to you who lives here?" the guy responds.

Ahh, shit.

Logan narrows his stare, and it's clear this conversation is going nowhere. "Hi," I say, stepping around my brothers while ignoring the pissing contest that seems to be going on. "I'm Cassie and these are my brothers. We were told there was a room for rent here?"

"Yeah," he says. "For you?"

"Yes," I reply hesitantly. "I thought a girl lived here?"

"I do. I do. I do," comes a feminine voice from the hallway. "Move out of the way, moron. You're going to scare her away."

A petite brunette pushes between the door and the big guy and jams her elbow into his ribs, forcing him to take a step back. "Hi," the girl smiles, extending her hand toward me. "I'm Brianna and this is my twin brother, Bobby. And yes, I'm looking for a roommate, and no, this big boofhead won't be here," she says, indicating to the now scowling *boofhead* behind her.

"I'm Cassie," I smile, already knowing I'm going to like this girl. "These are my brothers. Sean, who's basically married. Logan, who thinks he's a comedian. And Carter, the designated manwhore and self-proclaimed God's gift to women," I say, pointing each of them out, not that she'll remember who's who. No one does. After all, they're the spitting image of each other.

Carter reaches around me and offers Brianna his hand while also giving her his dazzling smile and wink, the one he saves for special occasions. Bobby the boofhead groans as his sister instantly blushes and takes his hand. "Don't," I cry out, slapping Carter's hand out of Brianna's reach. "He shook hands with Bronny the showgirl, mid-performance, and I'm yet to see him wash his hands."

"Ugh," Brianna cringes, glancing at his hand as though it's infested with herpes before stepping slightly further away from Carter.

"What?" he shrugs. "I'm saving the smell for later."

Both Brianna and I cringe, but she manages to look past my brother's foul tendencies and steps out of the doorway. "Come in," she says. "I'll give you a tour and then you can decide if it's the right fit for you."

Feeling hopeful, I follow her inside, and we head down the hallway while the boys linger in the living room, sussing out Bobby. "So," I hear Logan start. "You're an athlete?"

I drown out their conversation as I follow Brianna into the kitchen.

She shows me around, and within seconds, I fall in love with the place. "So, you're a senior then, I'm assuming?" she asks as she heads into what would be my bedroom.

"Yeah, a senior. I just moved back to Denver from New York. You?" I ask as we step into the room to find a small bedroom, fully furnished with a double bed.

"Yeah, senior too," she replies. "Do you like it so far?"

"I do," I grin.

"Good," she smiles back at me. "I don't see the point in having a car here. So, the garage would be all yours."

Feeling at home already, I turn to her with a beaming smile. "I'll take it."

Her eyes bug out of her head, relief shining in her eyes. "Really? Thank God," she breathes. "Do you have any idea how hard it's been to find a good roommate? Bobby has run off everyone that's come to the door. You're the only one he let pass through."

"Seriously?" I ask as we make our way back to the guys.

"Yeah, he's a bit protective," she explains. "I'm sure by the way your brothers all showed up, you know a little something about that."

"Damn straight, I do," I laugh as all four sets of male eyes land on us.

She leans into me, both of us staring right back at them. "Do you think it will ever stop?" she whispers as the boys eye us curiously.

"Not a snowball's chance in hell."

Sean lets out a huff and glances at his watch. "I'm assuming you like it here since you're not running for the hills," he says hopefully.

"Well, I'm guessing that Brianna isn't a crazy person or isn't going to kill me in my sleep. So taking that into account, yes. You can start unloading the truck," I tell them with a proud smile. For the first time since moving back, I'm starting to feel excited about this change.

"Thank fuck," Carter breathes as he turns on his heel and heads out to the truck with an agreeable Logan and Bobby behind him.

Sean, the sensible one as always, fixes me with a hard stare. "Don't forget to sign the rental agreement," he says before turning toward the door to help the boys, only he stops in his tracks and glances back at me, his lips pressed into a tight line. "On second thought, I might take care of that for you."

I roll my eyes and call to his retreating frame. "I'm a big girl, Sean. I can take care of it on my own."

His scoff is heard from all the way out at the truck, and all I can do is ignore him before turning to Bri with a wide grin. "Where should we start?"

Between the four boys, the Dodge RAM is unloaded in no time, and my new room is completely set up.

"You all good?" Logan asks as he places the last of my things down on the dining table.

I take a quick look around and realize that everything is done, apart from putting my clothes away and making the bed. Though I know for a fact these idiots aren't going to help with that. "Yeah, I'm all good," I tell him as he pulls me into a big bear hug.

"Be safe, Cassie Bear," he tells me, holding me a little tighter than ever before. "I have to head back to the city tomorrow, but the boys will be around if you need anything."

"I know," I grumble as he lets go and makes room for Sean and Carter to say their goodbyes.

Brianna disappears into the fridge and brings out a celebratory bottle of wine while I watch in amusement as Bobby and the boys exchange numbers.

"This is going to be interesting," Brianna says as she comes up beside me to watch the comical performance.

She hands me a glass of wine and we clink our glasses together. "It sure is," I agree, taking a sip.

"We'll come to watch a few games when we can," Sean tells Bobby as he claps him on his large, beefy shoulder and steps out the door, throwing back a wave as he leaves.

A sinking feeling begins to settle in the pit of my stomach as I know there's only one game on planet earth that my brothers would go out of their way to watch.

"Games?" I whisper to Brianna, who I notice is far too occupied blushing at Carter as he follows Sean out the door and winks at her again.

Just freaking great.

"Bye," I call out as the door closes behind them, leaving me with Bobby and Brianna in my new home.

Bobby is staring down at his phone when his head suddenly snaps up to me. "Wait . . . your brother, Logan?" he questions as his eyes widen in excitement. "He's not Logan Waters? As in NHL, Colorado Thunder, pro hockey player Logan Waters?"

"Ahh . . . yeah," I confirm as that sinking feeling gets worse. "You know hockey?"

"Yeah, you could say that," he scoffs, raising his eyebrow at me as if I should know who he is.

Brianna rolls her eyes at her brother. "My twin brother here is on the college hockey team, the Denver Dragons," she explains. "He considers himself to be top shit. Though personally, I think his ego is slightly getting in the way."

"Whatever," he scoffs, walking forward and knocking his sister in the arm. "Jax and I are gonna be campus legends this year. Especially when we bring home that championship."

My whole world crumbles in on itself at the mention of *his* name. How the hell did I get into this situation? "You know Jaxon?" I ask as my heart rate picks up and my hands begin to sweat, unease rocking through me.

"Yeah," he responds, looking me over with narrowed, curious eyes. "My best friend and team captain. Why? Are you one of his many conquests?" he asks with a knowing wink and cheesy grin.

Oh, no, no, no. The one person I need to avoid this year, and I've just moved in with his best friend's twin sister. *Great move, Cass.*

"Ahhh, something like that," I respond, glancing away before he catches the fear in my eyes. "He's someone from my past, and I'd love it if he could stay there."

"No worries, babe," Bobby laughs. "Jax doesn't make a habit of repeat performances. I think you're good," he says, not realizing how his casual comments about Jax's sex life tears my heart to absolute shreds. He pokes around in the fridge and pulls out a Gatorade before grabbing a hockey bag from the counter. "Anyway, I'm out of here. Got to hit the gym. Nice meeting you, Cass. Let me know if you need anything."

"Uhh, thanks," I smile as he makes his way to the door. "Oh, hey," I call after him. "Can you not mention any of this to Jax?"

"Sure," he laughs, then makes a cross over his chest like a fifth grader. "Your secret is safe with me." Then just like that, Bobby disappears through the front door and lets it slam closed behind him.

"Right," Brianna starts as she grabs my nearly empty glass of wine and heads into the kitchen for a refill. "I know I just met you, but I saw the pain behind your eyes when Bobby was talking about Jax," she says as she hands me back my glass. "I know there's a heartbroken story there, and I have a feeling you're in need of a good vent."

"I swear, you must be my soul sister," I laugh.

"Good," she smiles, "Plonk your ass down on that couch. I'll order Chinese, and once you're finished spilling the beans on Jaxon, you can tell me all about Carter, and I can steal his number from your phone."

"Oh, Jesus," I groan. "I'm going to freaking love you."

CHAPTER 2

JAXON

My alarm screeches on the bedside table, and I sit up with a groan as I fumble around in the dark, trying to shut the damn thing off.

"Mmm, what time is it?" a feminine voice grumbles beside me.

My head whips in the direction of the chick beside me, my eyes straining to see in the early morning darkness, but there it is. A butt-naked silhouette of the girl I fucked last night.

Goddamn it. They should know the routine by now.

They strip, they get the screw of their life, they get their bragging rights, and then they get the fuck out. They don't get to sleep in my bed and cuddle in the middle of the night. That isn't me. There's no deviating from the plan. Well, on second thought, I may have strayed from the plan a few times, but only because I passed out and had no say in the matter. Which is clearly what happened last night.

"Hey," I call to the girl and give her a nudge. "Time to go, honey."

"What?" she moans, rolling over and giving me a nice view of her full tits. "It's the middle of the night."

"So? I got shit to do," I say, throwing my blankets back and getting up. I move around my room in the dark, attempting to find my shit. I flip on the light switch and frustration gnaws at me, realizing she isn't making a move. "Get up. You should have been gone hours ago."

"But . . . I thought I could help you start your morning off real nice," she purrs, stepping out of bed and fixing her sultry stare on me. She moves across the room, stepping right up in front of me before pressing her used body up against mine. She trails her nails down my naked chest and grabs my dick. "Come on, Captain. Come back to bed. You can take me any way you want."

Grabbing her by the waist, I spin her around and she lets out an aroused moan. I walk us back toward the foot of my bed before pushing her down on my mattress. She scrambles to her knees, her ass high in the air, determined to get the railing of her life.

The girl looks back over her shoulder, watching me intently as my hand presses down on her back, forcing her to drop her chest to the mattress, her already wet pussy perfectly on display.

"Is this what you want?" I ask, slowly running my hand up the back of her thigh and narrowly missing her center. "You want to be a fucking whore for me?"

"Yes," she whimpers into the sheets, her hands balling into fists, anticipating what I might do next. "God, yes."

I slide my hand over her ass, getting a good look in the process. "Is this where you want it?"

"Yes," she breathes, pushing her ass back into my hands.

Mmm, fucking tempting. "Right here? Hard? Fast?"

"God, Jaxon. Yes," she groans, rotating her hips as if to entice me more. "Give it to me."

"You know what I want, babe?" I murmur.

"What?" she whimpers. "I'll do anything."

"I want you," I start slowly, "to get the fuck out of my room like I asked you to five minutes ago." She gasps but I continue on. "Thanks for the offer, babe. But now you've made me late for my boys."

I grab my running shorts and shoes while the girl watches me in shock, and not bothering with a shirt, I head straight for the door. Let's face it, it's only going to end up tucked into my shorts by the end of my run. "You better be gone by the time I'm back," I call over my shoulder as the door closes behind me.

The girl lets out a frustrated cry before screaming out what a jerk move that was. And yeah, she has a point, but all the chicks around here know my deal. And if they don't, that's not my problem. But I'll repeat it for those who don't understand. I, Jaxon Payne, do not do repeat performances.

At least, not anymore. I've only ever allowed one chick in, and I ended up shattered. Joke's on me, but there's one thing I can count on—I will never let it happen again.

After quickly changing in the bathroom and taking care of

business, I rush down the stairs before slipping out the front door to meet my boys at the track.

"Woah, Captain. Have a sleep-in, did ya?" Bobby teases the second I come into view, glancing at his bare wrist and making a show of checking the time.

"You fucking wish," I grin as I jog to meet up with them.

"Where you been then?" Xander, our newest recruit, asks.

"Fucking chicks, man," I tell him. "They just don't get it. I'm here for a good time, not a long time."

"Damn straight," he murmurs and holds out his fist. "Hit it and quit it."

"Fuck, yeah," I laugh as I bump his fist. "Eat it and beat it,"

I chuckle as I take off, leading the group in our daily morning run. The boys laugh along as they fall in behind me. "Hump it and dump it," Aaron adds, turning this from a passing comment into the shit show of the century, each of them now wanting to put in their two cents.

"Nail and bail," the new sophomore calls out.

And so it begins. Player after hockey player adds their own saying, trying to outdo the guy before. But let's face it, they're no match for me.

"Fuck it and chuck it," someone in the back says.

Xander laughs behind me. "Hit the crack and don't look back."

"Blow your load and hit the road," comes from Shorty, which I must admit, has me holding back a grin.

"Please," Bobby scoffs. "You're all fucking amateurs."

"This is going to be good," I laugh to myself.

Unable to help himself, the grin cracks across his face before he's even started. "Ejaculate and evacuate," he announces proudly, making the boys double over in laughter and crown him the king.

Needing the boys to get back on task and concentrate on their run, I take off a little faster, knowing without a doubt they'll do everything to keep up. Without fail, each of them zips their lips and gets serious about training.

We loop around campus twice before stopping back at the track and getting started on some drills for agility and speed. Anything to help us take out the championship once again. We run sprints and work on footwork before looping around campus and finishing where we started, giving us each enough time to head home, grab breakfast, and have a shower before our morning classes. And then we'll finally get our first on-ice practice for the season.

I can't fucking wait.

I get home and rush through breakfast before dashing up to my room, all too pleased to find the chick from this morning has disappeared. I walk in and kick off my shoes, only to notice my phone sitting neatly in the center of the made bed.

My brows pull down in suspicion as I grab my phone and unlock it. I find the picture gallery app open with a new video making my stomach sink.

My eyes widen in shock as I hit play to see the chick from earlier finishing herself off with a wicked grin across her face. I consider keeping the video for my spank bank before realizing if something like this were to be connected to my name, I'd lose my shot at the NHL. I hit delete on the video and double-check that she hasn't sent it out from my phone.

All good.

With a shake of my head, I throw my phone down and head to the bathroom for a shower. I emerge not long after, and before I know it, I'm sitting in my business class, scrolling through social media and waiting for the lecture to finish.

The day drags by, but I finally end up in the locker room, suiting up for practice, and I couldn't be more fucking ready.

"Payne," Coach Harris hollers from the door of the locker room. "Get your ass in my office. Five minutes."

"Yes, Coach," I reply, even though he's long gone.

I get my skates on and grab my stick and helmet before taking them out to the ice. Leaving them by the barrier, I make my way up the long hallway to Coach Harris' office.

"What's up, Coach?" I ask, barely knocking on his door before pushing through.

He looks up and gives me a quick nod. "Take a seat, kid," he says, waving toward the chair opposite his desk with his pen and a stack of paperwork residing in front of him.

I do as I'm told but can't help noticing last season's *Boys of Hockey* calendar up on the wall, open to the page of last year's captain, Miller Cain, in the ice rink gym. Coach sees what's caught my eye and groans. "Really, Coach? Didn't realize you were into that kind of thing."

"Cut the shit, Jaxon," he says, rolling his eyes as he leans back in his chair. "Dani put it up and kept putting it up every time I pulled it down. It got to the point where I couldn't be fucked anymore," he explains. "God, I miss that little spitfire."

"I hear ya. Now, what can I do for you?" I ask, anxious to get on the ice.

"I'm just making sure you have your head screwed on this season," he starts, watching me all too closely. "I don't want any repeats of last year. You were a loose cannon, and we can't afford any fuck-ups if we're going to defend our trophy."

"I agree," I tell him straight out. "Miller was the best captain this team had in years, and I'm going to do everything I can to follow in his footsteps. You can count on me, Coach."

"Good. If you're going to go pro then I can't be dealing with stories about my captain getting wasted at parties and having threesomes in his friend's spare room," he warns, pointing out a particular incident from last season.

Embarrassment floods me, but I quickly shrug it off. "Yes, Coach."

"Now, I'm not saying you can't enjoy yourself. After all, this is your senior year of college. I just need you to stay in control and think about the consequences of your actions. You have a future to think about now. Understood?"

I nod, itching to get out of here. "Understood."

"Good, now get your ass out on the ice. You have drills to run."

"On it, Coach," I say as I escape his office and consider his words, only to realize that for the first time, I honestly mean it. I will do anything it takes to make sure I sign a contract at the end of the season.

Even if it means my manwhore, drunken, partying ways are over. Well, to a certain extent at least. After all, I'm still a man.

Opening the barrier gates, I step on the ice and glide out into the center, feeling my blades cut through the ice. I instantly feel at home. Nothing is more natural to me than this.

"Gather round, boys," I call out and watch in amusement as the team creates a semi-circle around me and takes a knee. I go through the warm-up portion of our session and get a freshman to grab the pucks and pull the goals into place. I explain the few drills we'll be running and dismiss the boys to get started. They do as they're asked without hesitation, getting stuck into their work and doing me proud.

I fall in line with the boys, pushing them to their limits and encouraging the stragglers. I do everything in my power to ensure I have the best team at my disposal this year.

Following training, the boys and I collapse into the locker room, absolutely exhausted from our massive first day. Bobby takes a seat next to me as he leans down to untie his skates.

"Great session, man," he says, sweat dripping from his hair. "It's going to be a killer season."

"Yeah, I hope so," I say, leaning back to rest against the locker as I try to catch my breath. "What are your plans for tonight?"

"Bri's making dinner," he explains.

"Oh, yeah. She on the menu?" I ask, taking a minute before standing up and pulling off my sweaty jersey.

He ignores my question, and I smirk in response. He knows I would never touch his sister, but the overprotective brother in him will never quit. "She finally got a roommate," he tells me.

"Bullshit," I laugh. "There's no way you actually approved of someone. Bri's doomed to live alone the rest of her life."

"Seriously," he grins back at me. "Though I don't think I really had a say in the matter. Bri fell in love with the chick straight away. I swear, they've known each other for three days and they're already joined at the hip," he tells me with an affectionate smile, one only his twin sister can bring out.

"Shit," I say. "That's great and all, but is the chick hot?"

"Smokin' hot, but she's too good for your sorry-ass," he tells me, dropping his pants and standing before me in nothing but his birthday suit. "You'll be keeping away from this one."

"Come on, man. I'll just test the waters. Just dip one toe in," I grin.

He bursts out laughing, barely covering his junk. "Fuck, man," he says, grabbing his things for a shower. "You have no clue how fucking ironic that is."

"Huh?" I ask, completely lost, but all I get is a secretive smile and a shake of his head before he disappears to the showers, leaving me as curious as ever about Brianna's new roommate. But not curious enough to investigate tonight. I'm too fucking exhausted.

After rushing through a quick shower, I grab my things and glance around at the boys. "C'ya bright and early, boys," I call out, making my way to the exit.

They all give me exhausted responses and pathetic waves but I don't bother to bust their balls on it. After all, I'm feeling just as worn out as they are.

I head out of the locker room and jump in my truck. In no time at all, I'm pulling up at my door, scarfing down a quick dinner, and collapsing in bed. Just so I can do it all over again tomorrow.

CHAPTER 3

CASSIE

Two weeks I've been here, and to say Brianna has managed to pull me out of the depressing fog I've been living in over the last six months would be a major understatement. No matter how hard she tries, she won't be able to dull the ache that took residence in my heart six months ago when Dad passed, but at least she has the ability to help me look forward to my days.

The night I moved in, I spilled my guts to her. I told her about my dysfunctional family and about Dad's heart attack before tackling the crazy lives of my idiotic brothers. I shared with her the memories of my mom, who we lost to breast cancer two years ago.

Then I had to go and tell her about the brown-haired, blue-eyed boy that moved in next door when I was twelve years old. How we were inseparable for six years until I broke his heart at eighteen. How I fell madly in love with him and how, still to this day, he's the only man I have ever, and will ever love.

He taught me to ice skate on the frozen lake that ran behind our properties, held my hair back when I threw up after stealing as much liquor as we could from the triplet's stash, and stayed right by my side, holding me when we heard the news of my mother's cancer.

He was my rock, my soul mate, and I made the biggest mistake of my life by leaving. But here I am, three years later, occasionally still in one piece. That boy I watched grow into a man has turned into a completely different person, one I no longer recognize, and I have only myself to blame.

All I can do for him now is stay out of his way. I'm sure I'm the last person he would want to see, especially now that he has so much going for him. He's the Captain of the Denver Dragons and is heading straight for a contract to the NHL. He's getting everything he ever wanted, and I swear to God, I am so damn proud of him.

For the past two weeks, I've managed to avoid him like the plague. The first time I saw him on campus, he was flirting with some girl who was busy writing her number on the back of his hand. My heart stopped and so did my world. Seeing him for the first time after so many years threw me straight back to the day I left. My eyes began to water and my legs wanted nothing more than to run to him, so I turned my back and walked away, even though it nearly killed me.

Each and every class I've stepped into, I instantly scanned the room like a crazy stalker making sure he isn't there. By the end of the week when I realized I was safe, I was over the moon.

The next time I saw him, I was prepared and managed to duck out of his line of sight just in time. But stepping into the gym to see him sweaty and shirtless, to see his muscles have developed, turning him from a boy into a grown-ass man was enough to stop me in my tracks. He's fucking beautiful.

I'm lucky he was in the middle of a set and was concentrating on his workout, giving me enough time to gawk before disappearing right back through the door. The only good thing that's come from this is I'm now running outdoors and absolutely love it.

Jaxon tried to find me at the beginning of the term. And by *me*, I mean Brianna's new roommate. I received a text message from Bri saying he was on his way, and I managed to get out just in time. Although, getting out meant slipping through the back door, jumping over the fence into the neighbor's yard, and walking around the streets for a good forty-five minutes until Bri texted to say the coast was clear. I'm assuming she managed to keep him out of my room and the garage, as my car and the family photo I have on my bedside table would have given me away.

I know he hasn't seen me around campus yet because he hasn't stormed up to me and demanded answers. But that's assuming he actually still cares and, judging from the endless supply of pussy he has on speed dial, my guess is that I'm old news. He probably forgot about me the second he got the taste for the single life.

The thought shatters my heart just a bit more, but that's the price I pay for my mistakes. All I can do now is watch him from afar and pray he finds someone who will love him the way I did . . . and still do.

Brianna hated the way I looked when I came home after I saw him, so she suggested I find something to pass the time. We searched for part-time jobs that would keep me as far away from him as possible, which is how I found my shift at the college library. To say that I freaking love it would be an understatement. There's no way Jaxon would ever be caught dead hanging out in the library. Well, any of the hockey guys for that matter. It's become my safe haven. The fact the other employees are awesome is just an added bonus.

As I walk into my Human Sciences and Movement lecture on Friday morning, my eyes instantly scan the room, just as they always do. Deeming the room Jaxon-free, I head up a few stairs and find the spot I had taken the week before. I sit down and put my bag on the ground beside me, pulling out my pens, notepad, and phone, and placing them all neatly on my tiny desk.

I start scribbling lyrics into my notepad, completely unaware that I'm even doing it. It sort of happens like the way someone would bite their bottom lip or hum a song to themselves. Writing lyrics is my secret habit. Well, *secret* is probably the wrong word for it, but it's not something I flaunt anymore. Not since . . . *him.*

For the past three years, my writing has been dark, not the same as the happy-go-lucky shit I used to write. Now, it centers around heartbreak and loss. I've kept my work close to me, fearing someone might actually realize just how broken I really am.

An incoming text has my complete attention as I wait for Professor Macintosh to show up and get started on his lecture.

Sean - You busy this weekend? We're thinking breakfast then visiting the 'rents.

My heart breaks at the thought of having to visit both my parents at the cemetery, but I haven't had a chance to check in with them since being home. There's no way I'm skipping out on this opportunity. Not to mention, after being away from my brothers for the past three years, there's not a chance in hell they will let me.

I hit reply.

Cassie - I have a shift at the library tomorrow. Can we make it Sunday?
Sean - Sure kid. We'll pick you up at 8.
Cassie - Don't be late.

I put my phone on silent as Professor Macintosh walks through the door and calls the room to attention. I see another incoming text message from Bri but don't get a chance to check it before the professor launches into his lecture. I throw my phone in the bottom of my bag, turn to a new page in my notebook, and concentrate on the lecture. I want to be an awesome physiotherapist one day.

"Alright," the professor says toward the end of the lecture, walking from one side of the room to the other. "Check your emails and you'll find your first assignment for the semester."

He waits a moment, watching as we all fish our phones out of our bags or pockets before bringing up his email. I have just a few seconds to skim through it before he launches into a detailed explanation that has me feeling pretty damn confident, a million ideas already circling my brain. "You have three weeks to complete this assignment," Professor Macintosh continues, earning a few groans from around the room, but the timeframe doesn't bother me. I'm a dedicated student and will most likely have it done with plenty of time to spare.

He shushes everyone as he walks to his desk and picks up a clipboard. "I'm sure you would have all noticed by now that this is a partnered project," he starts, making everyone burst into chatter as they begin deciding who to pair up with. "Your peers within this room one day may very well be your colleagues, and I know I don't need to go into the importance of developing the skills to communicate appropriately with those who are not considered one of your BFFs," he says, rolling his eyes at the ridiculous saying. "So, with that in mind, your partner has already been chosen for you. Stand up as I read your name, so your partner can see who you are. You should make arrangements following class to meet up and collect each other's contact details."

Professor Macintosh gets straight into it, ignoring the groans coming from around the room. It doesn't take long before I hear a familiar name. "Bobby Lucas." A smile spreads across my face. I hadn't realized he was in this class, and I find myself spinning around to seek him out. "You'll be paired with Cassandra Waters. Please stand."

Relief blooms through my chest, realizing I have a partner who has his head screwed on properly, and I quickly stand with a big cheesy grin on my face. Bobby stands up the back, grinning right back at me and he gives me a stupid salute before dropping his hand back to his side. My gaze follows the movement and my heart comes to a stop the second I see the person sitting beside him. The very person who looks like he's seen a ghost.

My eyes lock on his, and I lose my breath, my whole world burning to ashes at my feet.

Shit.

My stomach drops, and the smile is wiped from my face. Dropping back into my seat, I face the front of the class, waiting for the professor to hurry up and finish pairing off the rest of the class. My eyes remain focused on my desk as my heart threatens to beat right out of my chest. My hands shake, his face the only thing in my mind as I hastily begin shoving things back in my bag, ready to haul ass out of here the moment we're dismissed.

I hear his name called, but I don't have the guts to turn around or to even figure out who his assignment partner is. I feel his eyes drilling into me, like some sort of intense laser beam.

The clock counts down. One minute to go and I'm out of here. I'll make my escape before he has the chance to catch up to me, and then I can figure out what the hell to do. Maybe I could transfer to a different class or drop the subject altogether?

Thirty seconds to go.

My stare is heavily focused on the clock, and I grab my bag off the floor.

Ten seconds. Five. Four. Three. Two.

Panic tears at me and I go to push up out of my chair when two strong arms come down around me, landing on either side of my desk and caging me in as his body leans over me, leaving no room for escape. His heavenly, familiar scent wraps around me and breaks me in two.

Jaxon. My whole fucking world.

Three years. Three long-ass years since I've smelled him or felt him so damn close, and all I can do is breathe him in. Words escape me as with every new breath, a million heartbreaking memories come right back with it.

Out of the corner of my eye, I see his head hanging close by mine, his eyes closed as he tries to control his breathing. His hands on my desk turn into fists, and I can practically feel the rapid rate of his heartbeat.

Jax doesn't say a word, just hovers over me as the class empties out around us.

A sob desperately wants to break free from my throat, but I hold it in. "Cass," he breathes my name ever so quietly, his tone filled with everything he's refusing to say. The sound of his pained voice and the subtle brush of his sweet breath against my neck has a single tear falling from my eye. It spills down my cheek and onto the desk beside his clenched fist. I watch with bated breath as his thumb strikes out, wiping my tear off the table. He always hated it when I cried, and always said it broke him more than it broke me.

I go to look up, to apologize to him, to say all the things I've held back for the past three years, but just like that, he's gone.

I watch as he clears the last few steps and disappears through the door, leaving me behind just like I had done to him all those years ago.

Taking a shaky breath, I force myself to get in control. My hands shake as I grab my bag from my lap and stand on wobbly legs. Putting one foot in front of the other, I move until I have enough control to run.

I fly through the door and, not stopping to check on Brianna, I crash into my bed, squishing my head into my pillow as the tears begin to consume me. The need to write comes over me, but my hands shake so violently that it's impossible. Sobs rip from deep in my throat, and before I know it, I'm curled under Brianna's arms, her soothing words in my ear.

How the hell could I have been so stupid to assume I could avoid him all semester? Sure, I knew there would be an odd occasion where we might end up at the same party or bump into each other on campus. I had prepared myself for that. But this . . . Being in the same class, seeing him all the time, becoming friends with his inner circle . . . I need to be more careful.

Damn it.

Now that I think about it, I should have known. Of course someone with the dream of getting into the NHL would take courses to help his own understanding of human anatomy and its limits. It's just my luck that those classes are very similar to the ones I'm taking on the road to becoming a physiotherapist. All those times I thought about Jax at college, it was always on the ice or in the gym training. I never thought about the classes he would be taking. Shame on me.

Brianna allows my tears to run their course before she gets the balls to question what happened. She grabs a tissue for me to wipe my eyes, and I gather the strength to finally talk about it.

"I'm so sorry, babe," she says, latching onto me and holding me just that bit tighter the second I've finished getting the words out. "It sounds like what you two had was pretty intense."

"Yeah," I whisper, thinking back on those years when we were so deeply in love. "From the moment I met him, we were attached at the hip. We were each other's world until one day, I . . . I just left. He has every right to be mad at me. Hell, it was three years ago and I'm still mad at me."

"How do you know he's mad? Maybe he was just shocked to see you," she suggests.

"Oh, he was definitely shocked, but I don't know. I can just tell when it comes to him. He's mad. Furious, even."

We both sit in silence as she allows me to catch up with my thoughts and eventually, I fall into a fretful sleep.

I'm awoken a few hours later to the sound of the front door closing, and I sit up and wipe my swollen eyes. I get out of bed and trudge into the bathroom, only to catch sight of myself in the mirror. My eyes are all puffy and red with smudges of mascara all over my face. My chestnut hair looks like some kind of bird's nest, and my nose is still red and slightly runny.

Gross.

Quickly stripping off, I jump into a relaxing shower. I scrub my hair for good measure, then step out and wrap a towel around my body. Hearing Brianna in the living room, I head out to find her fussing around with food in her gym shorts and tank, making me realize she must have ducked out to the gym not long after I zoned out. "Hungry?" she asks.

I glance over at the clock to see it's five in the afternoon and realize I haven't eaten since my cold toast at breakfast. "Starving," I reply, moving over to the couch and plonking down in my towel.

"Feeling better?" Bri asks, handing me a plate so I can start digging in.

"Yeah, actually," I say with an apologetic cringe. "Sorry I put you through all that."

She shrugs off my apology and digs in. "Don't be stupid. That's what friends are for. Just know, when your brother breaks my heart, I'll expect something damn special from you."

"Oh, jeez," I laugh, "You better stay away from Carter then because I can guarantee it will most certainly end in heartbreak. He's a player, through and through."

"Noted. So . . . I have a bit of a confession," she says, nervously.

"Yes?" I ask.

"Well, Bobby called me to check if you were okay. He saw what happened in class and apparently, Jax was in a foul mood. So, he sort of put together that maybe you were a little something more than just one of his conquests. He was worried, so I filled him in on the crucial details," she explains. "I hope that's okay."

"Yeah, it's fine. He was bound to find out sooner or later. And with me having to partner with him for the assignment, I'm assuming he would have had the whole story within a few days," I say. "The only reason I wanted it kept quiet was because I didn't want to upset Jax. This school was his home before it was mine, and I didn't want to mess with what he's got going on here. But now he knows, there's no point shying away from it."

"Fair point, but I am sorry. I feel shitty about telling him, even though I know you can trust him. Bobby is one of the good guys," she promises.

"I know. Don't stress about it. But speaking of your brother, I'm going to need his number so we can organize some time to get this assignment done."

"Oh, sure," she laughs. "You get to have my brother's number, but I don't get to have yours. The double standards in this room are blowing me away."

Rolling my eyes, I get up and quickly grab my phone from my room before heading back down the hallway. "Hey, I have a message from you," I say, stopping in the hallway and checking it.

"Yep," she responds in a smug tone.

I hit open on her text.

Bri - Babe, heads up. The boys' training schedule just got messed around. Pretty sure they're heading your way. Good luck.

"Oh, shit," I say. "Why didn't you tell me you had tried to warn me?"

"Well, I kind of thought it wasn't really the right time for *I told you so,*" she says.

"Yeah, maybe," I laugh as I drop down beside her on the couch while typing out a text to Bobby.

Cassie - Hey, sorry about class today. When are you free to get this assignment done? Cass.

Passing the phone to Bri, I let her enter Bobby's number before I hit send. Not even two seconds later, the front door opens, and Bobby pops his big head through the door, the sound of his incoming text ringing in his pocket.

"Good timing," I say as he comes through the door, making Brianna and I grin like idiots when we see the bottle of wine he's brought along.

"Yeah, I saw Bri leaving Micky's with take-out. So I thought I'd see if there was any left, and I figured you girls could use this," he grins as if he's some sort of knight in shining armor coming to save the damsels in distress.

"That we could," Brianna says, springing up off the couch and grabbing the bottle before disappearing into the kitchen.

Bobby strides through the living room, making his way toward the couch when he meets my stare. "Was he okay?" I ask with a cringe, not needing to clarify who I'm talking about.

Bobby takes over Bri's spot on the couch and gets stuck into her half-eaten dinner. "Yeah, he will be. He's all out of sorts for now," he says around a mouthful of takeout. "I think he's just blindsided and shocked. He wasn't expecting to see you like that, but he'll work it out in the gym. The asshole probably needed a little warning and time to prepare before seeing you again."

"Yeah," I agree quietly, falling back into my own thoughts.

"Nope, none of that," Bri says, dancing back into the room and handing me a glass of wine, scowling at her brother as she realizes he's just annihilated the rest of her dinner in three easy forkfuls. "We're going to forget today even happened. Are you in?"

"Hell yes," I declare, grabbing the glass and throwing caution to the wind. It's been a shitty day so the least I can do is not remember it tomorrow.

CHAPTER 4

JAXON

What the fuck is Cassandra Waters doing here in my school, and in my goddamn Human Movement class for that matter? This is supposed to be my senior year. I'm the fucking king of campus. The last thing I want or need is Cass coming in and screwing it all up.

My mind is blowing up with so many thoughts that I can't even think straight. The one thing I am certain about is that I am fucking furious. After three fucking years, she shows up here without a damn word? No fucking explanation about where she's been this whole goddamn time?

Fuck.

Question after question takes over. How long has she been here?

Why is she here? Why isn't she in New York like she's supposed to be? Where the hell is she staying? Why haven't I seen her on campus? And the one which is making my brain steam, why the fuck did Bobby look at her like they knew each other?

Fuck. It's barely been twelve hours since I stood over her, and the chick is already messing with my head. I promised Coach Harris that there will be no fuck-ups this season. I need to get this shit sorted. I have a career on the line.

I've been tossing and turning since the second I got into bed, and when I realize sleep isn't going to come, I throw my blankets off and sit up in bed. Grabbing my phone, I let out a sigh when I see it's only 3:45 in the morning. The only thing that's going to calm me down is getting on the ice, apart from confronting Cassie and getting some goddamn answers out of her, but I don't think that's a good option right now. The rink doesn't open until six, and even then, the figure fairies have it booked out all day, so I go with the next best thing.

Pulling on some clothes and my runners, I take off like a bat out of hell. I push through the front door, letting it slam closed behind me, not caring who the fuck it wakes up inside. I breathe in the fresh air as I try my hardest to concentrate on the feel of the concrete path under my feet, and I push myself harder, but the thoughts of Cassie still remain.

With each new step, I find myself back in that classroom, waiting for Professor Macintosh to call out my name while a blonde bombshell a few rows down was busy eye fucking me. I had my whole day planned out. I was going to skip my next class, take the blonde home and screw her until she couldn't walk, then I was going to train and spend the night partying with my boys.

Until my whole world came to a standstill when I heard the name that's been haunting me since I was twelve years old. It used to give me a different sort of rush, but now all it does is make my chest ache for all the things that could have been.

At first, I thought my mind must have been playing tricks on me. There was no way Professor Macintosh had gotten that right. Maybe I'd misheard him or some prick was pulling a twisted prank on me. There's no way Cassandra Waters would be back in Denver. She left over three years ago and never looked back.

My heart stopped when I saw that familiar wave of chestnut hair. Then the goddess had to go and turn around, blinding me with that perfect smile. The smile I still think about every night before falling asleep. The smile that could bring me out of my worst depression and give me the strength to keep pushing on. The smile that could easily drop me to my knees.

I saw the exact moment she noticed me beside Bobby. That beautiful face of hers fell, that smile dropped away, and that sun-kissed skin immediately turned white. I would have given anything to take away her pain, but my anger and frustrations took over.

My eyes didn't move from her for one second as I watched her jam her bag full of her things and wait for the clock to count down. I knew she was planning to run, but I was going to beat her at her own game. I stood up when my name was called and still have no idea who my partner is for that stupid assignment. All that mattered was Cass.

I took my seat and watched the clock right along with her. With ten seconds to go, I saw Professor Macintosh scowl at me as I started making my way down the stairs. Her body shifted, ready to run, but she wasn't going to make it. I stepped up behind her and slammed my hands down on either side of her.

That same fruity smell of her shampoo was nearly enough to paralyze me. I took a deep breath in and was assaulted by the feeling of home as my mind jolted back to the past. "Cass," I whispered as I hovered over her, the desperate need to bring my arms in and hold her.

I clenched my fists to regain some sort of control, but it was shattered the moment I saw a perfectly round teardrop fall from her cheek and come crashing down on the table. My thumb struck out without thought and wiped away her spilled tear before I was out the door like a lightning bolt.

Why does she get to cry about it? She's the one who left. She's the one who ran.

To say my afternoon was shit is an understatement. I went home, punched a hole through my wall, and nearly got into a fistfight with Bobby during training. I spent my night trying to work my frustrations out at the gym, but here I am at just after four in the morning and the frustrations are still riding high.

I shake out my head and push myself to my limits, concentrating solely on my footfalls against the pavement. A runner ahead catches my eye, and I move to the side to allow room for the person to pass. As the person comes nearer, it becomes startlingly obvious who it is. "You've got to be shitting me," I groan to myself as I continue on.

Cassandra grows closer, her head down and earphones in, completely oblivious to me coming her way. Anger takes over me. Does she have any idea how dangerous it is for a woman to be out here at this time of the morning alone, especially with the way she looks in those little shorts?

No matter how furious I am with her, I can't help the protective nature that comes over me whenever she's around.

I try my best to zone it out and concentrate on my run, but I can't take my eyes off her, watching as she notices my movements, her head snapping up. Her eyes widen as she recognizes me and quickly drops her gaze back to the ground, doing her best to ignore me, but I know my presence affects her when she nearly fumbles and eats dirt.

I eye her as she passes, and I get smacked in the face with that damn fruity shampoo again. Even with her chin tilted down, I can still see her red, swollen eyes and the dark, sleepless bags lingering beneath them. I want to be happy knowing that she's suffering just as much as I am, but the thought kills me.

My eyes close for a moment as I try to continue, but I know there's no point. I can't bear to leave her knowing she's out in the dark running by herself. "Shit," I mutter to myself as I turn on my heel and begin running behind her, looking like a fucking dirty stalker.

Her back stiffens, clearly knowing I've turned around, but I stay a few feet behind, making sure she's okay while keeping my eyes firmly focused on her glorious ass that I've missed so damn much. We must be another ten minutes in when she comes to a screeching halt, doubling over with her hands on her knees, struggling for breath as sobs come tearing from her chest.

My heart aches as I stop behind her, completely unsure of what to do. The girl I used to know would want me to swoop in and save the day, be her knight in shining armor and tell her I forgive her, but I'm not the same guy I used to be. I slowly begin to walk her way, trying to give myself time to think of what the hell to say while getting my emotions in check, but she pulls herself together and takes off again.

I follow behind for a little while longer when she turns down a familiar street, then down a very familiar driveway. What the hell? Pieces of the puzzle begin falling into place. "You're Bri's new roommate?" I scoff, feeling like an absolute idiot as she reaches for the door handle.

She turns back to me, her eyes roaming all over my face and body before they focus on my eyes. She gives me the smallest nod before pushing through the door and closing it behind her. "Fucking Bobby," I grunt as a new wave of betrayal comes over me.

Needing to get this shit sorted, I take off in his direction and find myself at his door, my fist pounding against the hardwood. "Open the fucking door, Bobby."

The moment the door opens, my fist slams into his face, nailing him in the jaw. He falls back a few steps before catching himself, his hand clutching his face. "What the fuck?" he growls, rubbing his jaw.

I push past him and make my way into the kitchen to grab a bottle of water from the fridge. "Cass is Bri's new roommate," I state.

Anger grows behind his eyes as he gets in my face. "Tell me you weren't just stalking my sister's house in the middle of the fucking night?" he growls. "What the fuck were you doing there?"

"Calm down. I was out running. Cass was too. I followed her home to make sure she was safe. How the hell was I supposed to know I was following her to your sister's place?"

"I told you Bri had a new roommate," he argues.

"You failed to mention who the fuck it was."

"She asked me not to. I assumed she was some chick you fucked, and when I asked if she was, she just said *something like that*. How the hell was I supposed to know she's the chick you've been in love with since you were a fucking kid?" he growls, his hands flying up in frustration.

"I'm not in love with her," I throw back, slamming the bottle down on the kitchen counter.

He rolls his eyes and scoffs. "Yeah fucking right. I can see it in your eyes. The second you saw her, everything changed. In all the years I've known you, you've never reacted like this over some chick."

I want to argue, but I know the fucker is right. The proof is right there for the world to see. I lean up against the counter and hang my head as I try to get my emotions under control, concentrating on my breathing. "Sorry 'bout your face," I grumble.

"No drama. I should have told you her name."

Yeah, I definitely agree with that, but there's no point in mentioning it. I move into the living room, take my water bottle with me, and collapse onto the couch.

"Dude, you probably don't want to hear this, but you know who her brother is, right?" Bobby asks, his eyes lighting up in excitement.

"Yeah," I laugh, rolling my eyes. I should have seen this shit coming. Of course the bastard idolizes Logan Fucking Waters. "Who do you think taught me to play?"

"Fucking hell," he scoffs, shaking his head in disbelief. "How have I known you this long and never known that?"

"You may not have noticed, but I don't talk about home or anything to do with her, period," I murmur.

"Yeah, no shit," he grunts under his breath. "I worked that out."

We sit in silence for a short while before Bobby gets up. "If you're all good, man, I'm going to head back to bed," he says, squeezing my shoulder on the way past. "You can crash here if you need," he adds, disappearing before I can give an answer.

I lay back on the couch and pull a cushion behind my head, and once again the memories of Cassandra Waters come flying back. At least some of that rage seems to have dissipated.

Finally falling into a proper sleep, I wake hours later when the boys start messing around in the kitchen. I sit up on the couch and stretch out my cramped legs. "Yo, what's the time?" I call out to anyone who will answer.

"After eleven," someone replies. "Hungry?"

"Yeah." I get up to realize just how sore my legs are, no doubt from the intense run I put them through this morning. A run that had no stretch, no warm-up, and no cooldown. Rookie fucking error.

I sit with the boys to eat before Bobby decides he's forgiven me enough to give me a lift back to my place. "You owe me," he reminds me as I get out of his truck.

"I know, man," I say, studying the bruise developing on his jaw. I give him a quick nod and close the door behind me.

By the time I'm dressed and ready for the day, it's after one in the afternoon and the thought of seeing Cassie again has been eating at me for hours. I grab my keys, slip out the door, and find myself heading over to Brianna's place.

A weird kind of excitement I don't understand fills me as I get out of my truck and walk up the drive. I knock lightly on the door and wait a few agonizing moments for it to be answered.

Bri opens the door with a yawn wearing *Hello Kitty* pajamas. "Girl, it's after one in the afternoon. Why are you only getting out of bed now?"

She gives me an unimpressed look. "Not that it's any of your business, but we had a bit of a late night. I'm sure you can imagine why."

I let out a sigh. "Is she here?"

She doesn't answer, just looks at me blankly, clearly not wanting to give in. I'm sure I'm not her favorite person at the moment.

"Bri, come on," I beg, softening my stare and laying it on thick, knowing damn well she'll fold. Only when she doesn't bend under my stare, I realize just how pissed she really is.

"Stalk anyone lately?" she asks with attitude. "Oh, better yet, punch anyone lately?"

Yeah, I deserved that. "You know I'm the last person who would ever hurt her. She was running around the streets in the middle of the fucking night. Of course I'm going to follow her home. I would never have forgiven myself if something happened to her. Your brother, on the other hand, deserved what he got."

She lets out an annoyed huff but eventually, her walls begin to fall. "She's not here. She's working."

"Working?" I ask in shock. "She doesn't need the money."

My mind starts swirling. Why the hell would she be working? Has something happened to her family's money? She has a damn trust fund. Not to mention her brothers are loaded. Logan has a freaking multi-million-dollar contract with the NHL, Sean's one of the top criminal lawyers in the country, and who the fuck knows what Carter ended up doing.

Brianna gives me a dumb, pointed stare, and it suddenly clicks. She's working to avoid me.

"Where?" I ask with a sigh.

She lets out a resigned sigh. "Library. But she doesn't finish until seven."

I'm already opening my truck before she's even finished her sentence. There's no way I can wait around until seven knowing she's there.

I park in the library parking lot and hop out of the truck. The real challenge will be actually finding her in this big fucker we call a library. I head on in and search level after level, checking each row and study hall before eventually finding her on level three, sorting through piles of books and returning them to their positions on the shelves.

She grabs a book off the top of the pile and takes a look at the spine before searching the shelves for its spot. She finds it a few rows above her head and reaches up on her tippy toes to slide it in place, only she isn't quite tall enough. I walk up behind her, pressing my body flush against hers, and nearly falter at the feel of her body against mine. Then, before she realizes how fucking desperate I am for her, I bring my hand up and push the book into its position.

Cassie's body stiffens against mine, instantly knowing who stands behind her. "Can we talk?" I murmur, my hand falling to her hip.

She keeps her eyes forward as she slowly comes down from her tippy toes. "I'm working," she tells me in her velvety sweet voice. That velvety voice I didn't realize just how much I missed.

"Please," I whisper. "You owe me that much. Just one conversation."

She lets out a shaky breath and turns to face me, the movement causing her chest to press up against my rib cage. Her big brown eyes look up at me with tears beginning to pool, and it fucking kills me. "Jax," she sighs, regret heavy in her tone.

"I promise, I just want to talk," I tell her. "I'll come back when you're done and then I'll leave you alone."

She looks down at her feet as she thinks it over before finally meeting my haunted stare and nodding. "Okay," she whispers, ever so softly. "I get off at seven."

I step back out of her personal space and nod, letting her know I'll be back, before forcing myself to walk away. With nothing else to do to pass the time, I head to the gym. After a grueling workout, I get myself cleaned up and show up at six. Then like a fucking desperate fool, I take a seat in the back of the library, silently watching her work for the last hour of her shift.

As the clock ticks closer to seven, I notice her become fidgety and realize she's nervous, though I don't know why. We've been talking about anything and everything since we were twelve years old. Sure, it's been a few years, but I've seen this woman at her absolute worst and at her best. If anything, opening up to me should be as easy as breathing.

When the clock strikes seven, Cass says goodbye to the other girl working with her and grabs her shit from under a counter before hesitantly striding by me. She motions with a flick of her chin to follow her, and I get up, shadowing her through the library as she leads us into a long-forgotten study room, giving us the privacy we need.

There's still enough daylight coming through the window, so she doesn't bother to hit the lights as she passes them. I watch as she presses her back up against the wall, drops her bag, and slides down until she's sitting.

Following her lead, I take a seat beside her, leaving enough room between us so I'm not tempted to reach out and touch her. After all, I'm here for one reason and one reason only. To find the answers to the questions I've been asking myself for the past three years. But goddamn, not touching her is going to be the hardest thing I've ever done.

We sit in silence, neither of us knowing where to start. My eyes linger on her bag and spy the torn-up notebook poking out the top, causing a strange familiarity to pulse through me. I desperately want to reach out and pluck the notebook from her bag, knowing it would be filled with lyrics that would give me some sort of insight into what her life is like now. But I know she would probably beat me to a pulp if I tried. Those old notebooks of hers were always considered a forbidden fruit, something I desperately wanted but knew I could never have.

"How are you?" I finally ask, feeling like an idiot for giving her the benefit of the doubt and not bombarding her with the hard questions. After all, she tore my heart out. What's a little pain on her part?

"I've been better," she tells me, not wanting to give anymore. "You?"

"Confused," I admit. "What are you doing here, Cass?"

She studies her hands as she replies. "You mean here on campus? Or Denver?"

"I don't know," I say looking over at her, those big brown eyes tearing at my chest. "Both?"

Cass lets out a shaky breath. "I missed my family. It was time to come home," she explains, giving me a half-assed, rehearsed answer.

I nod, staring at the wall to keep from shaking the answers out of her. "So, you're back for good then?"

She hesitates before glancing at me, unease flashing in her eyes. "Is that going to be a problem?" she asks.

I shrug a shoulder, not able to give her a proper answer. "I guess we'll see," I tell her honestly.

Cassie gives a slight nod before moving along. "How are your parents?"

"Wouldn't have a clue," I admit with a shrug. "After you left, there wasn't anything there for me. I haven't been back since I started college."

"What?" she gasps, horror in those wide eyes. "You haven't gone home in three years? What the hell, Jax? I know your parents were assholes, but three years?"

"You don't get to judge me, Cass," I say, my stare hardening and having to force myself to try and calm down. "As long as I'm playing hockey, I'm nothing but a fuck-up. They haven't spoken to me since the day I accepted my scholarship. But you watch, they'll come running back to me when I sign with the NHL."

"Shit, Jax," she says with a sigh, her hand flinching at her side as though trying to keep herself from reaching out to me. "I didn't realize it had gotten so bad."

"How could you?" I grunt, feeling like a prick the second the words escape my lips.

"I guess I deserved that," she mumbles, focusing her eyes back on her hands.

I cringe, knowing that would have hurt, but I don't dwell on it. "How are your brothers?" I ask to keep her talking.

"They're okay, I guess. Sean's getting married in a few weeks," she says, a proud smile pulling at the corners of her lips.

"Sara?"

"Yeah," she smiles.

"And Logan?"

"He's good. Apparently, he has a new girl that we'll be meeting at the wedding," she explains. "He's been offered another four years in the league."

"Shit," I laugh in surprise. "Good on him. What about Carter?"

That proud smile quickly morphs into mirth. "Well, you know Carter," she scoffs. "Still the biggest manwhore around. Just like you," she quips with a hint of jealousy in her voice. Her comment stings, but

I don't let it show. "I'm waiting for the day some girl comes and knocks him off his feet."

"That'd be the day," I chuckle. "What about your parents?"

She falters, that beautiful smile falling away as pain rockets through her stare. She drops her gaze to her hand, and I look over at her, unsure of the sudden change. She blinks back tears and something inside me has me reaching for her hand. Her fingers instantly fold into mine, the movement feeling so right. "What is it, Cass?" I murmur quietly.

She looks up, her broken stare meeting mine. The heartache in her eyes kills me. "Jax," she whispers, gently shaking her head as the tears begin to pour down her face. "I'm so sorry. I thought you knew."

Dread settles in my stomach. I know without a doubt that whatever comes out of her mouth next is going to shatter every piece of my already fractured soul.

She lets out a shaky breath, and I give her hand a squeeze, prompting her to continue. "They're gone, Jax. They're dead."

CHAPTER 5

CASSIE

Jax reaches across and scoops me into his strong arms, pulling me down on top of him so I'm straddling his lap, and I fold into him as though this is exactly where I belong. He holds me close, looking at me with pain in his eyes, begging me to tell him this is a sick joke. "How?" he asks in a broken tone, his head falling to my shoulder, making no secret of the fact that all this time, he had no idea.

I take a deep breath, preparing myself to break his heart all over again. "Mom was nearly two years ago," I start with a shaky voice, but I push on. He needs to know. "The cancer came back, and she was gone within a few months."

He curses, the pain clear in his voice as he pulls me in tighter, urging me to continue. "Dad was taken by a heart attack six months ago," I murmur as the tears stream down my face.

We sit in silence, finding comfort in each other. "Fuck, Cass. They were my family too. I should have been there for them. For you."

I drop my head into the nook of his neck and breathe him in. I would have given my world to have been able to have his comfort on the tragic days I buried my parents. "I'm sorry," I cry as my lips move against his skin. "I miss them so much."

"I know, baby," he says as he removes his hands and brings them to lift my face to his. "There's nothing you could have done to change what happened," he tells me, holding me close enough to feel his breath against my lips.

"I could have come home more, been by her side," I whisper.

"She wouldn't have wanted that, and you know it," he says. I drop my forehead against his. "You should have called me, Cass. I would have been there."

"I hurt you. In the worst way. I didn't think I could."

"You were hurting. I would have come. No matter what," he murmurs.

Everything shatters within me, and the room falls to silence around us, each of us contemplating the depth of what's been said. Neither one of us move, desperately seeking out the comfort and familiarity the other offers, all while knowing just how wrong this is.

It could be minutes or hours that pass when he lifts his head and brushes his fingers down the side of my face. "Come on," he murmurs. "We still have a lot to talk about, but it's getting late. I'll drop you home."

At that, I finally look up and notice the room has fallen into darkness. I'm shocked to find how long we've been sitting here. "It's okay," I say, getting to my feet but feeling empty at the loss of his touch. I move back, giving him space. "I have my car."

"Okay," he murmurs as we walk out of the little room, only to find the rest of the library completely abandoned. Lights are off, the familiar whir of the computers gone, the librarian's desk empty, and of course, the front doors locked.

"Shit," I whisper. Jax double-checks the door while I peer through the window, my stomach sinking with dread. "Crap."

"What?" he asks, also peering through the window. "Still petrified of storms?"

"More now than ever," I cringe, turning away and heading for the windows in the computer lab, knowing that one tends to get jammed and is a bitch to close.

I climb up on the table and get to work trying to wiggle the window open. I hear Jax groan from behind me before grabbing my hips and moving me out of the way. "Watch out," he grumbles. "You're going to hurt yourself."

He steps up on the table, and with a bit of manpower, the window creaks open, bringing with it the noise of the raging storm outside. He shoves his head out the window and looks down. "It's a bit of a drop," he yells over the sound of the storm as the wind blows his hair around his face. "I'll go first and catch you at the bottom."

I step up beside him and peer out the window, my eyes growing as wide as saucers. There's no way I'm jumping out this window, especially in a fucking storm. "But—" I start before getting cut off by a crack of thunder.

"No buts. It's either jump out the window or stay the night here," he tells me, knowing I'm far too pussy to do either. Seeing the resignation in my eyes, he continues. "Be careful. The rain has made the windowsill slippery," he says as he climbs up, then before I know it, he launches himself out, and I gasp as he disappears into the dark night below.

"Shit. Jax? Are you okay?" I call as I search for him below.

"Yeah," he replies. "Hurry up, I'm getting wet."

"Ahh, shit," I groan as I pull myself up onto the ledge. I make the mistake of looking down into the nothingness just as a shot of thunder echoes through the sky, killing every ounce of confidence I had. "Fuck, Jax. I can't do it," I call down to him.

"Yes, you can. Now get your ass down here," he orders. "I'll catch you. I won't let you fall," he adds as lightning brightens up the sky. "Fuck," I hear him mutter under his breath, knowing the storm is only making this worse.

I peek over once again, the movement making my hair swirl around my face.

"Now, Cass," he demands.

Damn it.

"Fine," I snap before I close my eyes, scoot my ass to the edge, and launch myself over. A squeal rips from my throat as I fall through the sky, but moments later, two strong, warm arms are holding me up, saving me from imminent death.

"About fucking time," he grunts, making sure I find my feet on the ground. "I thought I was going to have to climb back up and push you out."

"Shut up," I say, reluctantly stepping back and dropping my hands from his strong, bulging arms. "You're drenched," I tell him, trying to cover up my unease, which I'm sure after all these years he can see right through.

"Yeah, I'm aware, but you will be too if we don't get going," he says, letting me off the hook.

With that, we both take off through the rain toward the parking lot. "You want me to follow you home?" he asks, though I know it's only because of the storm and his need to help a damsel in distress.

"I'll be okay," I tell him as we round the corner and come to a stop, both of us seeing the massive boom gate closing off the parking lot.

"Fuck," he curses. "We're going to have to make a run for it."

"Shit," I groan, turning to him. "I guess, I'll see you later?" I say, extremely awkwardly.

"Fuck that," he scoffs. "Like hell I'd let you run home at night by yourself, especially during a fucking storm. Your brothers would have my balls if they ever found out."

Shit. Don't think about his balls. Don't think about his balls.

"Fine," I grumble, knowing a losing battle when I see one. We both take off home, sprinting through the torrential rain, and before I know it, we're crashing through my front door and soaking everything in our path. "I'll grab you a towel," I say, taking off down the hallway, knowing Bri is going to kill me for this.

Jax follows behind me but stops when he gets to my room and pushes the door open. I rifle through the hallway cupboard, grab a towel, and step back into my room to find him with his back to me and my old acoustic guitar in his hands. The very guitar he had bought me when I was fourteen and finally admitted I wanted to make music.

"You've still got this," he says, turning slowly to look at me.

"Yeah," I breathe. "I could never part with it."

Jax turns it in his hands before gently placing it back down. He takes two steps, placing himself right in front of me, and pushes a dripping strand of hair off my cheek. His fingers run down the length of my face and down my throat, following my arms until he's gently taking the towel out of my hands. Rather than stepping back to dry himself off, he throws the towel aside.

His eyes search mine as he comes in closer, slowly tilting his face toward mine, almost as if asking for permission. I lift my chin, allowing my lips to softly press against his, bringing me home for the first time in three years. He kisses me tenderly, as though I'm a precious piece of crystal that could shatter in his hands.

My eyes close as my hands twine up his strong arms and come to rest behind his neck, my fingers finding purchase in the soft hair at the back of his head. Jax deepens the kiss, and a moan escapes me as his hands travel down my body and stop at the bottom of my shirt. He begins peeling the wet fabric off me, and despite knowing just how dangerous this is, I let him continue, my need for him like nothing I've ever felt.

He pulls the shirt up and over my head before trailing his hands back down my body and lifting me by the back of my thighs. My legs wrap around his strong body, and as he walks us toward the bed, his lips never leave mine.

Jaxon crashes to my bed, and his large body comes down on top of mine. Pulling my arms free, I get to work on his shirt, and he pulls back just enough to help remove the wet fabric. He reaches around me, unclasping my bra, his featherlight touch on my back causing tingles to shoot down my spine. He sits up a little higher and gives me an almighty view of his body as he slowly draws my bra straps off my arms.

His gaze sails over me, taking in every inch of my body as if seeing me for the first time. But I can't find it within me to watch his reaction. Instead, my eyes are glued to his body. A body that is now one of a man. A very sexy, very defined man.

I start at his strong shoulders and travel down to the muscled pecs, my mouth watering with desire. My hand rises and lands right in the center of his chest, feeling the strong muscles under my fingers, and I trail down toward his abs, my fingers feeling the sharp ridges that come with years of dedicated training.

He's a fucking Adonis. Perfect in every way.

I keep working my way down, past his glorious V, and take hold of his belt buckle. My gaze flickers up to meet his, making sure he truly wants this. His eyes are flaming with need, and I take that as my cue to continue. I rid him of his pants, and he comes back down on top of me.

Jax's lips find the soft skin of my neck and my back arches up off my mattress, my tits pressing against him. He works his way down, his hands cupping my breasts before sucking my pebbled nipple into his mouth, forcing another moan out of me. His free hand travels down my body and finds the button of my jeans. "Are you sure, Cass?" he asks. "I won't be able to stop. Not with you."

"Yes. I need to feel you," I breathe, knowing if he walked away right now, I would never survive. Jax looks me in the eye for another moment before bringing his lips down to mine, kissing me with unbelievable passion. My jeans and thong are gone from my body within seconds, and before I know it, Jax is settling between my legs, that thick, veiny cock more than ready to take me.

Reaching down between us, I curl my fingers around his hard cock, desperate to feel his velvety skin again. The second I do, I bite down on my lip, watching the way he draws in a deep breath. My God, he has grown.

His forehead presses to mine, a soft groan sailing through the room. "Fuck, I missed your touch," he breathes as his hand slips down between our bodies and his fingers find my clit. He applies just enough pressure, knowing exactly how I like it, before he rubs little, tight circles, making my fist tighten around him.

"Oh, God. Jax!" I pant into his mouth as he groans in satisfaction.

His fingers lower, exploring my body further to find me ready and waiting for him, and not a second later, he pushes two thick fingers deep inside my pussy as his thumb works my clit. A gasp pulls from the back of my throat. Just knowing that it's him doing this to me is nearly enough to make me come.

My grip tightens around his cock, and I work him just the way he likes, my thumb rolling over his tip as his fingers curl within, massaging my walls and making my eyes roll in the back of my head. My body arches up against him once more as I raise my legs to wrap around his hips. "I need you inside me," I beg, looking up at him.

He growls deeply, the hunger flashing in his eyes. "Condom?" he asks.

"No," I pant. "I need to feel you. Just you."

He lets out a slight groan and positions himself at my entrance. With a soft grunt of need, he slowly guides himself inside me, my body already screaming for more.

"Oh, fuck," I pant through the room as he keeps going.

Ever so slowly, he pushes the rest of his big cock deep inside me, completely filling me. "Fuck," he groans as I let out a desperate moan, my pussy clenching around him. He comes to a stop above me, dipping his head and gently kissing me. And with his lips on mine, he begins to move, real, real slow.

My nails dig into the tight skin of his shoulders as he begins to increase his pace, making me scream out for more. He speeds up and fucks me hard and fast, each of us so desperate for this release as we silently work out our frustration. Jax brings us both right to the edge before taking my hip and rolling us until I'm straddling him, taking his cock so much deeper.

Jax scoots up the headboard until he's sitting, giving us each a perfect view of the other, and I grip the frame of my bed, more than ready to ride him. He sucks my nipple into his mouth and grabs my ass with his free hand as I start to move above him. "Jax," I groan, throwing my head back while knotting my fingers into his thick hair. "I'm going to come."

"Not yet, baby. Hold onto it. I've missed this too much for it to be over yet," he growls, pulling me in tighter and biting me gently on the shoulder, making me clench around him. "Fuck."

"Jax," I cry out in warning, barely able to hold on as his hand comes down between us and presses against my clit, sending a jolt of electricity shooting straight through my cunt as I detonate.

My world explodes around him as I ride him like he's never been ridden before, my high shooting through my body and filling me with undeniable pleasure. My walls clench down, not daring to stop when I feel him come hard inside of me, making me feel like a fucking goddess.

I ride it out, his fingers digging into my hips, then when I finally come down from my high, I drop my head to his shoulder as we each desperately try to catch our breath. "Shit, Cass," he pants, his arms circling around my back and holding me close. "You were holding out on me all those years."

Jax looks up at me with a cheesy as fuck grin, and I can't help but laugh. "Look who's talking, stud."

He rolls his eyes, but things quickly turn serious as our minds return to us. "Come on. Let me get you cleaned up," he says, lifting me off him and taking me into the bathroom. I feel him beginning to leak out of me, but he reaches into the shower and turns on the taps.

Jax sets me down on my feet, and my knees shake as I let my rain-soaked hair rinse through the hot water before grabbing my soap and washing us off. "What does this mean, Jax?" I eventually ask in the quietest voice I can possibly manage, terrified of his answer.

He lets out a sigh and pulls me into him, and I know whatever he says is bound to tear me apart, but I deserve it. I broke him when I left. "Nothing, Cass," he tells me, not wanting to sugarcoat it and give me a false sense of hope. "You ended us three years ago with no explanation. You left me with nothing, and your brothers followed. How could I come back from that?"

I nod against his chest, completely understanding where he's coming from, as a tear falls from the corner of my eye. "Will you stay tonight?" I question, trying to mask the way my voice breaks, but I know he hears it. "You can go back to hating me tomorrow."

"I couldn't bear to walk out that door tonight," he whispers, his fingers brushing down the side of my face.

I nod once again, and he turns off the taps before reaching out and grabbing some towels. He wraps one around me before stepping out of the shower and pressing a feather-soft kiss to my temple.

We head back into my bedroom and climb into bed together, and Jax immediately pulls me against his warm body, holding me the same way he used to all those years ago. My eyes close, finally feeling at ease for the first time in three years. "Goodnight, Cass," he whispers into the dark.

He curls me in under his chin, and I rest my head against his chest as our legs become a jumbled mess. "Night, Jax," I say before drifting into the most peaceful sleep I've had in over three years.

soft knock comes at the door before Brianna pops her head through with a big-ass cheesy grin across her face as she eyes Jax's naked chest. "I knew it," she laughs quietly. "I fucking knew it. No one masturbates that loudly."

"What the hell do you want?" I groan. "It's too early."

"I just thought you might like to know that all three of your incredibly sexy as fuck big brothers are sitting in our living room," she says, enjoying watching the way Jax's body goes rigid beneath me. "I mean, I could probably stall Carter from coming down here, but you might have a problem with the other two," she grins. "Actually . . ." she adds as an afterthought, "what do you think their thoughts are on a foursome?"

"Are you fucking with us?" Jax questions, his eyes wide as he sits straight up in bed, taking the blanket with him and giving Bri a great view of my tits. He knows damn well that if he got caught in my bed, my brothers wouldn't hesitate to give him a beat down, despite the fact I'm a grown-ass woman.

"Nice rack," she applauds. "Now, get rid of your man."

"Fuck," I mutter, choosing to ignore her comments about Jax being my man, but liking it all the same. She backs out of the room, leaving me with an unsure Jax. "They're not going to be thrilled to see you naked in my bed. So you've got to go . . . preferably out the window."

"What?" he grunts. "How long are they hanging around? I can

wait til they leave and then fuck you all over again."

My cheeks flush, and despite being used to just how forward he is, there's nothing quite like it. "You know one of them is going to be suspicious and search my room. And besides, they figured you just didn't show for either of the funerals. None of us realized that you didn't actually know," I explain as he gets out of bed and searches for his clothes. "They've been wanting to beat your ass to a pulp for a while now."

He gives me a hard stare. "Do I need to remind you whose fault that is?" I wince and watch as he picks up his jeans to find them still soaking wet. "Shit," he groans, dropping them back on the floor.

I get out of bed and immediately feel his eyes on my body, and I do what I can to ignore it as I dig into my closet. I pull out Jax's high school hockey jersey, which should be long enough to cover the important bits, and toss it at his chest. "Here. This should work."

He straightens out the fabric and glances at his name across the back. "I wondered what happened to this," he muses.

"Yeah, well, now you know. But I want it back," I warn. "It doesn't matter what happens between us, I have custody of that jersey and you damn well know it."

He glances up at me, his eyes sparkling, and I know he's remembering the night I took it just as clearly as I am—the night we lost our virginity. "Got any sweatpants?" he asks, trying to keep us on track.

"Why? Afraid the whole campus is going to get a look at your dick?" I ask, smirking across at him with a raised brow. "There's really nothing to worry about. The majority of girls around here have already seen it. They know what you're packing."

He gives me an unimpressed look, but I see a flicker of guilt behind his eyes. A look that I can only detect through years of knowing him.

With a sigh, I give in. "None that would fit you," I grin, digging through my drawers to find my largest pair. He pulls them on, and I have to cover my mouth to avoid laughing too loud at the way they ride halfway up his calves, the waistband stretching so wide it looks as though it might tear in half. Hell, he better be careful. One small fart could have those bad boys disintegrating into ash at his feet.

Jax steps over to the window and opens it before turning back to me, a seriousness resting in his bright blue eyes. "We still have a lot to talk about," he tells me, giving me a gentle kiss on the forehead before looking me straight in the eyes. "You know, they both loved you so much. They would be proud of you," he adds, giving me a meaningful look.

"I know," I whisper before he ducks out the window and over the back fence as a heaviness sinks into my gut, feeling as though I might never see him again. Though, I know eventually he'll come searching for the answers he's still desperate to get.

With a sigh, I grab a nice outfit, throw my hair up and get ready to face my brothers, humming to myself for the first time in three long years.

"Hey," I snap as I walk up the hallway to see Brianna lounging comfortably in Carter's lap, his hand resting dangerously close to her vag. I narrow my eyes at them before focusing on the other idiots in the room. "I thought you guys were coming at eight? The sun has hardly risen."

"First of all, it's nine," Carter grunts, getting up before placing Brianna down gently on the couch and giving me a big hug. "And secondly, who the hell did you have in your bed this morning?" he adds, making Sean and Logan's heads whip in my direction.

"Ahh . . . what?" I ask.

"I've been playing that game since before you could walk, Cass," he explains. "Brianna was way too desperate to be the one who woke you."

Shit.

At that, Logan and Sean get to their feet and come to stand before me with their arms crossed over their big chests and matching scowls across their stupid faces. "Chill out, idiots. Bri and I have been doing naked yoga each night before bed. It's very relaxing and freeing. So, I've been sleeping nude if you really need to know. I bet you all would have loved walking in to see that, huh?"

Logan's eyes widen in surprise as he looks from me to Brianna. "You guys are lesbians?" he asks in shock. "Don't get me wrong, I'm all for it if you wanna bat for the other team, you know, pussy power and all that. I'm just a little surprised."

"What?" Brianna laughs. "When she says *naked yoga* she actually means naked yoga. You know, yoga in the nude. It's not a code word for kinky, lesbian sex," she clarifies. "Though, I have to admit, if I was going to go lesbian, it would be with Cass. I mean, you've seen her rack, right?"

I can't help but chuckle at the awkward discomfort across the boys' faces. I'm pleased to see my lie has at least gotten Sean and Logan off my back. They both start making their way out the door, Sean demanding I hurry up and get my ass in the truck. They think way too highly of me, and it almost makes me feel bad. *Almost.*

"You may have those idiots fooled," Carter whispers as we walk behind them, throwing his arm over my shoulder. "But I invented the naked yoga lie. I'll figure out who was here, and when I do, there'll be trouble."

"Oh, please. By the time you figure it out, you would have forgotten what your goal was," I scoff.

"Shut up and get in the truck," he demands, opening the door and ushering me in. I giggle as I step past him but do as I'm told. No matter how outrageous and foul my big brothers can be, they will always treat a woman like a lady, just the way my father raised them to.

"Alright, what do you want for breakfast, ass face?" Logan asks.

"Pancakes," I grin.

"You got it, dude," he replies before taking off down the road and eventually pulling into the first diner he can find.

Half an hour later, we're munching down our breakfast when Sean's eyes turn curious. "What?" I ask when he won't stop staring.

"I don't know," he says, as if deep in thought. "You seem . . . different or something," he adds, making the other two look at me in the same way.

"Probably the dick she got last night," Carter mutters, making me elbow him in the ribs. "I've noticed it has a way of relaxing a girl."

"Shut up," I scold. "There was no dick. And for the record, I feel better. I finally got a few things off my chest."

"Yeah," Carter scoffs. "Your clothes."

Everyone ignores his comments as Sean and Logan push for details. "Well?" they ask in unison, doing the mindfuck triplet telepathy thing.

"Jax found out I was on campus," I start.

Logan groans, cutting me off. "Ugh, what did that little prick want?"

"He just wanted to talk," I explain. "He has a few unanswered questions about why I left."

"Yeah," Sean scoffs, "and I have a few unanswered questions about why the fuck he didn't bother showing up to Mom and Dad's funerals. He might not have been blood, but they were his parents too."

Logan and Carter both grunt their approvals. "Stop it," I scold them as a wave of anger comes over me. "Have any of you seen him at home in the last three years?" I ask. "No," I answer, not giving them the chance to jump on the defense. "Did you check in with his parents only to find out they haven't spoken to him since the day he left for college? No. You all know damn well that I haven't spoken to him since I left, so did any of you call to let him know when Mom or Dad passed?" They give each other guilty looks, but I continue on. "No, you didn't. None of us did. So how was he to know? I had to break his heart all over again, telling him that the two people he actually considered to be his parents are now dead," I cry. "He didn't come to the funerals because he had no fucking idea they were gone. Which means you can all lay off and forgive him because he hasn't done anything wrong. He's just as torn up as we are."

They give their different versions of guilty curses, and I know exactly what they're all feeling because I'm feeling it too. Since the day Jax moved in next door at twelve, he became an unofficial member of the family. Hell, I'm pretty sure he was at the house more often than the boys were.

"He really didn't know?" Logan asks quietly, looking the worst out of all my brothers. Logan and Jax were the closest, especially when Jax started showing an interest in hockey and Logan took it upon himself to teach him all the tricks of the trade. To this day, their skating styles are still so similar it's scary.

"He had no idea," I tell him. "The last he heard, Mom was in the clear. He didn't even know the cancer had come back."

"Shit," Logan grunts.

"Come on, there's nothing we can do to fix it right now," Sean says, just as devastated. "Let's go visit Mom and Dad and then we can make good with Jax later."

Sean gets up and pays the bill while Logan slips out quickly to make a call, probably to the new girlfriend.

"It was Jax, wasn't it?" Carter asks as I scoot out of the booth.

"What?" I ask, a little confused.

"The guy in your bed this morning. It was Jax."

"Maybe it was, maybe it wasn't," I tease with a knowing smirk.

"Cass. Answer the damn question. Do I need to kick his ass or not?" he asks, following me out of the booth.

"If you're going to start getting protective over my virtue, then you should have kicked his ass back when I was fifteen," I grin, turning around and giving him a teasing wink only to see him stop dead in his tracks, his jaw hanging open and unsure how to respond.

I laugh as I push through the door, snatch the keys out of Logan's unexpecting hands, and climb into the driver's seat of the biggest truck I've yet to drive. I lock the driver's door behind me preventing any of my idiot brothers from ruining my plan. "Get in, fuckers," I holler out the window as I bring this beast to life and feel the rumble of the engine beneath me. "We've got a date with the parents."

CHAPTER 6

JAXON

I get up on Monday morning and meet the boys for our daily run. As usual, I'm the first one here, so I get some stretches out of the way.

"Hey," Bobby says, the next to arrive. "Where the fuck have you been all weekend?"

"Nowhere," I grunt.

"Really?" he smirks. "So, you weren't stalking Cass at the library and then fucking her all night?"

"I don't know what you're talking about," I say as the memories of Cassie's naked body riding me come slamming back to the forefront of my mind. The soft curve of her body. Her back arched as she threw her head back. The way she exploded around me, that tight cunt squeezing my cock. Fuck yeah.

"Oh, well, Brianna called yesterday. She said, and I quote, 'It was so fucking intense that I nearly came just from listening.' " I can't help but smirk, which has Bobby scowling at me. "Seriously? You had to fuck her with my sister in the house?"

I hate the way he describes it as a fuck. It was definitely not just a fuck. It was something more, something on a deeper level, a connection between two people. "Dude, sorry," I laugh, really not sorry at all. "I had no idea she was home."

He rolls his eyes but moves right along. "You really think going there with Cass was a good idea?" he asks.

Hell fucking yeah, it was.

"What's that supposed to mean?" I ask, standing a little straighter and turning to face him. Why's it his business what goes on between me and Cass? She's not his girl for fuck's sake.

"Dude, it's clear you both still have some sort of unresolved feelings for each other. I just don't think she's a one-night-stand kind of girl." He continues at the blank look on my face. "Does she want to get back together?" he asks. "Because you and I both know that's not who you are anymore."

Yeah, that's for damn sure. The person I used to be died three years ago, leaving behind a shell of a man with abandonment issues who screws random chicks to fill the void.

"I don't know," I shrug. "I doubt it."

"Do you want her back?" he asks slowly as his brow rises, curiosity gleaming in his eyes and once again making me wonder what the fuck it is to him.

"I used to, not anymore," I grunt. "I'm not the same person she once knew. A lot has changed since then."

"You know chicks, man. Sleeping with her is giving her false hope that something could happen between you. If you're not planning on getting back with her then you should back off," he suggests, probably so the fucker can make room for himself. "She's a nice girl and you're going to hurt her."

"Fuck man, it was one night. She knows what's up."

"You sure?" he asks, giving me a pointed stare as the rest of the guys reach us.

My mind swirls. The last person on earth I would ever hurt is Cass, but maybe Bobby is right. Perhaps sleeping with her wasn't the best idea, but what can I say? We were always so good together, especially when it came to sex. I can't say that I'm disappointed. She absolutely rocked my world Saturday night, just like she has a million times before. Call it taking a stroll down memory lane for old times' sake.

But . . . if I go back she might think that something could happen. Sure, there's a shitload of unresolved feelings, and sure, I might screw every brunette I come across just trying to get her out of my system, but when it comes down to it, Cass and I are over. She made sure of that three years ago and because of that, I'm done.

I'll get my answers and that's it. She's out of the picture for good. It will suck seeing her on campus, moving on, and dating other guys. But it's only one year and then I'm out of here, off to the fucking NHL.

"Yeah, man. She knows."

Or at least, she will.

I let out a sigh before taking off and putting an end to the conversation, and the boys fall in behind me, getting stuck into our training.

An hour and a half later, I'm pushing through my front door with Shorty and Aaron on my heels. Shorty and I collapse in the living room while Aaron detours to the kitchen. He comes back with three bottles of water and tosses one to each of us.

"Thanks, man," I murmur as my heart rate begins to drop back to normal.

"Mmm," he grunts, falling into the space beside Shorty and putting his feet up on the coffee table.

Shorty immediately falls into a deep sleep, and I roll my eyes as I pull my phone out of my pocket. My eyes widen as I check the time. "Shit," I hiss as I get to my feet and launch myself over the back of the couch. Aaron watches me with a questioning stare, and I decide to do him a solid and clue him in. "Our business lecture starts in twenty minutes, dude."

"Damn it," he groans, slowly getting to his feet then thinking better of it and collapsing back on the couch. "Fuck it. I can't be bothered today."

"Fine by me, but keep in mind, a skipped class equals a benched game in Coach's book and you can bet your ass he'll be checking up on it this year," I remind him.

"Shit." He gets to his feet again with a look of pure defeat on his face. Just as well, the kid needs as much time in a classroom as he can get. I think he took one too many pucks to the head as a kid.

With a satisfied smirk, I bound up the stairs and launch myself into the shower, before getting dressed and scarfing down some breakfast. Hell, I even manage to get to class before the professor begins his lecture.

From then on, the day drags by with images of Cassie's sweet ass circling my brain, which are then overtaken with devastating memories of her parents. By the afternoon, I welcome hockey practice with open arms. I step into the locker room and start grabbing my shit out of my bag to get suited up.

The boys are busy giving one of the freshman kids a hard time for striking out with one of the figure fairies out in the lot, and I can't help the smile that spreads across my face. This year truly is going to be amazing. Assuming I can get Cassie out of my head, of course. Give me a few weeks and a long list of fresh chicks to screw, and I'll be just fine.

I step onto the ice and the boys follow suit, instantly jumping into our routine and getting started on our warm-up. The boys are already working up a sweat and pushing themselves to their limits when a figure by the entrance catches my attention.

I bring myself to a stop, spraying an avalanche of shavings across the ice as I stare back at him.

What does this fucker want?

Coach notices the newcomer and watches him as though he's seeing a ghost before a bright smile cuts across his face. Coach makes his way to meet him, but the newcomer's stare is locked and loaded on me, daring me to step forward. Anger flares through me, and I clench my jaw as I begin slowly gliding forward.

Coach notices and with a nod, lets the scene play out. I rip off my helmet and make my way toward the edge of the barrier, completely unsure what the hell could be going on. Though I have one nagging idea that circles my head. I hear the sound of the boys' drills slowly come to a standstill before the gasps and shocked curses begin. But all that matters is the face staring back at me and the desperate need to pummel my fist into it.

"You lost?" I ask Logan as he watches me with a strange mix of unease and brotherly affection. I pull my gloves off and set them on the edge of the barrier just in case it comes down to a fight. After all, you never know with this guy. We've been known to get into it a few times, though for the first time, the playing field is finally equal.

He raises his chin and ignores my snappy attitude. "Sorry, kid," he says with his heart on his sleeve, stepping up before me to keep as much of our conversation as private as possible. "We thought you knew."

I cross my arms over my chest, knowing he's talking about his parents. Shit, the people I classify as *my* parents. I know this is not a conversation I want to have in front of my boys, but it's here, and it's happening right now whether I like it or not. "How could I have known? None of you fuckers have spoken to me in three years," I grunt, taking an angry breath as my voice raises. "Fuck, man. I haven't even been home since I left. How the fuck was I supposed to know?"

"We know that now. We all fucked up. Cass, too," he says, honesty shining through his eyes.

"Seriously?" I ask, not impressed.

"Shit, Jax. I'm trying to apologize here. Lose the fucking chip on your shoulder," he says, putting me back in my place, the same way he used to when Cass and I would get up to no good. "We fucked up. None of us reached out. We wanted to give you space when you left for college, and before we knew it, the cancer was back and we were all preoccupied. Our minds were solely on Mom and helping her get through it. We assumed that you would know. I don't know, I guess my thoughts were your parents would have said something. But then you didn't show, and you know how we get. We all took it as you telling us to get fucked."

"You're shitting me, right?" I practically growl, no longer giving a shit if the boys can hear me. "Had I known she was that bad, I would have been there every fucking day. You assholes stole that from me. *She was my mom too*. You guys were my brothers and Cass, well, who the fuck knows about that, but I would have been there either way. Instead, she passed thinking that I wasn't there for her. That I didn't care enough to come and visit her, and now I'm left with fucking no one! Each and every one of you turned your backs on me. I had nothing." By this stage, I feel like curling up into a ball and crying like a fucking bitch as all the old scars are torn wide open, right along with the new ones.

The thoughts had been running through my head since the moment I found out Cass' parents had died, and fuck, it feels good to finally get it out and be able to point my anger at one of the people who deserve it most. I thought I'd never see this guy again, never get the chance to let this out. Even though my heart still aches for them, it also feels like a weight is finally being lifted off my shoulders.

As soon as the words settle between us, the anger disappears with it, leaving behind only the ache of missing the people I loved as parents. As Logan notices the change within me, he steps forward and wraps his arms around me, pulling me in tight. "I'm sorry, brother," he says with sincerity as he holds me against him, not letting me go. "I don't know how, but I promise you, we'll make it up to you. I swear to you, kid. We were blinded by everything that was going on. We had no clue you were hurting so bad. We could have taken that away. We should have reached out, but instead, we stabbed you in the back in the worst way."

He lets me go, and I give him a slight nod, letting him know that I truly hear his words. He has made his peace, and now we can start working on mending that bridge that was torn down three years ago.

Coach watches on and can clearly see that whatever needed to happen here is done and makes his way over. "Logan Waters, what the hell are you doing in my training session?"

Logan instantly switches to his usual charming self and gives Coach a warm grin. "Thought I'd come and make sure you weren't screwing up the guys' chances of defending their title," he smirks.

"Watch it, Logan," Coach warns. "Just because you're a big hotshot now, doesn't mean that I won't still snap you in half."

"Like to see you try, old man," Logan replies fondly. "What do you say I get on and show these dimwits how a real man plays hockey?"

"Fuck me," Coach groans with a shake of his head before letting out a heavy sigh. "I'm going to regret this." And with that, he gives Logan a nod and turns away.

Logan grins before disappearing toward the locker rooms to get ready at the rink he called home for his whole college career. I can't help but feel a deep-rooted excitement pumping through my body. I grew up skating with Logan, and having the chance to do it again . . . fuck.

I skate back toward the boys when I pass Coach, and he stops me with a curious stare. "You know Waters?" he asks, clearly very fond of the dickhead.

"Sure do, Coach. We go way back," I say, pulling my gloves and helmet back on.

He lets out a frustrated sigh as he considers my response. "I should have known. Your technique is nearly identical. Bad habits and all."

I scoff, shaking my head, knowing he's fucking with me. "You know damn well my technique is near perfect. Not a bad habit in sight." Coach rolls his eyes, and with a smirk, I turn to face a bunch of little bitches, all starstruck by one of their idols. "Quit drooling," I tell the boys, "You've got drills to run, and please, for the love of all that's holy, don't make me look like a fucking dropkick in front of Logan Waters. I'll never live it down."

With that, the boys get straight back into training. After all, we have our first game of the season coming up at the end of the week, and these bastards need to be ready. Like Logan said, we have a title to defend.

Within seconds, Logan is on the ice and the boys kick it up a notch, but it doesn't take them long to realize they still have a shitload to learn. They may be kings here in college, but compared to the NHL, they're nothing but amateurs.

Logan kicks their asses while giving them as much encouragement as possible, the same way he had done for me when I was a kid. It's surreal having him share the ice with me again, but it feels right. Comforting, almost.

It's crazy to see in person just how much he has improved since the last time I played against him. Though, I guess that's expected when he's played for the NHL for the past four years. He gives the boys a few tricks of the trade, and I watch as Coach gives Logan the look of a proud father.

The session comes to an end and we pile off the ice. "You're a good choice for captain," Logan says as he takes off his skates. "I can see how much you've improved. You've got what it takes."

"Thanks," I nod as he stands beside me.

"I've got to run," he says, grabbing his things then looking at me hesitantly. "Look, I know it's not my place to say," he starts. "I have no idea what's going on between you two or what even happened three years ago, but Cass is all we have left. I know it's hard and probably really sucks, but look out for her, okay? Keep her out of trouble."

"You know I will," I say, getting up and giving him a quick goodbye. "See you around, man."

"Alright. Thanks, kid. I'll see you later," he says, pulling me in for a quick hug and clapping me on the shoulder. With a grateful nod, he turns toward the locker room door, gives Coach a quick goodbye, and disappears.

I stare after him, dumbfounded. I was not expecting my afternoon to turn out like this.

I've got my brothers back, kind of. While that road is still bumpy as shit, it's still there, and that's all that matters. A sense of relief comes over me, and for the first time in a long time, I start to feel content, like a piece of my heart has been returned to me. Almost like a missing puzzle piece has finally found its place.

CHAPTER 7

CASSIE

"**C**ome on," Brianna whines as she pulls a brush through her dark hair. "You've been sulking for days. Just tell me what happened already so I can make it better."

"You already know what happened," I shoot back. "And besides, I haven't been sulking."

"Whatever," she scoffs, dropping into the seat opposite me and pulling her legs up under her. "You've been a complete loser all week. And as for knowing what happened, there's a difference between witnessing the walls shake from the next room due to your intense screwing and actually knowing what's going on."

"Ugh," I groan. "If I tell you, will you leave it alone?"

She considers my question for the slightest moment. "No.

Probably not," she answers honestly.

"You're so annoying," I grunt, "but fine."

She squeals in excitement and grabs a cushion off the floor to get comfortable for story time. "There honestly isn't much to tell," I warn her.

"I don't care. I want all the juicy details, right down to how much things have changed in the downstairs area," she grins, holding up her hands and making estimations of the size of Jax's dick. But at least that means she's one of the few girls who hasn't had the pleasure of being screwed by Jaxon Payne.

"First of all, Jax is Jax. Do you think he would be as popular with all the sluts on campus if he was lacking in the equipment area?" I ask with a raised eyebrow.

"Hmm, I suppose not. Though there really isn't any point in having great equipment if the guy doesn't know how to use it."

"Trust me, he definitely knows how to use it," I say, unable to hold back my grin as all the steamy memories come rushing back, making me needy for more.

"Yeah, I kind of figured. You know, by the way you were screaming his name. I've faked many orgasms in my time, and I tell you, that was not fake."

"Oh my God," I grunt in embarrassment.

"Shit, I should have made some popcorn for this conversation," she muses. "But get on with it. I'm dying over here."

"Fine," I mutter, rolling my eyes. "So, he completely bombarded me at work on Saturday after some skank told him where to find me,"

I say, giving her a pointed look.

She shrugs her shoulders. "What can I say? The man is very charming. He does this thing with his eyes and, ugh, I caved like a bitch in heat."

I roll my eyes and continue my story. "Anyway, I was completely unprepared. I mean, I had everything figured out for if I saw him on campus, but I was not expecting him to show up at the library, so I froze."

I tell her how we talked in the back room about my parents and how we held each other searching for comfort. I explain getting locked in the library, jumping out the damn window, getting caught in the freaking storm, and my car getting locked in the parking lot, all to Bri's delight.

"Your life is like a movie," Bri comments.

"Jax insisted on taking me home. You know, Jaxon Payne, always the hero, making sure the damsel is safe and sound. So I said that I'd get him a towel, but instead of staying out here," I say, motioning to the living room, "he followed me down the hallway, found my room, and saw a few of the things that I'd been holding onto and . . . then he touched me."

"Oh, shit, I just got shivers. But you're going to have to clarify what kind of touch it was," Bri interjects.

I think back to that moment, how his eyes gazed into mine and he lifted his hand slowly, making his intention clear. I know without a doubt that I won't be able to explain this the right way, so I get to my feet. Bri looks at me with a confused, blank expression. "Get up," I tell her. She does as she's told but still watches me with an odd curiosity until I clarify, "I can't explain it, so I'm going to show you what happened."

"Yes," she says, pumping her fist in the air.

"Alright, you're me," I tell her then give instructions to take her hair out and squat down a little so the height difference between us would be correct. She gives me an excited nod and puts on a dreamy face as she bats her eyelashes at me. "I do not look like that."

"Shut up and get the show on the road."

I can't help but laugh at her excitement as I put on the show of a lifetime. I focus on her eyes, giving her the same lustful look that Jax had given me. Though at this point, I already had goosebumps covering my whole body. I take the two agonizingly slow steps toward her, letting her see his intentions as my eyes continue to bore into hers.

Finally reaching her, I tilt my head down before slowly raising my hand and gently pushing her hair behind her ear. My hand trails down the side of her face and down her arm as I shuffle my body closer to hers. "Holy shit," she murmurs. "You're going to get me all hot and bothered if you keep going."

At that, I crack up and step back out of her personal space. "Yeah, well imagine how I felt."

"Fuck. Yeah, you would have been screwed."

"Literally."

"I'm sorry. I know you don't want to hear this, but I've seen him in action, picking up countless girls, and not once has he looked at one of them the way you just looked at me. I hate to be the one to tell you, but that boy is still in love with you."

I shake my head before she has even finished her sentence. "No, there's no way. He made it pretty clear that it was a one-time deal. I broke his heart. No, I shattered it, and I have to deal with those consequences."

"Babe," she says, regret in her voice and sadness in her eyes. "I think there's still something there."

"There'll always be something there, but it's different now. It's not the same as it used to be. I don't know, it almost felt like the goodbye we didn't get three years ago," I explain. "And besides, he's so close to his dream of being in the NHL, he doesn't need me around screwing it up."

"Well, with all due respect to Jaxon," she starts. "He's a great player, but I'm pretty sure he needs a girl like you around to keep him grounded. He's most likely going to screw the wrong chick and get himself in trouble, then he can kiss the NHL goodbye."

"Probably," I grunt in agreement. "But there's no hope. I broke his heart in a big way, and I don't think he will ever forgive me for leaving him. Hell, I don't think I'll ever forgive myself."

"Okay, well, answer me this," she says, placing her hands on my shoulders and looking me straight in the eyes. "Are you physically and emotionally able to get through the day knowing he will never be a part of your life?"

"No," I sigh. "That's not something I can live with."

"Okay," she continues. "Are you still madly in love with him?"

I look her squarely in the eyes as I answer. "Yes, Bri. You know I am."

"Do you want him back?"

With a sad, resigned sigh I answer. "Yes. I want him back."

"Good," she smiles. "Then the new plan is to weasel your way back in. Go to every party. Make yourself known on campus. Become his best friend for all I care, but be present. The boys run every morning around campus and now, so do we. You need to show him that you are here to stay and that you will do whatever it takes to earn his forgiveness. Hell, even if we have to play dirty games. We'll make that boy sweat if we have to."

"Sounds like a great plan, Bri," I say with a sad smile. "But this is Jaxon Payne. Biggest manwhore on campus. He isn't the same guy he used to be, and that's my doing. Getting him back is not going to be as simple as that."

"It is that simple, Cass. I think the old Jaxon is still in there, and I'm sure after the other night, there's no doubt in your mind that he's still in there. He's just hurting, and he needs you to take it away."

"You really think that?" I sigh, already knowing she's right.

"Yeah, babe. I do."

"I don't know. I think it's a lost cause. I've screwed up too much."

"Look, the way I see it, you can sit around here, fucking around each week and avoiding him, or you can go out there and give yourself the best damn chance of getting your man back. Yes, you fucked up. Yes, he's angry and hurt, but you have this chance to earn his forgiveness and make things right. Or would you rather regret it in ten years when you're marrying Tom from accounting and having 2.5 kids?"

"Fuck you," I groan. "Why did I have to go and move in with the one person who could make me see reason? This sucks."

"So?" she asks slowly. "You're going to fight for him?"

"Yes, I'm going to fight for him," I say, mimicking her annoying voice and feeling like a complete dork saying it out loud.

Bri's face lights up like the Fourth of July. "Oh, hell yeah," she says, jumping up and running to the kitchen.

"If this backfires, I'm blaming you," I call after her.

"Get stuffed. The only way this is going to backfire is if you screw it up again, and there's no way in hell I'm about to let you do that. I'm telling you, that boy still loves you. It's your job to make him realize it," she says, coming out of the kitchen with a bottle of wine and a bag.

"What's that for?" I ask, eyeing the booze and bag suspiciously.

"We're going out this afternoon, and you're going to need this," she says, holding up the booze, "to make you do this." A wicked gleam lights her eyes as she hands me the bottle of wine and starts digging through the bag. "We're going to get your sexy on."

"Ahh, what?" I ask in confusion.

"When was the last time you got screwed?" she asks, then adds, "And I'm not talking about the pounding you got from the man of the hour."

I know she won't give in until I answer her question, so I take a deep breath and confess. "A while," I tell her. She looks at me with a raised eyebrow. "Okay, okay. A really long while."

With a smirk, she pulls out two tiny black crop tops and the tiniest little schoolgirl skirts. I'm completely confused until she pulls out a matching pair of hooker heels. I let out a groan, but she beams up at me. "That's right, bitch. We're going pole dancing, and you're going to remember what it feels like to be sexy. So, chug that wine and get dressed. We're leaving in ten." And with that, she disappears down the hallway and closes her door behind her.

Well, fuck.

Glancing down at the tiny clothes sitting on the coffee table, I let out a loud groan, hoping she can hear my frustration from her room. I crack the lid of the wine and take a big gulp. She was right, I'm most definitely going to need this.

Grabbing the clothes and the ridiculously high heels, I make my way to my bedroom and with another gulp of wine, I get dressed. After battling the ridiculous crop top for way too long, I stand in front of the mirror, the face staring back at me absolutely horrified. I look like a cheap whore. Just to add insult to injury, I put on the hooker heels and have to laugh. This is ridiculous.

Bri comes in at the sound of my laugh and gives me an approving whistle. I shake my head as I notice how her ass all but hangs out the bottom of the tiny schoolgirl skirt. "Oh, shut up. We look like a pair of hookers," I say, taking another drink of wine, only to have it taken from my hand as Bri does the same.

"No," she argues. "We look like a couple of badass bitches who are about to get you your man back."

With a shake of my head, I pull a tank over the top and grab a pair of sweatpants before switching out the hooker heels for a pair of flip-flops. I stuff the heels into my bag and wait for Bri to do the same.

"Ready?" she calls out from the kitchen.

"Yep," I murmur, grabbing the bottle of wine off my bedside table and heading out to meet her before locking up the house.

Since it's a beautiful day, we walk and become best friends with the bottle, and by the time we're pushing through the door of the dancing studio, the bottle is just about finished. Hell, now that there's alcohol pulsing through my system, I'm pretty damn excited about this. It's something I've always wanted to try but never had the guts to do.

We introduce ourselves to our instructor and she directs us to the other group of beginners, who have already started to rid themselves of their clothes. Bri and I follow suit and strip off our tanks and track pants while doing our best to hold in our tipsy giggles. I kick off my flip-flops and find my bag as Bri does the same, only to start wobbling as we try to pull on our hooker heels.

The second we're ready to go, we take a look at ourselves in the mirror, which covers the full front of the room. "I've got to say, Bri, I'm excited now," I tell her.

Her eyes glisten with excitement. "I knew you would be."

As the rest of the girls finish getting themselves ready, we crouch down around my bag and sneak another swig from the wine bottle. I stand up a little too quickly and realize I'm probably a little tipsier than I thought, but I honestly couldn't care less.

Bri notices the happy glaze in my eyes, and I giggle seeing the same look in hers. Yeah, this is going to be fun.

The instructor pumps us all up and says she's ready to get into it, then turns to put on some music as we spread out through the room and find ourselves a pole. Bri and I head to the back of the room to keep ourselves out of the limelight, knowing damn well this will only end in disaster.

Our spot is right by a massive window, but for once I can't seem to care. Instead, all we can manage to do is giggle like school girls at the intrigued faces of the men and women walking by.

Our instructor gets us started off with a sexy warm-up dance that has us swaying our hips, smacking our thighs, bending low, and shaking our asses. Even though we can hardly keep up with the moves, we're both having the time of our lives.

We watch as the instructor places a hand on her pole, positions her feet, and allows herself to spin around it. I gawk in awe. I know it's super basic, but I'm fucking impressed. Bri and I give each other a grin before taking hold of our poles and giving it a try. We both drastically fuck up our first time, but after trying it a few more times, we eventually get the hang of it.

Next, we move on to learning how to climb the pole, which manages to sober me up real fucking fast. I mean, damn, this shit is hard, but my determination is strong. So far it has proven to be an amazing workout, and I know my arms, stomach, and thighs will be killing me come tomorrow. Hell, I'll probably be feeling it by later this afternoon.

We're about an hour in when we start learning the really cool stuff, like flipping upside down and something the instructor calls a superman move, and I can't believe how much I'm enjoying myself. The majority of the booze has worn off, but I don't need it anymore.

There are women of all shapes and sizes in here, and not one has turned up her nose at another or watched another with lustful eyes. It makes me feel like this is a place I would happily come back to. The whole place is a vibe, and I'm grateful that Bri forced me into this.

I turn to Bri, who's currently upside down on the pole but struggling to find grip and slowly sliding down. "Thanks," I smile, knowing that without her, this never would have happened. I'd be sitting at home, sulking about Jax and how I haven't spoken to him in nearly a week. Instead, I'm here, upside down on a stripper pole, getting my sexy back with a plan to get my man back.

"What do you say about making this a weekly class?" She grins as she attempts that last move again.

"You've got yourself a deal," I reply before getting back into my own moves.

CHAPTER 8

JAXON

Bobby and I sit in his truck on the way to the ice rink for our first game of the season when we're stopped by the afternoon roadwork. "For fuck's sake," Bobby groans, looking out his window with a bored expression. "Why do they have to do this on a weekday and always at the worst time? What's wrong with weekends or nights?"

I nod my head, not really caring about his issues with the roadwork. They've been doing them for the past three months. It's not like he didn't know they would be here, and yet he still came this way instead of taking the back streets like I suggested. Though, I don't think an *I told you so* would be appreciated right now.

I gaze out my window as the jittery excitement for the first game of the season starts to take over. We're supposed to meet Coach Harris and the boys early so Coach can go over our game plan for the night. I'm sure he'll give us all one of his famous pep talks, which we know is going to consist of *Get out there and show them who has the biggest set of balls*. Throw in a few curse words, and it's just like the many he'd given last season and the seasons before that.

Movement in a store window catches my eye, and an appreciative grin crosses my face as I see a fine-looking ass up in the air. A tiny little schoolgirl skirt barely covers her ass, with a pair of legs poking out that I'd happily have wrapped around my face. "Fuck yeah, man," I grin, slapping Bobby across the chest and hoping my ability to appreciate this chick means I'm finally starting to put Cassie out of my head. "Class is in session."

He turns to look at what's caught my eye when the same appreciative smile takes over his face. The chick on the pole changes her position and makes her body slowly spin as she leans back, thrusting her perfect tits into the air for the men of the world to see.

Yes, please. This chick is seriously every man's fantasy, and I have to have her.

There's movement behind the girl, but I don't take my eyes off her as I wait ever so patiently for the girl to finish spinning to give me a good look at her face, so I can find her after the game and take her home.

"Is that?" I hear Bobby distantly questioning, but I can't be fucked to hear him out. After all, I'm on a mission.

A wave of chestnut hair finally starts to come into view, and I wait on the edge of my seat for my midnight snack to show her face.

And then finally, there it is.

My jaw drops before I have time to register anything else. "Oh, fuck no," I roar. I should have fucking recognized that sweet ass waving through the sky. After all, I've nailed it a million times before. I'm out of Bobby's truck and storming toward the dance studio before I even know what I'm doing.

The triplets would murder me if they knew I let her take this class for the whole fucking world to see. Fuck, not to mention how her father would be rolling in his grave. He'd haunt me for this.

Cassie's beautiful face finally connects with mine through the glass, and the giggly grin instantly disappears, replaced with shock and embarrassment. I must admit, seeing her this happy has my heart hurting, knowing I'm about to burst through her happy bubble. But there's no way I'm letting this shit go down.

I push through the door and head straight for her before she has a chance to get off the pole. There's movement behind me, and I realize Bobby has stormed in, his heavy stare locked further through the room. It must be Brianna. She's the only one who could get a reaction like that out of the guy.

Barely a second has passed before I reach her. "Wait. Jax. What are you—" I grab Cassie around the waist and pull her off the pole before throwing her over my shoulder. I grab a bag that I assume is hers and storm straight out the door while the instructor rolls her eyes, probably more used to this than any dance instructor should be.

I find Bobby's truck still sitting in the middle of the road—now the new reason for the held-up traffic—and I tear open the backseat before throwing Cassie in and slamming the door closed behind me.

I take a shaky breath and try to let go of the raging anger that rapidly courses through me as I get back in the front passenger seat. Bobby seems to be doing exactly the same thing as he gets in beside me, gripping the steering wheel with white knuckles.

I have no idea what possessed me to do that. She isn't my girlfriend anymore, and apart from the fact her brothers would rip me a new one, I just can't explain it. She's a free woman. If she wants to put her body on display for everyone to see, then that's her decision. It has absolutely nothing to do with me, but the thought of allowing that to happen has me shaking with rage.

I glance at her through the rearview mirror, and I can tell by the way she's silently fuming while clenching her jaw that she's about to burst.

Three, two, one.

"WHAT THE ACTUAL FUCK, JAXON?" Cassie yells at me from the backseat while Brianna gets stuck into Bobby. I turn around in my seat to look at her and nearly have to look away from the anger burning in her eyes. Although it's not because I hate to see her angry or upset, but seeing her this way, all feisty and ready to scream, is enough to have me wanting to fuck her right here and now.

"Look at yourself, Cass. You look like a cheap whore. I didn't realize you'd taken up residence on the street corner."

"Oh, shit," I hear Bobby grunt.

Her mouth drops in shock before the anger takes over once again.

She launches forward with her arms flailing around, trying to hit me, but she can't get to me because the headrest is in the way. A smirk crosses my face, which only has her fuming more. "Did you just call me a fucking prostitute, Jaxon Alexander Payne? And a fucking cheap one at that?"

Shit. She used the middle name. Maybe I took that one too far. "Cass," I sigh. "You know I didn't mean that, but look at yourself. What the hell do you think you're doing on that pole?"

"It's called having fun, Jaxon. Something I haven't had since I've been here," she snaps. "Besides, what's it to you? You're the last person I'd expect to have an issue with a girl on a pole. Isn't that your specialty now?"

I know there's no point in talking to her when she gets like this, so I turn on Brianna. "Has she been drinking?"

"Um, yes. How else do you think I got her to do it?" she throws back at me.

"Fuck," Bobby groans as he searches out his sister's eyes in the mirror. "You've been drinking too."

"So what?" Cassie practically growls. "Take us home."

"No." I shoot back, "You're coming with us."

"Why? You want me to dance for your boys?" she purrs, leaning forward and draping herself over the back of my seat. "You know, despite your comments, I'm not as cheap as you think. It'll cost them, but if they've got the dough, I'm willing to offer a good ride. I might even suck a dick or two if they're lucky."

My jaw clenches at the mere thought of Cassie getting with any of those bastards. "Fuck, Cass. We're not taking you home because I refuse to be late for the first game of the season, especially over this shit."

Cass and Brianna start grunting and moaning in the backseat and it's almost comical to watch. They're like a couple of kids throwing a tantrum. Cass peels off her high heels, tossing them around the truck and making sure to nail me in the back of the head before sliding her skirt down her hips while Brianna does the same.

Bobby and I give the girls a moment of privacy, and I'm pleased when I glance back to find them both in sweatpants and flip-flops. But they still have their little tops on. "Don't you have a shirt to wear?" I ask them.

"We do, but there's no point in putting them on. A cheap shirt isn't going to keep us warm in a damn ice rink," Cass informs me with as much attitude as she can possess, and I bite my tongue to keep from mentioning that at least the top wouldn't be showing the whole world how perfect her tits are.

Bobby lets out another unimpressed groan. "Pretty sure I have something in the back that you can wear, Bri," he calls over his shoulder. "I have my away jersey that Cass can throw on too."

With that settled, we sit in uncomfortable silence as we ride the rest of the way to the ice rink. What feels like a lifetime later, we pull up in a parking space, and I hop out to grab my shit from the back. I consider lending her my away jersey, but I'm far too selfish for that shit.

Cass gets out and purposely rubs her naked stomach across my body, making me yearn for her touch once again, leaving me no choice but to ball my hands into fists and shove them deep in my pockets.

Bobby holds out the jersey for her and she reaches across me to take it from him with her tight stomach brushing past me again. I take a step back to give her more room, but really, I think the room is for me. She pulls Bobby's jersey over her head and, looking at his name and number on her back, I've never wanted to tear clothes off her so damn fast.

Cass steps up to me and gives me a sweet, innocent look, placing her hand on my shoulder and stretching up onto her toes. "Have a good game, Captain," she whispers seductively, pressing a light kiss to my cheek and turning around to meet Brianna at the front of the truck.

Bobby gives me a knowing shake of his head as we follow the girls into the ice rink. "Fuck, these two are going to be trouble," he says. I nod in agreement, but I can't help but watch as Cassie walks before me. A scowl sits heavily on my face as I get another look at Bobby's jersey. It shouldn't matter to me, but I don't like it. It doesn't feel right. I know she isn't my girl, but if any chick around here was ever going to wear my jersey, it would be her.

We get through the doors and the girls disappear into the grandstands. Something screams at me to pinpoint where exactly in the grandstand she will be, but I shake the thought from my head. It's none of my business where she is and what she'll be doing.

We get into the locker room to find Coach going over the game plan for tonight. He looks up as we enter, and we hardly get a nod before his attention is drawn straight back to the clipboard before him.

Over the next ten minutes, the rest of the boys come dawdling in.

When it looks like everyone is here, Coach instructs me to lead the guys in a warm-up. We can't afford any injuries this season, especially injuries created by stupidity. We spend the next half hour running drills down the hallway to warm up and shooting pucks into a knocked-over trash can, which due to lack of space in the locker room, isn't as easy as shooting into the goal with the slick ice beneath it.

The noise from the grandstand grows, and it's almost game time. "Alright, boys," I say, getting everyone's attention. "Let's get suited up and show these people we're still the rightful owners of that big motherfucking trophy."

They grunt out their approvals as we make our way to our individual lockers to get ready. "Cover up, boys," comes a familiar voice from the doorway. "I'm coming in."

A grin spreads wide across my face before I even see her face. Sophie comes crashing in with Tank, Miller, and Dani on her heels, making a few of the freshmen gasp and attempt to cover their junk. Though we seasoned players know that Sophie is going to get an eyeful no matter what you do to prevent it. It's inevitable. "Sorry, guys," Tank says, with a grin. "They refused to stay in the stands."

"I wouldn't have expected anything else," I laugh as Sophie and Dani barrel toward me, knocking me into the back of my locker with the force of their affection. I wrap my arms around them both and pull them in tight.

"Jaxon," Dani exclaims with a grin. "I've missed you."

"Same goes, Dani girl," I laugh before passing the girls onto

Bobby. Soon the rest of the guys have all lined up, waiting for their hug from the girls.

"You guys mind getting your filthy hands off my girl?" Miller says, trying his hardest to look unimpressed, but the gleam in his eyes makes it obvious he's happy to be here.

"What are you doing here, man?" I ask, stepping up to him and clapping his shoulder.

"Had to come and see if you were good enough to follow in my footsteps or if I'd made a terrible mistake," he says with a grin.

"Dude, I'm so fucking amazing that you'll be kicked off your team so they can make room for me," I joke.

He rolls his eyes but cracks a grin. "What's up, dude?" Tank says, coming over. "You ready for this?"

"Born ready, man," I tell him honestly.

"Good. Don't let all our hard work from last season go to waste," he says.

"I got this," I say as he holds his fist up. I bump mine against his and follow suit with Miller.

The boys say a quick hello to Coach Harris, and not long after, the crowd is going nuts, ready to see their defending champions in action. The sound prompts Miller to call out for Dani, while Tank grabs Sophie and throws her over his shoulder. They make their way out, leaving us to get ready for our big debut.

"Alright, boys," Coach says, getting our attention. "This is it. The start of our season, and we are going to do it right. Last season's Dream Team came to see if you lot are worthy of playing under the title of defending champions, so do not let them down. Do not let yourselves down, and do not let your fans down," he demands as he looks each and every one of us in the eyes.

"Now, we know we're the best, the fans know we're the best. Fuck, the homeless guy outside of Micky's Bar knows we're the best, but there are a bunch of cocky pricks in the other room thinking they have a chance against us, thinking they can take our championship away on game one." The boys start booing and begin getting amped up with Coach's speech. "Are you going to let them?" he demands, making the boys shout out their protests. "Are you going to defend your title? Are you champions?"

"YES," the boys shout.

"Are you Dragons?"

"YES."

"Are you ready?" he finally shouts.

"YES," we roar, outdoing the sound from the grandstand.

With that, Coach looks at me. "You've got big shoes to fill, Payne," he says.

"I got this, Coach."

"Good, now lead your team out."

I step up to the locker room door and the boys fall in behind me. I walk up the hallway and finally into the arena. The crowd goes nuts chanting the Dragon's war cry. With an outstanding introduction from the announcer, we take to the ice.

My eyes immediately lift to the grandstand and fall upon Cassie, who still wears an annoyed scowl. She narrows her gaze at me before turning away, no doubt still pissed about the whole pole dancing thing. But honestly, what did she expect me to do?

A strange, familiar feeling settles within me, and I realize it's the same feeling I used to get when Cass would come and watch my high school games, being my own personal cheerleader. It occurs to me that even though she may have caught some of our games on ESPN, this is the first time she's seeing me play in three years, and something inside of me really wants to impress her. I want to let her know exactly the kind of man she tossed away.

The referee takes to the ice and we fall into our positions. I look up at Cass one last time to see her attention is now solely focused on me. She has always been a sucker for hockey, no matter how angry she is with me. She will always remain glued to the game until the final second.

The whistle blows, and our first game of the season is underway.

CHAPTER 9

CASSIE

The blood courses through my veins as I sit in the grandstand and wait for the referee to drop the puck. I'm already on the edge of my seat, and I hate myself for being so excited. I'd rather sit here and sulk about what a jerk Jax has been rather than drool at the thought of getting to watch him play again. Well, in person, at least. I've stalked a few of his games online and kept up with the headlines.

Jax looks up at me just moments before the whistle blows, the same way he used to when we were kids. But instead of a loving smile, I get a smirk, and I know without a doubt that he can see the excitement in my eyes.

That asshole.

If ever there were a time when I wasn't so obvious, now would be great. The smirk is mostly hidden by his helmet, making it too hard to tell what he means by it, but my guess would be it's a big *fuck you*, taking enjoyment in my misery.

I desperately want to look away, but I can't. I'm too intrigued by the game, or maybe it's Jax that has my attention. Either way, I'm screwed.

His eyes lock on mine for an impossibly slow and agonizing moment before he snaps his attention back to the game.

Relief rushes through me, and I hate that I feel this way. I should be stronger. I've been away from him for three years, yet he still has this ability to pull me in. I'm the moth and he's the flame. He hasn't spoken to me all week, and suddenly he thinks he has the right to manhandle me and remove me from my dance class? I should be fuming. I get why he wouldn't want me to be seen in a skimpy outfit and dancing on a pole, but he doesn't want me, so why is it his business?

But instead of raging and storming out of here, I sit like a good little girl, excited to see him play. What the fuck is wrong with me? I desperately want to go along with Brianna's *fight for Jax* plan, but I feel he's too far gone. I ruined my chances when I left, and now I have to deal with it.

Bri is so damn confident that I'm going to win him back, but I know the real Jax. When I left, I broke him, and I don't know if he will ever come back from that. Don't get me wrong, I'm going to try with everything I have, but I'm terrified that it won't be enough. On the other hand, after his little stunt today, I might wait a week or two before I really start to try.

The whistle sounds and the game is on, taking my inner thoughts and anger away.

It's not even thirty seconds into the game and my jaw is already on the floor. Jax is amazing, and I mean a-freaking-mazing. I've watched as many games as I could over the last few years, but they don't do him justice. Last season was all about the Dream Team, but here, seeing him in the flesh and witnessing for myself just how much he has improved, is incredible.

Jax effortlessly steals the puck from the opposition, and I'm reminded of the time he played that same trick on me. It was deathly cold and he'd convinced me to go for a skate on the lake that ran behind our houses. Just like all the times before, he had let me think I was winning before swooping in and stealing the puck away. And just like all those times, I can imagine him underneath that helmet, laughing and taunting the other player about how simple it had been.

I watch in delight as he loops around the back of the goal and comes flying up the other end. My heart pounds as an opponent comes right for him with the intention of slamming him into the wall, but Jax sidesteps the guy with some impressive footwork and continues on his way.

Two more come for him, but Bobby's got his back. Then moments before the collision, Jax flicks the puck to Bobby, avoids being nailed by the opposition, and gets straight back into his rhythm. With Bobby facing a similar situation, he slides the puck back toward Jax, who passes it on to some kid who's charging up the center of the ice. The kid shoots the puck right into the back of the net, and the buzzer sounds, signaling the first goal of the game.

I can't help but get to my feet and cheer, my hands flying up as I start jumping up and down with the rest of the crowd. "Who's that kid?" I shout to Brianna over the noise.

"That's Xander. He's a new transfer. I don't really know anything about him, but man, he has some skills," she says proudly before getting back to cheering for Bobby.

I catch Jax's eye, and a smile is somehow pulled from my body. He beams back at me, clearly overtaken by excitement, but that smile breaks my heart. It's the very same smile he used to give me and, for a moment, I pretend he's the old Jax, the one who unashamedly loved me. The crowd finally settles down as the referee gets set up to continue, and once again, I find myself on the very edge of my seat.

The game continues at the same pace with Jax and his team annihilating the opposition. Brianna and I spend the whole game cheering and booing at all the right times, and by the end of the game, my throat is aching. The boys have come out champions, and I couldn't be prouder, no matter how much I try to hide it.

As everyone spills out of the grandstand, I jump up to join the line. "Where do you think you're going?" Brianna asks as she kicks her feet up onto the vacated chair in front of her.

"Um . . . home?" I ask, a little unsure.

"And how do you suppose you're doing that? The boys drove us here, remember?" she smirks.

Ahh, shit. In all the excitement, I'd completely forgotten.

Taking my seat beside her, we wait for the boys to make their way out of the locker room. The longer we sit here, the more I dread the awkward conversation that's sure to come up between me and Jax, but if I'm lucky, he won't be there, and Bobby can just slip out to drive us home.

Hope starts to course through me as I watch the exit that leads from the locker room, and shortly after, the boys start trickling out. Unfortunately, Jax walks out right beside Bobby. Damn it, that's what I get for wishful thinking.

Brianna grabs my hand and pulls me along as she rushes down the stairs toward the boys. She gives her brother a beaming smile as she crashes into him with a massive hug. "Congratulations," she squeals, jumping up and down in his arms and accidentally nailing him in the chin with her big-ass head. They both cringe in pain as she steps back out of his arms. "Ouch," she whines, rubbing her head.

"Yeah, no shit," Bobby replies, lifting his hand to his chin.

"Ahh," I say, wanting to be anywhere but here. "That was a great game," I say to the boys but keep my eyes trained on Bobby.

"Great?" he laughs. "It was fucking legendary."

His attitude is infectious and has the awkwardness fading away, right until Jax turns around when a few girls all but throw themselves at him. My gaze falls to the ground, my heart shattering once again.

Bobby notices and does what he can to get my mind off the impossible. "So, what are you girls doing tonight?"

"Well, I was hoping you were going to take us home," I say, preferably without the tagalong and his new bitches.

"Ahh, no," Bri interjects. "We're going out, but it would be cool if you could drop us home to get dressed first," she adds, fluttering her eyes at her twin brother.

"No way in hell," Bobby scoffs. "I'm not your chauffeur. If you want a lift then it's either home or to Micky's with us. I'm not waiting around for an hour while you girls do all your girly shit."

I watch in delight as Jax's back stiffens when Bobby suggests we tag along to Micky's, and a grin spreads wide over my face. There's no way he'd hook up with some chick while I'm there . . . right? "You know what, Bobby?" I start. "I think we'd love to come to Micky's with you."

Bri's face instantly lights up, and she gives me a stupid grin, knowing exactly what I'm doing. "I think that's a wonderful idea."

"Cool," Bobby says, our conniving ways going straight over his head.

Jax slowly turns with tonight's hussy firmly clinging to his arm. The sight kills me, but I ignore it as he narrows those gorgeous blue eyes on me. Game on. "What are you doing, Cass?" he questions in a low tone, the suspicion radiating off him.

I look at him as innocently as ever. "What do you mean? We're coming to celebrate with you guys."

"Don't bullshit me. I taught you that trick," he says as if he knows exactly what I'm up to.

I shrug my shoulders. "Don't stress, Jax. If you don't want me there, that's fine. I totally get it," I turn my attention to Bri. "What about that new club we were talking about? I know it's a bit seedy, but it should be fun." I ask, she gives me an excited nod, and I turn to

Bobby. "Could you drop us there?"

The boys' faces drop, and Jax steps out of the hussy's hold and takes a step closer to me. "Fuck, no. We're not taking you there," he practically growls.

I shrug innocently as I take Bri's hand and start to turn away. "Okay, I'm sure someone around here is heading that way. We'll catch a lift. See you guys later."

"Wait," Jaxon growls at my back. I smother my grin before turning back around with my brows arched in question. "Fine. Come to Micky's then."

"Oh, okay, sure," I smile and turn to leave. "We'll meet you guys outside."

Bobby nods while Jax watches me go, realizing he just got played.

"Hook, line, and sinker," Bri laughs as we head out the doors. "How the hell did you know he was going to fall for that?"

"Come on, you have to give me more credit than that," I say, looping my arm through hers as we head through the parking lot. "I grew up with three overbearing, overprotective big brothers, and Jax grew up idolizing them. He's like a carbon copy of all three of them. It's simple math really."

"Screw the math, it's fucking awesome."

"As if you've never manipulated Bobby like that," I say as we finally reach his truck and drop the tailgate to sit up in the bed.

"Yeah, I guess," she says. "He's overprotective but not nearly as bad as your brothers. Bobby would usually just let me tag along and then drive me home or shove me in an Uber when he thought I'd had enough."

I shake my head at her and give her a wide grin. "Not anymore, sister."

We wait a little while longer and eventually the boys stroll out of the ice rink looking like they own the place, but at least Jax seems to have ditched the hussy. My gaze greedily travels up and down Jax's body before he has time to notice and damn, he well and truly has become a man.

The boys dawdle purposefully slow while Bri and I watch them with unimpressed scowls. "Hurry up, you lazy asses," Bri calls out, earning herself a smirk from Bobby.

I sit and watch until they finally make it back to Bobby's truck. We trade places with the boy's hockey gear and jump out of the back. Not a word is spoken until we're on our way. "Xander was on fire," Bobby comments to anyone who'll listen.

"Yeah, he was," Jax agrees.

"Could be a good choice for captain next year," Brianna says.

Bobby snorts while Jax turns around to face her. "Don't get ahead of yourself," he laughs. "It's only the first game of the season."

"Just saying," she says. "He looked pretty damn good from where I was sitting."

"Why? Are you interested in the kid?" Bobby questions, eyeing his sister through the rearview mirror.

"No," she scoffs then eyes me with a knowing grin. "I have my eye on a much, much bigger prize."

"Like who?" Bobby asks, rolling his eyes.

"None other than the wickedly sexy Carter Waters," she announces proudly.

Jax turns to me for the quickest moment before he breaks into the type of laughter that almost heals my shattered heart. "You're fucking with me, right?" he asks Bri. "The guy is the biggest player around."

"I know," she grins. "Challenge accepted."

Jax scoffs, knowing just how much of a challenge that really is. "So, you think you're going to be the one to tame the beast?"

"Hell, yeah," she announces proudly. "With all the girls he has been with, can you imagine how good he would be in bed?"

"Fucking hell. I don't want to hear this shit," Bobby whines as he pulls into the parking lot and turns to face me in the back. "Can you talk some sense into her, please?"

I hold my hands up in surrender and grin. "Don't look at me, I've already tried," I tell him. "She knows all about the kind of guy he is, but do you think that changed her mind?"

"Hell to the no, motherfuckers," Bri announces. "That man is exactly what this bitch needs. Now quit whining, you can consider me officially warned," she adds before opening her door and hopping out. "I'm ready for a good time."

Bobby groans as the rest of us pile out of his truck, and we walk to the door listening to the twins arguing over Bri's undying love for Carter. Bobby reaches for the door and ushers us all in, and the moment I see the place, I fall in love with it.

The bar is packed with Dragon's fans who all stand and cheer as Jaxon and Bobby walk through the door. The boys grin and a beer is thrust into both their hands.

We follow along as the boys lead us to a massive table at the back of the bar, and I instantly recognize the rest of the team. They all start saying their hellos when two faces at the table draw my attention. "Hey, you're Miller and Tank," I say with a star-struck smile.

"Yeah, hi," Miller smiles while Tank just nods his head. "You're a fan?"

"Sort of," I say, "I'm . . ." I look toward Jaxon before thinking better of it. "Nobody, just, yeah. I guess I'm a fan."

"Oh, whatever," Bobby says, already halfway through his first beer. "This is Logan Waters' little sister."

"Shit, I'd say you're more than just a fan," Miller says as the rest of the boys at the table go quiet and start gawking at me. "I played with Logan for two years before he graduated. He was always talking about his little sister. Cassie, right?"

"That's right," I say as a warm smile crosses my face thinking about that big goofball. "I hope it was all good things."

"Mostly," Miller comments. "He said you were trouble."

Jax scoffs at that and finds a seat at the table. "That'd be right."

Miller smiles and then introduces me to his girlfriend, Dani, who then pulls Sophie into the mix.

"Tell me you're not on a date with Jaxon and falling for his charms?" Sophie questions, well on her way to being drunk.

"No," I laugh as Jaxon's gaze pierces right into mine. "He's just my old neighbor who wouldn't let me and Bri go out clubbing after the game."

Dani nudges Miller and gives me a sympathetic smile. "Sounds a lot like someone else I know," she says, eyeing her boyfriend.

I laugh and get pulled down into a chair beside them while Bri drops down on my other side. After more drinks than we can count, we're just as drunk as the girls are.

I feel Jaxon's eyes on me the whole night, scowling each time I accept a new drink, but I couldn't care less. I'm having the best time, and Jaxon is here at the table rather than searching for the girl he's going to be screwing later. Besides, the more drinks I accept, the deeper he scowls, and goddamn, I'm enjoying getting under his skin.

Sophie orders a few bottles of tequila and enough shot glasses to go around the table. "We're playing *Never Have I Ever,*" she declares to the table as Tank groans in protest.

I've heard of it, however never actually played, but by the looks of it, I'm in.

Catching the look on my face, Brianna leans over and whispers, "It's simple. A question will be asked and if it applies to you, you take a shot. The person with the bottle asks the question," she explains. "So really, it's a good way to find out people's dirty secrets."

"Sounds good," I laugh as Dani starts filling as many shot glasses as possible.

"Okay, me first," Sophie says with a grin as she grabs the bottle from Dani then makes a show of thinking about her question. "Alright, never have I ever . . . been arrested."

And just like that, the game gets started. All the boys except for the freshmen grab a glass and down their shots as my mouth hangs open in shock. How the hell could so many of these guys have been arrested? And then it dawns on me that it's most likely for public drunkenness after playing games like this.

Dani stands next and turns her devilish grin to Sophie. "Never have I ever had a threesome."

"Babe," Miller groans.

"Oh shit," Dani laughs. "I forgot you used to be a whore."

He shakes his head before scowling and grabbing a shot along with Jax, Miller, and Tank. But when Brianna leans across the table and grabs a glass, Bobby's eyes widen in a mix of anger and shock. I turn to her with a raised brow, but all she does is shrug her shoulders and down her shot, proud of her achievements.

I do my best to ignore the fact that Jax drank to that too. I always assumed he'd gone full manwhore, but still kind of hoped he had some sort of innocence to him. Dani passes the bottle around the table to me, and I stand just as the girls had before me. Narrowing my eyes on Jax in pure curiosity, I say, "Never have I ever had a foursome."

Regret flashes in his eyes as both he and Tank reach for a shot and throw them back to the delight of the table. As the boys start congratulating them, Brianna turns to me and I see the question in her eyes. "I'm fine," I murmur for only her to hear, but we both know it's a lie. I'm absolutely shattered by how different he's become.

With a nod, she takes the bottle from my hands and stands before giving her brother an evil smirk. He groans knowing something embarrassing is coming his way. "Never have I ever gotten drunk at a wedding and accidentally screwed my cousin."

"Ahh, fuck." Bobby's eyes close in embarrassment and his head hangs as the rest of the table bursts into howling laughter. Reluctantly, he reaches forward and takes his shot.

The game continues, and I'm lucky enough to only have had to take three shots by the time the bottle makes it to Jax. He grabs the bottle and stands, eyes firmly on mine with a heavy curiosity within them. "Never have I ever only slept with one person."

Shit. This wasn't something I wanted to dive into with him quite so soon, but here we are.

Keeping my eyes locked on his, I reach forward and take a shot, welcoming the burn that comes with it. I'm probably the only one at the table who drinks, but I'm too distracted to look. His eyes widen in shock before a mix of guilt and relief takes over.

I rip my stare away from his but suddenly don't feel like playing anymore. He takes his seat and passes the bottle, and the game continues. Putting on a fake smile, I do my best to pretend like I'm enjoying myself, but it's impossible, especially with the weight of his eyes still on me. The rest of the game turns extremely sexual, so lucky for me, I don't have to drink anymore, and I just sit back and watch, feeling as though I'm about to crumble.

The game ends and Sophie demands that she wants to dance, and naturally, Brianna is straight on her feet, pulling me along with her. Groaning, I get up and immediately wobble, realizing that I'm drunker than I thought, and I put Jax to the back of my mind. I'm here for a good time, and I'm not going to let Jax's question bring me down.

Letting Bri drag me along, we move out onto the dance floor and the music takes me away. I feel the vibration from the beat deep within my bones, and we dance and drink for what feels like hours, both Bobby and Jax scowling at us with every chance they get.

CHAPTER 10

JAXON

I sit at the table watching Cass dance with the girls, and I have no idea what to think. Do I want to go dance with her, rub my body up against hers, and feel the way her body would relax into mine like it used to? Hell yes. Do I do it? No. I can't because I'm still fucking stumped by her answer.

How the hell could she have gone three years without sleeping with anyone else? More importantly, why? I mean, I get what chicks are like. Right after a break-up, they don't want to throw themselves back out there. I get it, it's respectable. But three years without jumping in the sack with anyone? That, I don't understand.

Don't get me wrong, I'm thrilled about her answer. Insanely relieved actually, but I just don't get it. She was quick to climb into bed with me last weekend. I just assumed she might have been like that with all guys now. Not that I really want to think about it. Has she been holding out for me? That's the only thing that makes any kind of sense in my mind right now, but that's ridiculous. She left me.

I must admit, her answer made me feel like shit though. My responses during that stupid game have hurt her, almost like I was rubbing it in, and then to find out she's only ever been with me. Shit. I wanted to be upfront with her, to let her know exactly the kind of man I've become.

Movement catches my eye, and I turn my head to find Xander getting up from the table with a strange look on his face. He glances at his watch then double-checks it as if he's late for something, but what the hell could he be late for when it's coming up to midnight? "I'm out," he announces to the table.

Bobby catches my eye, and I see the same thoughts running through his mind, but I'm not in the mood to dig any further. "Alright man," I say. "See you later."

He gives a curt nod and swiftly disappears through the door, probably to meet up with some chick.

The moment he's gone, my stare is back on my girl. Fuck. I mean . . . shit. I have no idea what the hell she is to me, but calling her my girl even though we haven't been together for so long still feels natural to me. She dances with the girls, and from the red flush on her cheeks, I know what she's going to do before she even does it.

I let out a groan moments before she makes her move, knowing these girls have the eyes of every man in the bar. Her hands start to rise and I start my countdown.

In three. Two. One.

She grips the hem of Bobby's hockey jersey and raises it high over her head before tying it around her toned waist. The look is fucking hot, with her little crop from her pole dancing class and the light sheen of sweat that covers her body. Add that to the messed-up hair and flushed cheeks and it reminds me of the Cass that was riding me on Saturday night. But it's not exactly something I want every dickhead in this place thinking about.

The overwhelming need to cover her up shoots through me, but I know that isn't going to go down well, especially after today's bullshit with the pole dancing. This is just one of those times I have to let it go.

To Bobby's dismay, Brianna follows suit and strips down to her small crop, and seconds later, both Sophie and Dani are dancing around in their bras.

"Fuck," Miller says with a shake of his head as he takes in his woman dancing half-naked across the bar. He gets up and takes a seat beside me. "What's going on, man?" he asks, knowing that going after Dani now is only going to end up with him receiving an ass-whooping.

I give him a sideways glance. "What are you talking about?"

"You're all torn up over this girl," he says, nodding toward Cassie on the dance floor. "And from the way that drinking game went, you two have history."

"A shitload of history," I admit.

"Dude, fucking spill already. I've known you a while now and have never seen you look at a woman like that. She's your girl, right?" he says as a group of guys starts approaching the girls.

"I don't know, man," I tell him. "She used to be. She was in high school. I would have fucking married her, but she left, no explanation, nothing. Just left."

"And now she's back," Miller says.

"Now she's back," I repeat, watching one of the guys come up behind her and put his hands around her waist to pull her into him. He tries to grind into her, but she pushes him away.

"Looks like she isn't going to be single for long, so you're going to need to figure your shit out, and soon," Miller says as the guy goes back for round two, this time pulling her in a little tighter. She turns around and tells him to go away, but he doesn't accept it, just keeps trying to grind his dick into her ass.

My stare hardens as I watch him drop his lips to her neck and lower his hold on her waist, moving further south. I see red. "Dude, you better intervene," Miller says, but there's no need. I'm already out of my seat.

I'm storming across Micky's with Bobby on my heels and probably the rest of the team, but I'm too furious to look back. The rest of the girls are way too drunk to realize Cass is in trouble, which only infuriates me more. I see the panic in Cassie's eyes as she tries to push the guy off her, prying at his fingers and trying to pull them back, but he sneers and tightens his hold as if he's getting off on her panic.

Cassie works out. She's strong, which only goes to prove how tight this asshole is gripping her. All I know is if he leaves a mark on her, there's going to be hell to pay. He starts to force his fingers into the waistband of her sweatpants, and I pick up my pace, shouldering past anyone who stands in my way.

Cass desperately looks around for help, and it's not long before she sees me coming and relief fills her watery eyes. As I grow nearer, I realize there's something off about this guy, something I can't lay my finger on, and I don't like it one bit. I step up in front of Cass, and as I raise my fist, she sees my intention and ducks down as best she can to keep out of the way.

The asshole notices me at the very last second, but he's too late to avoid it. My fist is already flying through the air toward his jaw. His eyes widen in shock as I connect with his face and he's sent flying back with the force of my punch, letting go of Cassie's waist in the process.

She falls into my arms, her body wrapping around me as I hold her close. Cassie gasps as she tries to control her breathing, the whole ordeal fucking with her head. "It's okay, you're safe," I whisper. A tear slides down her face and drops onto my shoulder, so I pull her back, wipe her face, then gently press a kiss to her forehead. "Come on. I think it's time to go."

She nods as the boys come and collect their girls, clearly having the same thought as me.

Cass grabs hold of Brianna, and I turn to let Bobby know I'm taking them home. He nods and offers to walk with us. After all, our driver is now extremely drunk off his ass.

We say our goodbyes and I lead Cassie out the door. The girls walk ahead of us as Bobby and I watch them from behind. We walk in silence as I re-run the night in my head. It was a risky move punching that guy and could have gotten me in serious trouble, not only with the college but with hockey. On the other hand, there was no way I was going to sit back and allow that douchebag to touch Cass. Besides, I have nearly a whole team of guys who can act as witnesses if needed.

I'm lost in my thoughts when I finally notice that Bobby has been slurring about the game and the shit he got up to at Micky's. I feel bad for tuning him out, but it's not like he realizes I'm not paying attention. Or if he does, he won't remember come morning. Instead, I focus on the girls' conversation in front of me.

Bri has her arm around Cassie's waist while Cassie's is thrown casually over Bri's shoulder as they struggle to hold each other up.

Bri tugs at Cassie's waist, and I watch in horror as she flinches in pain. My jaw tightens, struggling to hold myself back from turning around to find that prick so I can beat the living shit out of him. Bobby must have noticed Cassie's flinch as he places a hand on my shoulder, keeping me on track.

"I'm sorry," Brianna slurs to Cass as they both stumble up the pathway. "I should have been paying attention and now you're hurt. It's all my fault," she wails, big heaving sobs taking over.

"Don't be ridiculous," Cass soothes. "It's my fault. I shouldn't have drunk that much. I was the one dancing half-naked, and I'm the one who put myself in that position. At least, that's what moody back there's going to say the second you go inside," she adds, trying to whisper but failing while hooking her thumb in my direction.

"God, tell me about it. He really is moody," Bri agrees. "Kind of like a guard dog. You know, kind of rabid when you need it to be, but still loyal to its owner."

Cass bursts into uncontrollable laughter that has me scowling at her back and wanting to break up the conversation. But I know it's because of the tequila, and honestly, I want to see where the rest of the conversation goes.

The girls get their laughter under control, only to start again when Cass brings up the *Never Have I Ever* game. "I can't believe Bobby screwed his cousin," Cass laughs, making Bri snort back a giggle that has her choking on her own saliva. She stumbles a bit as she tries to right herself, but in doing that, she pulls on Cassie's waist again, making her hiss in pain.

Bri is oblivious to it, but I sure as fuck am not. My hands ball into fists, and I force myself to count to ten, trying to calm myself. "Speaking of that game," Brianna starts. "There would have been a million other questions you could have asked besides the foursome thing. I mean, there are a lot of other things I'd be interested to know when it comes to these boys."

"Believe me, I know," Cass replies, "But I wanted to know just how much of a manwhore he'd become. I assumed he'd been involved in a threesome, but I hoped not. Then he had to go and confirm it. So, I guess it had me curious."

"And now that you know?" Bri asks. "Does it make you feel any different?"

Fuck me, this conversation is like hitting the jackpot. I almost feel guilty listening in on what's clearly a private conversation, but when it comes to information about me and Cass, I'm going to take it any way

I can. With that resolve, I listen in closer, not wanting to miss a damn word.

"Ha," Cass scoffs, "ask me in the morning when I don't have so much liquor going through my body."

Damn it.

"Okay," Brianna laughs as we turn onto the girls' street. They walk in silence for a few steps when Bri turns her smirk on Cass. "You know, when you told me you hadn't been with anyone for a while, I didn't quite think you meant that the last guy was Jax, *three freaking years ago.*"

Like I said. The fucking jackpot.

Cass sighs and grins at Brianna. "You caught onto that did you?" she asks.

"Like I could miss that bomb," she laughs. "Explain yourself, whore. Though, I guess I can't call you that, huh? I bet you grew back your virginity . . . Unless you were going hard with a big-ass dildo and vibrator. I know I would have been."

Even though I can't see her face, I can just imagine how she would roll her eyes before answering. "I mean . . ." she sighs. "Sex means something to me. It's about a connection between two people, whether it's hot and heavy or slow and sensual. For me, if there's no connection then sex is off the table."

I've never heard so much bullshit in my life. I know Cass right down to the bone, and I know without even looking at her face that she's lying right through her teeth.

"Okay," Bri scoffs, as we near their driveway. "That's the lamest answer I've ever heard. What's the truth?"

Shit. I underestimated Brianna. I take my hat off to her, and I must remember to thank that little she-devil.

Cass groans. "Fine," she huffs. "I tried. I really did. I had the guy right there where I needed him. He was gorgeous, huge, rock-hard cock with abs to kill, plus a cocky smile. But when it came down to the crunch, I couldn't do it. I chickened out like a little bitch." She takes a breath and leans her head against Brianna's shoulder. "How can I sleep with another man when I still have Jax in my head?"

Fuck me. My mind spins. She left three years ago without a damn word. I assumed it was because she was done and needed an easy way out. But if that was the case, why the hell is she still struggling to forget about me?

"Babe," Brianna says with a sigh. It's a moment before her next question comes and I must commend her, she is on fire tonight. "Why did you even try? With the other guy, I mean?"

Cass scoffs as she reaches into her tiny crop to pull out their house key and finally starts to lower her voice as Bobby and I inch closer to them. "I'd heard the stories about him, you know, becoming the Carter-in-training, and I guess it made me realize that he had moved on and was officially done with me. It hurt, so I wanted to inflict the same kind of pain on him. But it backfired, like really, really bad," she says with an embarrassed smirk. "I got a reputation for being the girl who doesn't put out."

"Shit," Brianna laughs. "You don't need to worry about that here. I think the whole campus knows that isn't true."

A triumphant grin spreads across my face. Fuck yeah. That night last week was fucking amazing, and I don't care who knows it. I'd be proud to let them all know this woman rocked my world.

The door is pushed open and Brianna waltzes in without a backward glance. Cass stops at the door to say goodbye while Bobby struts straight past and collapses onto the couch, falling into an instant sleep.

"Um, well, thanks," she says, twisting her hands together. "You know, for walking us home and for that guy."

"No problem," I say as she starts to yawn and stumbles back into the brick wall of the house. Shit. "Come on."

I lead her through the house to her bedroom before rifling through her drawers and pulling out her pajamas. I order her to get dressed while I go find some painkillers and a glass of water for the morning. When I come back to her room, I find her in her bra and undies, struggling to get her feet through the hole of her pants.

With a sigh, I step up to her and start to help.

My gaze roams over her body, and I find her waist is red and raw with a small scratch marring her perfect skin. "Wait here," I tell her before disappearing into the bathroom to find some kind of soothing lotion. I come back to find her laying on the top of her bed, already curled up into her pillow, and I sit down beside her and start rubbing the lotion into her bruised skin. She hisses in pain and I do my best to make this as quick as possible.

"I'm sorry," she murmurs. "I shouldn't have drunk so much."

"No, you shouldn't have," I agree with a grunt.

"I don't know what I would have done if you weren't there," she says with a yawn, tears lingering in her beautiful brown eyes.

I pull her blankets over her and watch as her eyes start to flutter. "Go to sleep, Cass."

"Can you stay?"

With a sigh, I get up and lean over, placing a kiss on her forehead. "That's not a good idea and you know it," I tell her before turning and walking to the door, though I don't miss the deflated look in her eyes. A look that absolutely kills me.

Standing by the door for a moment, I watch as her eyes close and she drifts into what I hope is a peaceful sleep. "Goodnight, Cass," I whisper into the darkened room before I turn to leave.

I'm nearly through the door when I hear her pained whisper. "I *knew*, Jax. I'm sorry. I was scared."

I stop dead in my tracks, my heart racing.

No, there's no way.

I turn back to look at her, but her eyes are closed. "What did you know, Cass?" I push, lowering my tone, making it so that she can't ignore me.

Her eyes open just a sliver, studying me in the dark. There's heartbreak in her gaze, and it kills me to know exactly what she's about to say. "The ring, Jax. I knew about the ring."

And just like that, it all makes perfect fucking sense.

Without another word, I turn my back and leave.

CHAPTER 11

CASSIE

"Fuck, babe, you can really sing," Brianna says as I come strutting out of my room with an overnight bag, making me pause in horror, my eyes widening. Shit, I hadn't even realized I'd been singing. I must have been doing it in the shower, but I'm not ready to tell this secret yet. "Wait, where the hell are you going?"

Thank God. I give her a pointed look, cluing her in that she's being an absolute moron. "Sean's wedding, remember?" I say. "I'm pretty sure I've told you this a million times."

"Oh, shit," she says with a guilty look. "I forgot that was this weekend. I was hoping for another pole dancing class."

"There's no way we would be able to get away with that," I laugh as I open the internal garage door and dump my bag into my car. "The boys probably have their little freshmen wanna-be's staking out the dance studio in case we happen to come by."

"Yeah, I don't doubt that," she agrees with a heavy sigh. "But what am I going to do all weekend? Bobby's still pissed at me."

"Seriously? It's been two weeks."

"Yeah, I know. I think he's just shocked to find out that I'm actually a lot more like him than he had ever hoped," she laughs.

"I mean, you kind of blindsided him with the whole threesome thing."

"Shut up," she grins. "It was awesome, and I'd totally do it again."

"Ugh," I groan. "Let me know how that goes for you."

Bri gives me a salute as I head back to my room and do another look to make sure I have everything I need before heading back out to the living room. "Okay, I've got to get going," I tell her. "Have a blast without me, but don't even think about finding a new best friend, otherwise I'm going to delete Carter's number from your phone."

"Fine," she groans as she throws her arms around me and squeezes the living daylights out of me. "Have fun. I'll let you know if any brooding hockey captains come around to apologize."

"Yeah right," I scoff. "I'd pay to see the day that happens. It's already been two weeks since I told him, and he hasn't said a word. I didn't even get a scowl during class."

"Oh shit. That bad, huh?"

"Yep," I shrug.

"Maybe he just needs a few more days to sulk," she says, trying to keep me positive. "We can put the *Fight For My Man* plan into action after that."

"Okay," I laugh. "It's not going to be easy though."

"Nothing worth having ever is."

With a roll of my eyes, I drop into my car. "See you tomorrow night," I call out the window before I start backing out of the garage.

A thought enters my mind and I quickly stomp on the brake before Bri gets the chance to scurry away. "Hey, you haven't been in my room, have you?" I yell through the open window. "I'm down for you sharing my shit, but if you're gonna be scrambling through my clothes, at least put them away nicely."

Bri looks at me like I'm deranged. "Why on earth would I be going into your skanky-ass room?" she questions. "I haven't touched your clothes. Besides, mine are way hotter than yours. If anything, you're the one who needs an ass-whooping here."

I flip her the bird in response, then resume reversing out the driveway. Bri follows me out and gives a wave before heading back in, probably to go back to sleep for the rest of the day. But in reality, she's nursing last night's hangover so she can head out tonight with her girlfriends and do it all over again. At least I was sensible enough to be the sober one last night.

Flicking on the tunes, I drive the twenty short minutes to my family's home, a mix of happiness and sadness pulsing through me.

The thoughts of coming home to the place that holds my memories of Mom and Dad and of course, Jax, frightens the living shit out of me. But this is the one place I feel closest to my parents. I'm pretty sure the triplets feel the same way, hence why Sean is having his wedding on the property. You know, besides the fact that the property is an amazing estate, perfect for hosting weddings and functions. If we hired it out, we'd make a killing, but I couldn't stand the thought of our family home being used that way.

Driving past Jax's parents' home, I scowl in that particular direction before turning into my driveway. I stop at the gates and enter my code, waiting as the massive metal gates slowly open to allow my entry.

I hit the button for the window and drive down the tree-lined driveway, breathing in that familiar smell of home. My eyes widen in amazement as I get to the house, finding parking attendants and delivery trucks scattered around the whole yard. Men and women in all sorts of different uniforms go about in a rush to prepare my home for Sean's wedding.

Delivery men are busy lugging beautiful white chairs through the door while some poor bastard is chasing around a couple of swans that have broken free of their travel cage.

Ladders and tables are being unloaded from the back of a truck, and I pull around it to drive up to the front door. A smirk pulls across my face as I bypass an older man struggling to untangle fairy lights, only to have another man in a penguin suit stop by my door and offer to assist me with parking.

I hop out of my car and grab my things before handing the keys over. My parents used to throw extravagant parties all the time, which were always amazing, but we've never held a wedding here before. I must say, so far, it's absolutely shocking and beautiful at the same time.

Mom would have loved every moment of it.

I walk up the stairs leading to the entrance of our family home and make my way through the open double doors. The house is in absolute chaos, but an organized chaos, and I need a moment to take it all in.

Dumping my things at the bottom of the stairs, my curiosity gets the best of me. I head on through the house toward the back room, where I'm assuming the reception will be held, and bingo, I'm right.

The double doors are held open by massive white vases that contain the most amazing flower arrangements, welcoming the guests into the room, and as I glance through, I suck in a gasp. White tables and golden chairs surround me, and dazzling fairy lights and beautiful flower arrangements offer the room a breathtaking ambiance. To the side of the room, a wide space has been set aside for a dance floor. The fairy lights trail around the pillars throughout the room, and I just know that come nightfall, this is going to be the most spectacular sight I've ever seen.

Mom really would have loved this.

The big chandelier in the center of the ceiling has white drapes flowing from the center all the way to the edges of the massive room, taking my breath away as I slowly make my way through. The glass bi-fold doors that enclose the room have been opened completely to a second dance floor, which overlooks the garden and lake.

Walking out on the balcony, I peer over the wide lake and find where the ceremony will be taking place. Taking in the chairs and the stunning altar by the lake, my eyes begin to water. This wedding is going to be nothing short of spectacular, and I know without a doubt that Mom and Dad are looking down on Sean and Sara today.

Turning back to the reception hall, I find a well-dressed lady running around like a mad woman, clipboard in hand and earpiece firmly attached. She spots me and gives me a blank stare, which immediately puts me on edge. "And you would be?" she asks as politely as possible, though, I can see the annoyance in her eyes at having been disturbed.

"You must be Rebecca?" I ask, realizing this is the frustrating wedding planner Sean has had to deal with. "I'm Cassie, bridesmaid and the groom's sister. Also part owner of this estate," I add, just to put the bitch in her place and remind her whose home she's in.

"Oh," she says, a little shocked, the annoyance fading from her features and replaced with a fake smile. "And a beautiful estate it is. However, there isn't time to waste. The boys are on the second level while the girls have taken up the third." She glances down at her clipboard. "You should have roughly ten minutes to say hello to your brothers before you are required for hair and makeup with the bridal party."

"Wonderful." I give her a curt nod and exit the room in search of my brothers, grabbing my things from the bottom of the stairs before making my way up them. If Rebecca hadn't told me the boys were on level two, I would have figured it out pretty damn fast. The noise coming from that level is just ridiculous.

I knock on the door of the loudest room to have none other than Carter appear. "Little sister," he beams excitedly, clearly already wasted. "You made it." He pulls me in for a hug while Sean and Logan appear behind him.

Logan closes the door, and we all stand out in the hallway, the boys as happy as ever while I'm being squished in between their muscles. I hear more loud noises from behind the door before something smashes, and I look up at Sean. "Tom is smashed and running around naked. You know how he gets," he explains about his best friend. "You probably don't want to go in there."

"Yeah," I say. "I think you're right about that."

"Has anybody seen Cassandra?" Comes a high-pitched yell from above.

"Damn it," I groan. "I think I'm needed."

The boys laugh, knowing just how much I hate the torture of getting my hair and makeup done. "Run along, young one," Carter smirks.

I flip them off before heading up the stairs, quickly ducking into my old childhood bedroom to grab my bridesmaid dress before pushing through the doors to the massive bridal suite. The room is in chaos. The girls are sipping champagne in little silk robes, all color coordinated, of course, while they sing along to music and get their makeup started. Sara, the bride, sits with her feet up on a stool, getting a pedicure while the hairdresser works on a beautiful up-do.

"Cassie," she squeals as I make my presence known. "How are you?"

"Good," I say, walking deeper into the room, a smile spreading wide over my face. "Have you seen the place? It's absolutely stunning."

"No, I haven't," she smiles before gripping my arms, her eyes widening. "Tell me they got the swans?"

"Yes, I saw some idiot out front struggling to get the bastards out to the lake. Quite funny actually," I laugh. "The poor swans were being assholes and ganging up on him, but they seemed really happy in the lake. You know, once they got there."

Her face melts into joyfulness. "Oh, thank God."

I'm about to say hi to the rest of the girls when some lady snatches the dress out of my hand and scoots me over to a chair. Within a few seconds, she rips my ponytail out of its hair tie while someone else comes at me with a face wipe. I let out a sigh and give in to the torture. This will go quicker if I just tune it all out and try to enjoy myself.

Someone shoves a champagne flute into my hand, and I get lost in the music while the people around me start the pampering process, and I'm forced to admit that it's really not so bad. I could definitely get used to this.

An hour later, we start getting into our gowns, and with my hair and makeup done, it takes my breath away. The silver strappy gown sticks to me like a second skin and drops between my breasts, showing off the perfect amount of cleavage.

My gaze follows the line of the dress down to where it flares with the slightest train. I know the second the sun reflects off the material, it's going to sparkle like a Cullen and take my breath away. I slowly turn in the mirror to get a look at the back, and a grin stretches across my face. The dress dips right down and scoops just above my ass, showing off my sculpted back.

With a smile, I slip on my heels and give myself another once over.

I feel like a glamorous celebrity about to take the red carpet. The last time I felt or looked this good was my senior prom where I had the man of my dreams on my arm. How things have changed.

The photographer comes around, and that's another event on its own. It takes forever, and I feel like my feet are already going to fall off, but I smile and do it for my big brother. We get pictures pretending we're getting dressed, pictures of the makeup artist touching up our already perfect makeup, and of course, pictures of girls helping the bride into her dress. Next, we head all over the property, getting every shot possible, and I dread the time between the ceremony and the reception when we're going to have to do it all over again with the boys. But of course, I'll smile for my big brother.

We're ushered back upstairs where Sara's parents are waiting, and we're given the half-hour call. I slip off my shoes and take a seat to wait patiently. The wedding planner comes up and gives us the rundown of how the ceremony is going to work. Who is going to walk down in what order, who holds Sara's bouquet while she can't, blah, blah, blah.

Finally, it's go time.

Some guy in a suit ushers us down the stairs, and out a separate backdoor leading to a small gazebo area—an area that Jax and I had coveted as our own. I cringe at the memories that assault me seeing this place, but do my best to put it behind me. I can sulk all I want about Jax tomorrow. Today is Sean's day.

We're lined up, ready to go, and I listen as the wedding planner maps out the pathway to get down the aisle. From where we stand, we can't see where the ceremony is, but anyone who knows the property would clearly understand the path. Let's just hope the two girls before me understood what the planner was trying to say.

Shortly after the music begins, Sara's sister heads off, followed by her best friend and then me. With a breath, I take my first step toward the aisle, following the path I was told to lead. It doesn't take long for the ceremony area to come into view, but I keep my head down, terrified I might trip.

Once I reach the top of the aisle, I'm stopped by the photographer who takes a photo with a blinding flash before stepping out of my way and letting me continue.

Finally, I get a look at the groom, who looks at me with a huge, proud smile, but I also see a hint of guilt in his eyes that has my brows furrowing for the briefest moment.

I continue down the aisle and shift my gaze to Carter and then to Logan, who each give one another a sideways glance before glancing back at me with worried looks on their faces. What the hell is going on? My eyes continue scanning the line of groomsmen, expecting to see Tom, Sean's best friend. Instead, they land on the one person I did not expect to see here again. Not in a million years.

Jax stands up beside my brothers, looking as handsome as ever in his suit, his hungry eyes firmly on me. The pure shock of seeing him has me stumbling slightly before I right myself and slap on a smile. I force myself down the rest of the aisle, and instead of lining up with the other bridesmaids, I head straight to Sean and reach up on my tippy toes to place a swift kiss on his cheek.

To the guests, it would look like an innocent show of affection from a little sister to her big brother on his wedding day, but everyone standing before me on the groom's side knows better.

"What the fuck, Sean?" I say through my teeth as I smile and pull him in for a hug. "Are you trying to fucking kill me?"

"Sorry, Cass," he murmurs. "I couldn't picture today without him."

Sighing, I quickly glance at Jax, only to find those deep blue eyes already on mine. I flick my attention back to my brother before I get swept up with it all and grab the attention of Logan and Carter as well, knowing they would have known about this. "We're all going to have words about this later," I whisper before heading to my side to stand in line behind Sara's best friend.

Once firmly in position, I can't help but cast my eyes to Jax as I wait for the final bridesmaid to take her position. Jax watches me right back, and to say the moment is intense would be putting it lightly. From the look in his eye, I would say that for today only, he's willing to overlook our history and recent confessions and enjoy this time that we have as a family.

The music finally changes, letting us know the bride is coming, and I tear my gaze away from Jax. Looking up the aisle, I see Sara walking toward her groom with tears of happiness streaming down her face. I turn back to Sean and he's absolutely beaming as he takes in his bride, and I swear, I could not be happier. They are perfect in every way.

I tune out Jax and focus on the ceremony, and I'm glad that I do. Watching them publicly confess their love for each other and say their vows brings tears to my eyes that I can't seem to dismiss. I know marrying the man of my dreams is something that may never happen for me, but I'm so happy for Sean. Everything he has ever wanted is falling right into place.

At the end of the ceremony, the bride and groom walk back up the aisle with the bridal party following, which unfortunately has me partnered with Jax. He offers me his arm and I scoop my hand into place, once again being reminded of my senior prom.

"You look stunning," he murmurs to me as we make our way back up the aisle.

"Thank you," I say, "You don't look too bad yourself."

He casts his eyes down at me for a brief moment, and I see the raw emotion in his eyes. I know he's trying to tell me that this could have been us. *Should* have been us.

I desperately want to say something, to tell him that I take it all back, that I wish I never left, but all that comes out is a broken, "Sorry."

He turns his attention back to the aisle, putting a stop to any conversation.

We make it to the end where hugs, kisses, and congratulations are passed around. Jax releases my arm, but a force is pulling me back to him. I know he needs a moment before he can deal with me again, so I give him what he needs.

Leaving to find my brothers, they both see me coming at the same time. Carter and Logan give each other wary looks before turning to face my wrath. "You should have told me," I scold them. "I must have looked like an idiot stumbling down the aisle."

"Well, to be honest, telling you would have been an awful idea," Logan says. "And watching you squirm was far too enjoyable."

I ignore his comments as my mouth drops open. I stare at him in shock. "What planet are you living on?" I laugh. "How could it possibly be an awful idea? Are you insane?"

"Honestly, it's quite simple," he tells me.

"How so?"

"Had you known, would you still have attended the wedding?" he asks.

I look at him like he's lost his mind. "Of course I would have."

"But?" Carter says, giving me a pointed stare.

I roll my eyes, knowing exactly where this is going. "But I would have complained about it."

"Exactly," they say at the same time, doing that freaky triplet thing where they read each other's minds. "Come on," Logan says, always on team Jax. "You know it felt right having him here."

I cast my eyes around and take him in, speaking with my grandparents as if talking with long-lost friends. My grandmother pulls him in with open arms and he goes willingly, making my chest ache in the good kind of way. "Yeah," I admit. "It's right having him here. He's family."

Needing to get my mind off Jax, I make my way around the crowded guests, taking a few moments to say hello before the photographer whisks us off for another photo shoot. Though, with the boys here, this round of photos is somewhat more comical than the last.

CHAPTER 12

JAXON

Fuck me. I don't understand why chicks insist on getting all these damn photos taken. It's ridiculous. My only saving grace is that Logan's here and has already had a few too many drinks, otherwise, the boys and I would have thrown in the towel a long time ago. Especially considering the ever-growing tension between me and Cass.

It's almost nightfall when the wedding planner comes around to tell us it's time to head up to the reception. Carter and Logan take off with Tom, while Sean sweeps his bride up and throws her over his shoulder. She squeals and beats on his back as he takes off after the boys. The girls scream for him to put her down, saying some shit about messing up her hair and chase after them, leaving me and Cass behind.

She gazes after her family fondly before realizing we're left alone together, and her smile becomes forced. She pulls her heels off and holds both of them in one hand, along with the hem of her silvery dress—a dress that I wanted to tear off with my teeth the moment I saw her in it. She's fucking radiant today with her chestnut hair done up and natural makeup. She didn't go all out like the other girls did, and she looks absolutely breathtaking.

Cassie starts walking to the house for the reception, and I can't help but fall in beside her. I don't know what makes me do it. Maybe it's the day, maybe it's how beautiful she looks, or maybe it's the look in her eyes that tells me she's still in love with me. I don't know why, but I quietly slide my hand into hers, my fingers lacing through hers just like I've done a million times before, and it feels like coming home.

She looks up at me with wide, questioning eyes, and all I can offer her is a sad smile. She takes it for what it is and turns her attention back to the grass, but she doesn't dare let go. We walk the rest of the way back to the house hand in hand before I gently pull mine out of hers. She doesn't look back at me, just continues walking until she stands among the other bridesmaids, putting on a brave face.

I don't know how this all happened. All I know is that Sean called me a few days ago and told me it wouldn't be right if I wasn't standing up there with him. And I have to agree, being here feels like being with family again. I hated it the second he told me that I shouldn't tell Cass I was coming, that it would just make her overthink and panic, and he was right. That's Cass to a T. However, it made me feel as if I was betraying her trust somehow, blindsiding her. But either way, I'm here now, and I wouldn't change it for the world.

I watch as she mingles with the girls and accepts a glass of champagne, though she only sips at it as the other bridesmaids throw theirs back. I guess she wants to remember this night. An arm falls over my shoulder as a big body leans all of its weight on me. "You've got it bad, brother," Logan says, a knowing glint in his eye.

"Shut up," I say, pushing him off.

"Why the hell would I do that? Stirring you up is a favorite pastime of mine. I couldn't possibly skip an opportunity like that," he says. I roll my eyes and turn my attention back to Cass as she throws her head back laughing. "You know," he says, taking on a serious tone. "She's still yours. All you have to do is forgive her." With that, he walks away, leaving the thought swirling in my head. If only it were that easy.

The reception gets underway, and I take my seat at the bridal table. Night has fallen and the room is completely lit up. I must give credit to the bitch of a wedding planner because she has done an incredible job.

The room is packed. There must be at least two hundred guests here, and I find myself scanning the room. I notice my parents and my jaw clenches. What the fuck are they doing here? There's no way Sean would have invited them. They'll be here purely for the social climbing opportunities, and I make a note to steer clear. I don't need to be dealing with that shit today.

Logan hovers by me, and I glance over at him, watching the way he smiles at some chick at a table to the left. She's a cute blonde, and I realize this must be his new girl, so I make a note to introduce myself and stir as much shit as possible. I'm sure Carter will happily join me in that venture.

Things get going and soon enough, we're demolishing hors d'oeuvres and main meals before moving right along to speeches.

Sara's best friends get up and give a speech that has the bride and the majority of the women in the room in tears, but it's all made better when Logan and Carter stand to make their dedication to their brother. The whole room is in stitches and hangs on every word they say as they confess their brother's misguided activities of his past. The boys finish it off with a few touching words about their parents which has Cass discreetly wiping a tear.

The moment the speeches are finished, the band takes to the stage, and the crowd starts conversing and moving around the room. I watch as Cassie excuses herself from the table and steps out into the fresh air.

I'm moving away from the table before I even realize what's happening. I follow her out the side exit and find her standing at the edge of the patio looking out into the night, the soft breeze gently catching in her gown.

I step up behind her and watch as her body tenses as she feels my presence. I gently wrap my hands around her waist and pull her back against my chest, feeling at home as she relaxes against me. "Are you okay?" I ask.

I feel her take a deep breath as she slowly turns in my arms. "You don't need to do this, Jax," she says, making my heart slowly break.

Without hesitation, I look down into her big brown eyes. "I want to."

She searches for something in my eyes and eventually must be satisfied by what she sees, then with a sigh, she wraps her arms around me. Cassie leans her head down against my chest, needing to be held, and I pull her in tighter, gently swaying her to the music flowing through the open side door. I soothe her as best I can and remind her that her parents would have loved to be here.

After a short while, she slowly pulls her head back from my chest without stepping out of my hold. "I truly am sorry, Jax," she says, looking up at me with those gorgeous eyes. "I never should have left."

I search her eyes, the same way she had done to me before, though I have absolutely no idea what I'm searching for. "Why'd you go?" I ask, desperately needing an answer to the question that's haunted me for three long years.

A tear trails down her cheek as she takes a shaky breath. "I was scared," she starts. "I was there that day. You showed up with a ring and talked to my dad."

"No," I cut in, confused. "You were gone. You were with that girl from school."

"No, Jax, I was home. Millie had a flat tire and was running late. I didn't bother telling anyone because it wasn't going to be a long wait," she explains. "But then you came and you were so sure of yourself, of our future, and it freaked me out."

"Fuck, Cass," I groan, letting her go and putting space between us. "Don't tell me you left because of that."

"No," she begs as more tears escape her eyes. "Just hear me out, please."

I turn away from her as I attempt to get my thoughts in order before turning back and allowing her to continue. She takes another shaky breath. "I was confused after graduation, and I didn't know what I wanted to do with my life. I needed a change. So I was talking to Mom one night, and she told me as long as I was happy, it didn't matter what I was doing. She joked that I could have been a truck driver for all she cared, as long as I was happy. Somewhere along the line, I had gotten it in my head that getting out of Denver was the key to that happiness."

She needed a change? What the hell? We were weeks away from heading to college, what more of a change could she have needed? "Why didn't you talk to me about this?" I snap. "Fuck, Cass. If you wanted a different college or city I would have gone with you."

"I know," she snaps back.

"What the hell, Cass? This doesn't make sense."

She lets out a sigh as she looks back up at me. "I knew you would follow me anywhere, and I couldn't let that happen," she explains. "Things with your parents were bad, and I knew you wanted to get away, but you needed to be here. Your dream is to be in the NHL. You needed to go to college and use your scholarship. This was your shot. I would have never forgiven myself had you thrown that away to follow me while I searched for what I wanted."

I have no response. I can't even get my thoughts in order to figure out where to start.

"Say something," she cries.

"I can't, Cass. I have no idea what to say. You threw away our future because you couldn't talk to me."

She hangs her head, though I can't understand why. Regret maybe? Shame? "It didn't take me long to realize that I'd made the worst mistake of my life. But by the time I'd realized that, you'd already moved on. You were only a freshman, but you were already making features on ESPN and they made it clear what kind of reputation you had."

"So, the reason you left had nothing to do with the conversation between me and your dad?" I ask.

"No," she breathes. "It just made me realize how serious you were about us."

"You're sure?"

"Yes, Jax. I'm sure," she tells me with the slightest bit of annoyance in her voice at having to repeat herself. "I had to get away, and I couldn't let you give up your future for me."

"Babe," I sigh, stepping up to her and pulling her into my arms. I bury my head in her neck and breathe her in. Her arms wrap around me and she holds me tight, needing the closeness. "All this time, I thought you left because you were done with me. That you were over it, over us."

She pulls me back and looks into my eyes. "Never," she says. "How could I ever be over us when I'm still so madly in love with you?"

"Fuck," I say, getting frustrated with the situation. If she had only talked to me and let me in on what was going on in her head, this whole thing could have been avoided. "So, if you were so unhappy, why didn't you come home?"

"I couldn't," she sighs. "I had already hurt too many people by leaving, and I didn't want to make that worse by letting them know that

I wasn't happy. I made the biggest mistake of my life, and I was too stubborn to admit it."

Fuck. This woman is my kryptonite.

I crush my lips down on hers, making her gasp for air. She kisses me back and it feels amazing. It's different from the night we shared a few weeks ago. That was desperate, needy, and a mess of confused emotions, but this . . . This is something that comes from the heart. Something I'm not even sure I know how to describe.

We could have been kissing for seconds or it could have been hours, but she eventually pulls back and rests her forehead against mine. "What's happening between us, Jax?" she asks.

"Honestly, Cass, I have no idea," I tell her as my hands tighten on her waist. "I still care for you. Hell, I might even still love you, but I'm not the same man you once knew."

"Yes, you are," she insists. "I know you are. The old you is still in there, it's just clouded by the girls, the reputation, and this persona you have as the captain, but that's not you. I know it's not."

"I don't know, babe. I have to think about this. You tore me to shreds when you left," I tell her honestly. "I can't just forget about that."

She looks up at me, tears in her eyes. "I don't know how I will ever make it up to you."

"I don't know either, Cass. I just . . . I guess I just need time to sort this out. To figure out where my head is."

"Okay," she whispers, a little unsure. I lean back against the railing and pull her into me as we silently listen to the party within.

It's not long before we hear a voice in the distance. "Found her," Sean calls out to someone behind him and begins to approach. "Uhh, sorry guys," he says hesitantly, clearly not wanting to disrupt anything that could be going on out here.

"It's fine," Cass says, stepping out of my arms to face her brother. "What do you need?"

He cringes and glances at me before turning back to Cass. "I was hoping for a favor?"

"Sure," she says, automatically.

"Well, our first dance is coming up, and well . . . we were hoping you might sing?" he asks, cringing once again. My brows furrow. It's a simple question, one we all know she will accept with ease. So why the hell does he keep cringing?

"I . . . I don't know," Cass replies, making my jaw drop as I stare at her. "You know I haven't sung in a while."

What the hell? Cass hasn't sung in a while? That's as crazy as me not playing hockey. Singing is a part of who she is, it doesn't make sense. Sean glances at me once again before turning back to Cass. "It would really mean a lot if you could do it. I know it's hard, but it would mean the world to me and Sara."

With a sigh, she looks down at her feet and quickly wipes a tear away. My eyebrows furrow before she looks back up at him with a smile. An extremely fake smile at that. "Okay, yeah. Sure. No problem."

"You're sure?" Sean asks.

"Yeah. I'll be okay," she nods. "Now, get lost."

He gives her a tight, grateful smile before disappearing. "Um . .

. you're not singing anymore?" I ask, completely blindsided by this revelation.

"No," she sighs. "Not since I left."

"What the hell, Cass?" I ask, alarmed. For as long as I can remember, she wanted to be a singer and musician. That was before she discovered she wanted to be a physiotherapist, but the singing never stopped. It's her passion. She used to joke that she might have even loved it more than me, though I'd always pin her down and tickle her until she took it back.

"I just can't do it," she responds with a shrug.

"Stop bullshitting me and be straight. Why aren't you singing?"

She turns back to me. "Because I'm a mess. I sing when I'm happy, and I haven't been happy in a long time," she explains. "It hurts."

I'm quiet for a short while as I consider her answer. "You're still writing though?" I ask, remembering the old notepad I saw sticking out the top of her bag that day in the library.

"Yeah, I'm still doing that," she admits. "But it's not how I used to write, it's . . . I don't know. It's different. Darker."

With a nod, I let her off the hook and bring an end to her interrogation, knowing I'm somehow going to have to help her through this. I have no idea how I'm going to do it but I know I won't stop until her heart is no longer hurting. I can't stand an unhappy Cass. "Come on," I say. "We better head back inside."

"Okay," she whispers as we turn and head back to the door. We're walking back into the room when she stops abruptly before me. I follow her eyeline and notice she's staring at my parents talking with

Sara and Sean. "What the hell are they doing here?" she asks.

"What else?" I scoff. "Social climbing."

We watch as my mother leans in and gives Sara a tight hug and kiss. "I don't think Sara has any idea who she is," Cass mentions.

"Probably not," I mutter, my hand involuntarily taking her waist. "Mom would be telling her what a wonderful wedding it was and how spectacular she looks."

Cass scoffs, "And Sara would be thanking her for coming, keeping it polite in case they're friends of Sean's," she murmurs. "If only she knew."

We watch as my father holds a hand out to Sean, who takes it in his own and gives it an extremely firm shake. Once Sean releases his hand, it goes straight behind his back where he shakes it out, clearly in pain, but the fake smile doesn't fade from his face.

"Don't stress, they'll be leaving soon. They just needed to show their faces at the wedding of the year," I tell her, hoping they're not ruining Sean's night.

"They haven't changed," she grunts as we head back to the bridal table.

"Never will," I murmur.

The party kicks up, and soon enough, the emcee announces the first dance and introduces Cass to the stage, and the crowd applauds as they gather around.

Cass nervously adjusts the microphone as Sean and Sara get into position. Her eyes flick to mine, and I give her an encouraging smile, even though it's selfish. All I want at this moment is to hear that magical voice of hers once again.

The music starts and she belts out the opening lines of "At Last" while Sean and Sara dance and sway to the beautiful song. Her eyes remain locked on mine, and I watch as another tear falls from her eyes, reminding me once again that this should have been us.

CHAPTER 13

CASSIE

As the song comes to an end, I feel empowered. I still can't believe my stupid brother and Jax convinced me to do that, but either way, I am so glad they did. Singing on a stage again felt amazing, and I can't for the life of me understand why I stopped.

Well, I know why I stopped, and it was necessary at the time, but tonight something feels as though it has clicked back into place. Like a piece of my soul has returned to me.

They gave me the hardest song on the planet to sing, not because of the notes or the runs, but because of the lyrics. My eyes sought out Jax's as the lyrics poured out of me, and at that moment, only the two of us existed.

I look out at the crowd and am humbled to see them all come to their feet and applaud for me. Even Sara and Sean turn to face the stage, Sara with a beaming smile while Sean watches me with love in his eyes and mouths, "Thank you."

"You're welcome," I mouth back with a little nod before giving a slight nod to the crowd and making my way off stage.

Elation pulses through me as the emcee invites the rest of the bridal party and the guests to join the bride and groom on the dance floor. I'm hardly back to the table before Jax sweeps me up in his arms and turns me around to head straight back to the dance floor.

A waiter walks by with a tray of champagne, and Jax scoops up two glasses and hands one to me. "Enough of the serious bullshit tonight. We're partying now."

Undeniable happiness tears through me, and with a grin, I take the champagne flute and throw it back. "Let's do this," I say.

The band makes way for a DJ to take their place, and he cranks the music right up the moment he takes the stage. Drinks float around, and all the older guests hit the road, leaving us young ones to celebrate a great night.

We dance and party the night away, and I'm stolen from Jax by an extremely drunk Tom when the emcee asks all the couples to hit the dance floor. "Kiss Me" by Sixpence None the Richer comes on, and all the couples around start making out on the floor with a bit of dirty grinding involved. I try my hardest to bat Tom away, but I end up slapping a hand over his mouth to hold him off, though that only has him making out with the palm of my hand while I'm laughing like a hyena.

"Would you mind not defiling my little sister?" Logan deadpans as he and Carter finally come to rescue me. They drag Tom away as he confesses his undying love for me over the sound of the music and promises he will be back to rescue me from the torturous clutches of my evil brothers.

With that, I find another glass of champagne and search the room for Jax. I find him trying to avoid being groped by an older woman looking for a young stud to show her the time of her life. I walk right up to them and drape myself over Jax who instantly puts his arm around me.

"Sorry, love," I say to the lady while roaming my eyes greedily up and down his body. "I think you'll find this one is taken tonight."

Jax looks down at me, lust burning in his eyes, before turning his attention back to the lady. "I think you'll find more luck over there," he says, pointing out the senior's table. She gasps in outrage before Jax sends her a wink and whisks me off.

I lead him outside and start walking out into the yard. "What are we doing?" he asks with a grin.

"I have an idea," I tell him. "A really stupid idea."

I lead him toward the break in the fence between our two properties before he starts to grow wary. "Are you going to explain this idea anytime soon?"

I turn back to him and give him a charming smile, which I know he sees right through for the mischief it is. "I'm getting all our old shit back," I explain.

"You mean, you're breaking into my parent's house?" he clarifies.

"Eh," I shrug, "tomato, tomahto. Are you in?"

A grin spreads wide over his face as a twinkle appears in his eyes. "Hell, yeah."

Before he has finished his sentence, I grab him by the hand and rush through the hole in the fence. We run around the perimeter of the property, trying to keep in the shadows of the trees, then pass the pool house and sneak in between the two buildings before heading for the back door.

I mean, we don't have to break in. I'm sure we could simply knock on the door and walk right in, but with the way things are between Jax and his parents, it would just be easier to avoid them altogether. Besides, this way seems a lot more exciting.

Jax bends down and lifts up an old plant pot and, sure enough, he comes back up with a key and a wicked grin. "Bingo."

He unlocks the back door to his family's estate, and we sneak in as quietly as possible. Though with us both as drunk as skunks, I'm pretty sure we're heard all over the house, but here's to hoping.

Jax roams around the house acting like some kind of assassin, and I have to bite down on my lip to keep from laughing too loudly. We head up two flights of stairs until we come to the level with his room. We tiptoe across the landing and down the hallway, just in case his parents are close, and push open his bedroom door.

He walks into the room and looks around as if he has never seen the place. I gently close the door behind me and watch him with hooded eyes. He turns around, catching my gaze, and stills as he watches the way I reach up and gently pinch the thin strap of my silver gown, letting it fall down my shoulder.

After slipping the strap off my other arm, I let my gown drop to the floor before stepping out of the material, leaving me in nothing but a pair of panties and my high heels. Hunger flares in his eyes as I stride toward him, and he looks at me like a starved man, ready to devour every inch of me.

Moving into him, he takes my waist as I reach up and grasp the tie at his neck before gently loosening it. Jax allows me to slip the tie over his head, licking his lips in anticipation as those blue eyes flame with need. Turning him around, I tie his wrists behind his back, and once I'm satisfied that he won't be able to get free, I lead him to the armchair and push him down onto it.

Neither of us says a word as the sexual tension grows between us, and I turn my back on him and flick my heated gaze over my shoulder, causing butterflies to swarm through my stomach. I suck in a breath and watch the way his gaze sails over my body as I slip my thumbs into the waistband of my panties.

Ever so slowly I drag them down my thighs, bending until I reach my ankles and showing him absolutely everything I've got on offer. Jax groans, adjusting himself in the armchair as his cock strains against his pants. I straighten back up before stepping out of my panties and turning back to face him.

Intense hunger slams through my chest, and I'm already wet for him, but I'm not nearly done teasing him yet. I stride back toward him and that hungry stare comes back to mine, full of need. My knee comes down beside his strong thigh on the armchair, and I pull myself up until I'm straddling him, and after letting out the softest groan, I start to dance for him.

Feeling his long, thick cock through his pants, I grind down against him as I grab his shirt and tear it open, listening to the buttons as they hit the floor. Slipping my hands inside, feeling his warm skin beneath my palms, I push his shirt back over his shoulders and chest.

I've said it before, and I'll say it again. He's fucking gorgeous. So sculpted and defined, his body fitting perfectly into mine.

Jax groans as my hands begin roaming over his body and I drop my face to his, capturing his lips in a deep kiss before reluctantly pulling back and sliding off his lap. Holding his stare, I latch onto his belt buckle and quickly undo it before whipping it off and dropping to my knees.

His eyes become hooded with anticipation, and he raises his hips to help me remove his pants, allowing his cock to spring free. My tongue rolls over my bottom lip, so ready to take him and tease him until he comes in my mouth.

His breathing grows heavy, and he watches my every move as I wrap my hand around his cock and slowly start working my fist up and down, my thumb rolling over his tip. The hunger slams through me, and I simply can't wait any longer.

Moving up higher on my knees, I move in between his strong thighs and then finally draw him into my mouth. His tip hits my tongue and I lap up the bead of moisture that waits for me. I'm a greedy whore just for him, and I love every fucking second.

Jaxon's eyes close in satisfaction, and the pleasure on his face as I take him right to the back of my throat leaves me with the best feeling in the world. My tongue rolls over his tip as my fist tightens at his base, moving up and down, matching the pace of my bobbing head.

I tease him slowly before I start picking up my pace. "Fuck, Cass. Untie me," Jax begs.

I slow my movements and meet his stare, letting him see just how hungry I am for him, then shake my head, a grin pulling at the corner of my lips. His muscles bulge in his arms and I have no doubt he's trying to get himself free, but knowing he won't break free of those binds anytime soon, I keep playing.

With a sly, seductive grin, I get back to work.

Up and down, tighten and groan, I give it to him just the way he likes it, and just when I've got him on the edge, a cocky grin tears across his face and he flies up off the armchair. Jax stares down at me on my knees and drops the tie beside me on the carpet before reaching down and lifting me with ease.

An animalistic growl tears from the back of his throat as he slams my back against his bedroom wall, and I immediately lock my legs around his waist, pulling him into me. I should have known a simple tie wouldn't be enough to keep him from taking me.

It's like a fight for dominance, and I've never been so desperate. Putting me out of my misery, Jaxon lines that thick cock up with my entrance and slams himself deep inside me.

"Oh God," I groan, my eyes rolling with undeniable pleasure as he begins to pound into me, my arms entwining around his neck. "That wasn't . . ." thrust, "part of the . . ." thrust, "plan."

"I figured," he grunts, his jaw clenched as I grip onto him for dear life while getting thoroughly fucked. "I made my own plan."

I can't help but laugh. After all, this is exactly how I intended we would eventually end up, but as he rocks his hips and takes me from a new angle, my eyes roll to the back of my head and my laugh quickly morphs into needy moans.

Jaxon thrusts hard and wild, the intense need and sexual tension so fucking heavy in the room. He's relentless and raw, and within seconds I feel my orgasm creeping up on me. "Oh, fuck," I pant, my nails digging into his skin. "I'm gonna come."

"Squeeze my cock, baby. Let me feel you."

His words are my undoing, and I come hard, my orgasm blasting through me like a stick of dynamite exploding. My high rocks through my body as my walls convulse around his cock.

"Fuck, Cass. So fucking tight," he growls, dipping his head into the curve of my neck, his lips moving across my skin. He soon finds his own release, shooting hot spurts of cum deep inside my pussy.

His forehead drops to mine as we desperately try to catch our breaths. "Next time, I'm using handcuffs," I tell him as he releases my legs and helps me find the floor.

Jax laughs and raises a brow at me, his voice thick with desire. "You think handcuffs are going to stop me when the alternative is burying my cock so deep in your sweet cunt, I could puncture a fucking lung?"

I smirk up at him, and with a roll of my eyes, I step out of his arms and dash into his bathroom. After cleaning myself up, I head back out to find him with his pants on, searching through his wardrobe for a new dress shirt, and with a satisfied sigh, I slip my dress back on and get busy taking what's rightfully his.

The room is filled with old memories, some good and some bad. I even notice there's quite a lot of my stuff in here. Jax finishes in his wardrobe, and I find all his old jerseys. With a smile, I grab one of his empty hockey bags out of the top of his closet and start loading it up.

I turn around and find Jax sitting on his bed, watching me with an amused smile on his handsome face, and I give him a pointed look. "Are you seriously just going to sit there? This could be one of your only chances to get this shit back."

"Good point," he grunts, getting to his feet and grabbing all his old watches and anything that was special to him.

I search through his bedside table and find a small, black velvet box, and I sit on the edge of the bed and slowly pry open the lid. A beautiful white gold engagement ring stares back up at me and I find myself struggling for air.

The bed dips beside me, and Jax reaches for the box, taking it in his hands and giving it a look over himself. "I have no idea what possessed me to leave this here," he murmurs, the heaviness in his tone speaks volumes. "I had gone to ask your dad permission because we were going to be living together on campus, and I needed him to know my intentions. I was going to wait a year or so before I asked you because we were way too young and you would have had my balls for asking so soon."

I reach over and take his hand in mine, unsure of how I could possibly comfort him right now. We sit in silence, both staring at the ring that would have been our future, when we hear a noise coming from the hallway.

"Shit," Jax curses, standing up and pocketing the ring. "Come on, we have to get out of here."

I get up and cross the room as he grabs the bag packed full of old mementos off the bed. I gently open the door, peeking my head out into the hallway, the same way I used to when I'd sneak in and out of his room as a teenager. The coast is clear, so we duck out the door, sprint down the hallway, and fly down the two flights of stairs. Jax flings open the back door, and we run out, chuckling like a bunch of school girls, but he quickly drops the bag and heads back in.

"Jax?" I ask into the night but get no response.

He comes out moments later with as many bottles of his dad's expensive liquor as he can possibly carry before smirking and offloading them to me. He picks up the hockey bag and we dash away, feeling as though that was the biggest victory I'll ever experience—in more ways than just one.

We hurry back over to my property and ditch his bag upstairs before heading down to the reception to find the party still in full swing. We walk in with matching grins and are instantly cornered by Carter. "Where did you two disappear?" he questions.

"Oh, you know," I say. "I just had to seduce Jax in the middle of a break-in."

"What?" he asks, his jaw dropping to the ground. I give him a wink and turn to leave, but I see Jax pull the expensive bottle of liquor out from behind his back with a cheesy as fuck grin. The boys whoop and shout, and once the majority of the guests leave, the real party gets started.

It must be at least four in the morning when Jax carries me up the stairs and helps me out of my dress. I pull on a tank top before climbing into bed, while Jax loses his clothes and scoots in beside me. He throws his arm around my waist and pulls me in tight, the move coming so naturally. I guess that's what happens after sleeping together for so damn long.

His fingers draw little circles over my hips, causing need to bloom deep within me, and I press my ass back into him. He slides my underwear down then rolls me to my back as he hovers above me. Jax settles between my legs, and as he dips his head and captures my lips with his, he slides his thick cock deep inside me.

He thrusts into me as though he'll never touch me again, and I curl my arms around his neck, holding him as tight as possible. This isn't the intense, drunken, needy screw from earlier in the night, and it isn't the wild *I've missed you sex* from weeks ago. This is slow and sensual, filled with raw emotion, and it speaks right to my heart.

I look up at him as though he's my whole world, and the need to tell him what I'm feeling fills my veins, but now isn't the time. Not unless I want to see him bail and then spend the rest of the night alone. "I know," he tells me, reading me better than I can read myself. "Me too."

It's enough to put my mind at ease while he works on putting my body at ease. A moan slips from my lips, and he smothers it with his kiss, the raw passion between us filling me with unconditional love.

I raise my hips to meet his thrusts, taking him deeper, and it doesn't take long before we're coming together. He drops his head to mine and presses a gentle kiss on my lips. "What is it about you, Cassandra Waters?" he groans against my lips.

I smile against his lips, feeling content and at peace for the first time in three long years. "I could ask you the same thing."

He looks into my eyes as he considers something before sliding out of me and pulling my back against him, spooning me once again. "Goodnight, Cass."

"Night, Jax," I whisper into the darkness as a yawn takes over me.

He pulls me in tighter and drifts into a peaceful sleep, his arms bringing a safety that I've craved since the day I left.

It must be at least an hour later when I feel Jax pull away from me. He climbs out of bed and pulls on a pair of pants, and I listen as he takes a few steps toward the door and pulls it open. "What's up?" he asks, his voice thick from sleep.

"I was just checking in on Cass," Sean says. "I figured she would be here with you."

"Yeah, she's fine. She's out like a light," Jax explains.

"Yeah, good. It looked like she enjoyed herself tonight," he says, a hint of concern in his voice.

"Better believe she did," Jax laughs, the fondness in his tone making something heal in my heart. "I haven't seen her like that in a long time. It was nice."

"Yeah, sure was, man," he says. "Listen, I actually wanted to talk to you."

"About what?" Jax grunts in confusion.

"About Cass, the real reason she's home," Sean says, making me stiffen in bed. What on earth is he talking about? I'm home because the boys asked me to come back. Because with Dad gone, they needed me close, somewhere they could easily watch over me like the overprotective big turds they are.

"Go on," Jax says cautiously, and I can tell by the shift in his tone he suspects that I've lied about something.

"Shit," Sean sighs. "Look, I'd really appreciate it if you didn't mention any of this to her, but me and the boys sort of manipulated her into coming home." I hear the cringe in his voice, and I can imagine what his face would look like at this moment.

"Huh?" Jax grunts, amusement in his voice, prompting Sean to go on.

"She wasn't happy in New York. We had all gone to visit, but it never got better, and we knew the best thing for her was to come home. Then after Dad died, we guilt-tripped her, saying we needed our baby sister home. We had all talked about it and agreed it was best for her to go to Denver and see you again. You're what makes her happy and we knew, whether it was intentional or not, you'd take her pain away."

Jax is silent for a moment, but I'm a different story.

I shoot out of bed and storm up to my big brother, pushing him in the chest, not giving a shit that he's still celebrating his wedding. His eyes widen in shock, either too tired or drunk to have noticed me earlier. "You lying sack of shit!" I scream at him. "All of you. You're nothing but dirty, lying douchebags!"

"Shit," he mutters under his breath.

"Shit?" I hiss. "That's all you have to say?"

"Yep. What else can I say?" he says with a nonchalant shrug. "We don't regret it. Look at you, you're smiling again. For fuck's sake, Cass, you even sang tonight. Don't you see that?"

Tears well in my eyes, the raw emotions giving me whiplash. "It should have been my decision to come home," I tell him. "I wasn't ready."

"That's where you're wrong, little sister. We had to step in. You're way too stubborn to have admitted it to yourself. If it were up to you, you would still be rotting away in New York, not living. You would have died there, Cass. Fuck, you were dead. You were nothing but a fucking shell. Jax brings you back to life."

"He's right," Jax cuts in as the tears begin to spill. "You should have come home years ago."

I give him a look that would scare the dead. "Whose side are you on here?"

He raises his brow at me and gives me a stupid look. "Uhh, theirs," he says as if I should have known, but really . . . I should have.

I flick my attention back to Sean, and all I can do is stare at him as I admit defeat. He's right, but that doesn't mean I have to like it.

"Look, I have to go," he says before a grin rips across his face. "We have a flight leaving in three hours and I still need to consummate my marriage."

"Gross," I grunt as Jax puts his arm around my waist and pulls me to him.

"Night, kiddies," he winks before backing away.

"Just so you know," I call after him. "I love you, and I've had the best night, but at this very moment, I really hate you."

"Got the message, loud and clear," Sean smirks with a salute as Carter and Logan walk by on the opposite side of the landing.

"Oh, and I hate you fuckers, too," I call out to them. They give me confused looks, but I slam the door closed before they can question it.

"God," I groan. "They're a bunch of jerks."

Jax just smiles at me and drags me back to bed. "Come on, you can whine and bitch them out tomorrow. For now, I need to feel your body against mine."

How could a girl possibly resist that offer? "Okay," I say, climbing back into bed, letting Jax pull me against him. He whispers goodnight in my ear and plays with my hair until I have calmed down enough to finally fall back into a peaceful sleep.

CHAPTER 14

JAXON

*S*tanding in front of the mirror, I take myself in. I'm a fucking mess of nerves. My hands shake, I'm fidgety, and my heart is threatening to beat right out of my chest. I take a deep breath and hold it in before blowing it out, the same way I do right before a big game.

I check my suit in the mirror and grab the little box off the vanity as I double-check that I've done everything. After all, I want to make a good impression. I've shaved, remembered deodorant, and even shined my goddamn shoes.

It's either now or never. I'll never be able to scrounge up the nerve to do this again. I fire off a quick message to Cass, just to make sure she won't be home.

Putting the small, black velvet box in my pocket, I rush down the stairs before I have the chance to back out. I head out through the front door without a backward glance, ignoring my parents who call after me, wondering what the hell I'm doing *in a suit.*

I consider cutting through the fence to next door, but I want to do this right. Instead, I walk the whole way up the driveway, cross to the next property, and walk back down to the house before climbing the front steps and hitting the doorbell.

I wait for a short moment before Cassie's dad answers the door, Brad Waters. "Mr. Waters," I greet with a nod, while silently shitting myself. I mean, fuck. Why does this have to be so nerve-racking?

He stands before me in silence as he takes in my attire. "Shit," he sighs, skipping over the fact that I addressed him formally, which I haven't done since he ratted me out for it when I was twelve. "Either someone died, or you're here for something else. To be honest, I'm kind of hoping you're on your way to a funeral."

"No, sir," I say, proudly. "No funerals in my immediate future."

"Hmm," he grunts, not impressed. "There's about to be."

With a grin, I ignore his quip. "May I come in?"

He steps out of the way to allow me to pass. "I don't know why you didn't just sneak through Cassie's window like you usually do." My eyes go as wide as saucers. Shit, I didn't realize he knew about that. What the hell was I thinking coming here? He's going to chew me out for sure. "Relax kid. If we had a problem with it, we would have said something when it started four years ago."

I don't know what to think about that, or even how to respond, but I take it in stride and follow him into the house. Brad leads me through the kitchen and grabs a beer before passing one to me. We walk into the good living area and he offers me a seat, which I take gingerly and wait until he's comfortable before getting started.

"Wait, I'm not ready," he cuts in, holding up a hand with a gleam in his eyes. He gets up and steps out the open door before hollering up the stairs, "Boys, get your asses down here. Young Jaxon has something he'd like to discuss with us."

Ahh, shit. Now I'm fucked.

Brad walks back into the room and sits silently before me, watching me freak out as we wait for Cassie's older brothers to come down.

Each of them enters with smirks on their faces. But once they take me in, those smirks quickly morph into deep scowls. "Fuck me," Carter says, as the boys flank their father and turn on me.

"Alright, kid," Brad says. "Now I'm ready."

I let out a shaky breath before getting to my feet and pulling the box out of my pocket. I open it up to reveal a white gold engagement ring and place it down on the coffee table between us.

"Well," Brad says, ripping his eyes off the ring to focus back on me. "I'm honored, but you're really not my type. Besides, I'm not sure my wife would approve of me having a boy toy."

The boys chuckle at his response, and it's deathly clear where they get their humor from.

"Sir," I say, looking him in the eye. "I have known Cassie since the day I moved in next door, and knew I wanted to be with her since the second she punched me square in the nose and got blood all over my parents' carpet. As you know, next year we're heading off to college, and we'll be living together. So I'm coming to you to make you aware of my intentions. I'm not some kid who's messing around with her or would ever hurt her. Cassie is it for me, and it's important that I let you know that."

Brad slightly raises his chin to me with respect and I continue. I eye the boys before focusing back on their father, so they know they're included when I ask this question. "Sir, I would like your blessing to propose to your daughter."

He takes a deep breath and wipes a hand down his face. The boys give each other knowing glances, but I focus my attention on Brad. He slowly rises from his seat and makes his way over to me before holding his hand out. I reach to shake his hand but he pulls me into a bear hug instead. "Son, I have known for years that your intention was to marry my Cass, and you have both mine and Cathy's support."

"Thank you," I say as he releases me.

"My only concern is your age. You're just a kid. Hell, Cassie's just a kid, too. I know your relationship is heading that way, but there's no rush."

Sean nods before offering his two cents. "I think what Dad is trying to say is that Cass would have a fit and kick your ass if you asked her now."

"Yeah, I know," I tell him. "My plan is to wait. I just wanted you to know my intentions before we moved in together."

"Thanks, son," Brad says, a big cheesy grin across his face and pride shining brightly in his eyes. "Welcome to the family, Jaxon."

"With all due respect, I feel like I've been a part of the family since I was twelve," I tell him honestly.

"Shit," Logan laughs. "Looks like the old man is about to cry of happiness."

I wake with a start, and it takes me a moment to realize I'm still in Cassie's childhood bed. I have to admit, it's a bit eerie dreaming about the day I asked for Brad's blessing right after I'd been at his son's wedding, the girl in question sleeping in my arms.

Maybe it's being in this house again, or maybe it's just Cass, but I'm starting to think and feel things I haven't felt in a long time.

Desperately needing to clear my head, I get out of bed and head downstairs for breakfast. The place is a mess, but not a soul is awake, apart from the clean-up crew who are running around as though their lives depend on it. I know Cass and the boys won't be up for hours, so I fix myself a bowl of cereal and make my way into the media room to catch up on last night's game.

An hour passes before I decide it's time to make my way back to campus. I go back up to Cassie's room and give her a kiss on the forehead. "I have to go," I tell her. "We'll talk when you get back to campus."

She mumbles something in her sleep and with that, I grab my things and my filled hockey bag of shit we rescued from my parents' house and head downstairs. The bag is thrown in the back of my truck when I spy Cassie's car across the property.

A grin pulls at my lips as I skip back up the stairs two at a time and break into her old recording room. I start dismantling as much of the important stuff as possible before I take it down bit by bit and load it into the back of my truck. I can't resist going back to her room to give her another kiss before finally leaving. She mumbles another goodbye and snuggles deeper into her bed. I gently close the door and soon find myself climbing into my truck.

After getting back to campus with a plan to spend my day working out and going over some assignments, I promptly fall asleep on the couch, not waking until nearly nightfall.

I have a lot to think about where Cass is concerned, especially after everything that happened at the wedding, and so I did the only thing that helps me sort through my head in times like these—practically kill myself in the gym. The moment I returned back to my place, I promptly collapsed on the couch, which is where I've stayed ever since, assuming Cass wouldn't be back on campus until late afternoon.

Bobby had taken one look at me, smirked, and said, "Looks good on you." I gave him a blank stare, denying that I knew what he was talking about, but it is pretty damn obvious. I have Cass back in my life, in a strange, together-but-not-really-together kind of way, and for the first time in years, I'm starting to feel settled within myself. I've not been as grouchy or dying for the party lifestyle like my reputation suggests. I haven't chased after pussy or even acknowledged them when they attempt to climb all over me. I just don't feel the need anymore. There's no longer a void that needs filling.

For the first time in a long time, I feel like myself. Clearly, Bobby has noticed.

"So," I hear Bobby say, and I realize he's sitting on the opposite couch watching ESPN. Why isn't he doing that at his own place? "Ready to talk about it yet?"

Ahh, fuck.

I send a scowl his way as I sit up on the couch. "Don't know what you're talking about."

He nods toward a cold beer on the coffee table, and I reach forward and take a sip. My stomach clenches with the idea of more alcohol, and I place it back down with a cringe. "Quit pussy footing around," Bobby demands. "How was the wedding?"

"Good," I grunt, not offering much more than that. He gives me a pointed stare, and I let out a resigned sigh. "Fine," I say, telling him what he really wants to know. "Cass and I talked and sorted some shit out."

"And?" he prompts.

"And? I don't know. She still wants to be with me, but I'm not sure I can trust her not to up and leave again," I tell him. "I just can't go through that again. Why do you think I've avoided this shit with chicks all these years?"

"Honestly, dude, I think you've avoided it because you've been holding onto hope that Cass would come home. Or at the very least, have been waiting for someone who could even resemble the kind of person she is," he says. "Even though you never would have discovered anyone like that because you don't give any of them the time of day."

"Seriously?" I mutter, giving him a blank stare. "The kind of chicks I've been with are not really the type of women who are interested in a relationship. They're after the bragging rights, which I was more than happy to give to them."

"And what about now?" he asks.

"Now?" I repeat with a sigh. "Now, the thought of being with another woman makes me feel sick. Like I'm betraying Cass in some way. It's ridiculous because we're not even together."

"It's not ridiculous," Bobby says, channeling his inner Dr. Phil. "You're in love with her, and you know as well as I do that if you were to be with someone else it would hurt her. It only makes sense for you to want to protect her from that."

"Yeah, I guess. But it doesn't change the fact that she's the only one I want in my bed. I just have to make sure I can trust her now."

"Holy shit, Jaxon Payne has seen the light," Bobby sighs

dramatically as he raises his hands to the heavens. "I never thought I'd see the day."

"Shut up, man," I say, grabbing the cushion off the couch and launching it at him.

He catches it with lightning-fast reflexes, which is one of the reasons he makes such a great hockey player. "Are you planning on going over there to talk with her?" he asks. "Because if you are, I may as well head over, too. I'm fucking starving."

I think it over for a moment before shaking my head. "Nah, man. She probably isn't back from her place yet. She most likely stayed to help clean up a bit, and knowing her, she probably needs a bit of space to sort through everything that happened last night."

"Yeah, okay. I better go and scrounge up my own dinner then," Bobby grumbles.

With a lift of my chin, Bobby strides out the door, and I take a page out of his book. Getting up, I find myself something to eat before settling back onto the couch and watching the game, which is exactly where I stay until I fall asleep again.

I wake on Monday morning and just know that it's going to be a good week. All the pieces of my scrambled life are finally falling back into place. There are only a few odd ends left to fit back together.

Rushing out the door, I meet the boys for our morning run, and we get straight into it. I lead the pack with Bobby by my side, the rest of the boys following behind.

A smirk plays on my lips as two petite brunettes come jogging toward us on the opposite side of the road. Bobby and I recognize them instantly, but they're too lost in their conversation to realize anyone is around.

Bri notices us first and nods her chin toward us, prompting Cass to look up. A grin tears across her face as she focuses her heavy stare on me. I jog across the road and the boys follow so we're heading straight for them, and I watch as her eyes sparkle with happiness.

I adjust myself on the path so I'm running right in her way and stare her down. Heat rises in her cheeks, and I know she's thinking about the night of the wedding. More specifically what we did in my old bedroom. Hell, I haven't been able to stop thinking about it, too.

Cassie's bottom lip gets lost between her teeth, and the overwhelming need to pin her up against a tree and fuck her right here fires through me. Fuck the boys, I don't care who's watching. I just need to have her.

Knowing I'll never be able to concentrate on my training like this, I push the thought from my head, but the closer we get, the wider my smirk becomes. Cassie narrows her stare on mine, reading me better than I could ever read myself, and she releases her lip, her flirtatious gaze turning into a deep suspicion. She starts shaking her head, but it's too late. We're right on top of them now.

"No, no, no," she squeals.

Cassie tries to sidestep but I move with her, bending low and wrapping my arms around her legs as our bodies collide. She lets out a shriek, but before she even knows what's happening, she's thrown over my shoulder and I continue my run as though I don't have a squealing woman hanging over me.

Bri turns and runs with us while Cass kicks and pounds on my back, begging to be released. I can't help but laugh as I smack her on the ass. "Would you put me down, you big turd?"

My laugh takes over, and I have no choice but to stop and put her down before I hurt us both. I place her back on her feet and she narrows her eyes at me in annoyance, but I step into her personal space and stare down at her. The irritation in her eyes quickly fades, turning into a desperate, hot need.

She parks her fists on her hips as I lean into her and kiss her deeply, and I grin as she becomes putty in my hands. She kisses me back, and I almost forget we have an audience before I release her with a wink. "Gotta go, babe," I say, taking off with the boys and leaving both Cass and Bri staring after me, dumbfounded.

A chuckle from beside me has me glancing at Bobby. "Fuck man, you got it bad."

With a roll of my eyes, my fist shoots out and collides with his shoulder, completely throwing him off the path. But he's right. I do *got it bad.* I got it so fucking bad.

The rest of the day flies by, including hockey training, and when we break to head to the locker room, Coach hollers across the ice for me to join him in his office.

I step off the ice and make my way to Coach Harris' office as quickly as possible. I'm keen to get this meeting over and done with since I have got myself some plans for tonight. "What's up, Coach?" I ask, flopping down into his chair. With all my hockey gear still on, I barely fit into the seat, awkwardly folding in on myself as I focus my attention on Coach.

"Just checking your head is in the game," he says with an accusing tone.

I'm instantly on edge. "It is," I insist, feeling better than I have all season. "All my games have been spot on. I haven't missed a beat."

"Chill out, kid," he says with a grin. "You're right. Your games have been flawless, your training sessions with the boys are fantastic, and your dedication to your role as captain is commendable."

"Huh?" I grunt, confused why I've been pulled in here.

"What I'm saying is that anything hockey related is near perfect, but don't act like I don't pay attention to you boys once you step off my ice. Your head is a mess," he accuses.

"Nah," I deny. "I'm all good."

He gives me an annoyed look and gets straight into it. "You're running three times as much as the others, you've logged a shitload of hours in the gym, you've stopped your wild partying, and the moment you step off the ice, you sink away into your head," he says. "Now, I know I may be getting old, but fuck me, Jax, I can clearly tell you're distracted by something. You have three seconds to tell me, or you'll be on during the next figure skating session doing your drills."

Damn it.

With a sigh, I look up at Coach. "There's a girl."

"Ahh, fuck," Coach groans. "Why is it always a girl when it comes to you assholes?"

"Yeah, my thoughts exactly," I mutter. "She's kind of the girl I've been in love with since I was twelve."

His head snaps up and he gapes at me as though I just told him a big blue alien appeared in his locker room and fucked Bobby up the ass. "What?" he grunts, wide-eyed.

I lean back in my seat, feeling like this meeting is about to be a little longer than intended. "We were together for six years before she up and left for New York without a goodbye, and now she's back," I explain.

"I'm not seeing your problem," he tells me. "It was years ago."

"Yeah, well . . . I keep accidentally falling into her bed."

"Right," he says with a nod. He takes a breath, thinking it through before dragging his hand down his face. "The way I see it, you both have some unresolved issues that you need to sort out before you run yourself into the ground or ruin a game."

"Agreed," I say.

"Good, now get out of here," he says. I get up from my chair and turn to leave, but he stops me in the doorway. "Jax," he says with a more serious tone in his voice. "If you're still in love with this girl after years of being apart, then I dare say she's the one for you. You'd be a fool to mess that up."

"How do I trust that she won't leave again?" I ask, hoping he might have the answers to all of my problems.

"Faith, Jaxon," he says. "You know as well as I do that trust is earned, not given. Maybe she just needs the chance to earn yours back." With that, he gives me one final nod and turns his eyes down to the paperwork on his desk, excusing me from the room, not realizing just how heavy his words are on my shoulders.

Heading down to the locker room, I quickly kick off my skates and start pulling off my training gear, my mind once again a rush of thoughts. After three long years apart, I am still madly in love with Cassandra Waters. But how the hell can I be sure she won't leave? The first time was devastating. Going through that again … Well fuck, it'd kill me.

I find Bobby in the locker room and sit down beside him to take my skates off. "All good, man?" he asks, referring to my meeting with Coach.

"Yeah, he just wanted to bust my balls a little," I explain with a grunt, grabbing my shit for a shower.

"Heading home?" he asks as he stands and picks up his hockey gear.

"Nope," I say with a wide grin.

He shakes his head and strides for the doors with a hasty goodbye to the rest of the guys as I grab a towel and head into the shower. After all, I don't want to smell like a dirty locker room when I'm sliding into Cass later. Stepping into the shower, I let out a sigh as the warm water rushes over my sore muscles and realize that maybe Coach is right. Maybe I am overdoing it a little.

Movement catches my eye, and I turn to see Xander walking out of the showers, trying to pull a shirt on. His arm raises above his head and my gaze is drawn to the massive purple bruise across his ribs. In fact, there are smaller cuts and bruises all over him.

What the fuck?

"Dude?" I say, stopping him in his tracks. He turns to look at me and instantly realizes what I've seen.

"It's nothing, man," he says with a shake of his head before pulling his shirt the rest of the way down and leaving the room. I think about going after him, but I'm naked and not really in the mood to get my ass whipped by twenty towels for leaving the showers in my birthday suit.

I finish off my shower wondering who the hell could have done that to him, and more importantly, why? If he was in some kind of trouble, he knows he could come to us. We would back him up, or we'd at least try to resolve the issue and prevent it from happening again. If he gets caught fighting, especially on school grounds, he'll be kicked from the team. That kid is too valuable to lose.

Stepping out of the shower, I wrap a towel around my waist before heading back to my locker and pulling on a pair of jeans and a shirt. I promise myself to look into this thing with Xander—or at least try. The kid is a black sheep, and if he wanted to tell us something, he would have done it already.

With a sigh, I grab my things and jam them into my hockey bag before searching my locker for my phone. Glancing down at the screen, I scoff at the missed call from my dad, knowing he would be questioning me about taking that shit from my old room. I swipe the notification away and bury my phone in my pocket. I don't have time for his shit. I have much better things to be doing right now, and they all involve sliding into my girl and hearing the way she screams my name when she comes.

CHAPTER 15

CASSIE

Brianna and I sit in the living room after a long Monday, me with my notebook scrawling out lyrics, while Bri scrolls through social media, searching for anything worthy of her attention.

I scan over the last few pages of lyrics I've written, making a mental note to stop throwing my bag around so much. The pages look worn, some even a little ripped, which has my brows furrowing. I've always thrown my bag around with my notebooks in it and they've never quite looked like this. It's almost like someone's been smashing my notepad against the side of the house.

Putting it to the back of my mind, I continue scanning the lyrics and notice a change in my writing between now and New York. It almost seems lighter in a way, much like it was before I left for New York. I flick back a few more pages and compare the differences. It's soothing, still full of darkness, but there's a healthier contrast. A light at the end of the tunnel.

The moment I left for New York, my lyrics were all about heartbreak, but then my parents died and a dark depression slipped into it. I feel as though being home has begun to heal me, cleanse me from within, and I know exactly how that happened.

Brianna starts spilling out the latest gossip about who knows what while trying to talk over the sound of the TV, which neither of us is paying attention to. There's a knock at the door, and we look at each other with confusion lacing our features.

"You invite anyone over?" I ask.

She shakes her head, giving a very unladylike shrug. Though, ladylike is not something Brianna has ever claimed to be.

"So I'm assuming I have to answer it?" I grumble as I get up from the comfort of my couch.

"Yuuup," she sings as her attention falls back to her phone.

I trudge to the door and open it to find a very handsome man standing at my door with a pizza. How very romantic. "Are you lost?" I smirk as I position myself in front of the door and lean against the frame to block his entry.

The sight of him standing at my door has my heart warming, especially the fact that he feels he can just come and drop by unannounced like he used to. Like he feels he belongs here.

"Not me," he replies with a twinkle in his blue eyes.

I stare at him, trying to keep a straight face. "What are you doing here, Jax?" I question, though the intrigued tone of my voice is a dead giveaway.

He shrugs his shoulders. "You know," he says as if he doesn't have a care in the world. "I was in the neighborhood."

"Right," I reply, leaning against the doorframe so I can cross my arms over my chest. I watch as his eyes dart to my now pushed-up cleavage and grin as his eyes heat with excitement. "You just happened to have a pizza on standby in your truck?"

"Your mom would have been the first to bitch me out had I shown up empty-handed," he explains.

"Very true," I smile, thinking of all the times Mom had done just that. "I thought you were on a strict diet for hockey?"

"I am," he says. "This is for you."

I eye the pizza and take a deep breath, taking in the heavenly aroma, just knowing he would have bought me pepperoni. "And what are you going to eat?"

He lets out the smallest chuckle as he steps into my space, a seductive smirk crossing his features as the twinkle in his eye returns. He slides an arm around my waist and pulls me into him, sending a surge of electricity pulsing through my body. I lick my lips and my bottom lip disappears between my teeth. I'm practically panting before he's even spoken. "You."

Jax's eyes darken as my body reacts to him. I feel him hardening as I press myself against him, trying to relieve the ache he's managed to cause in the last thirty seconds. He pushes me through the door and drops the pizza on the floor before crushing his lips against mine.

I moan into his mouth as he takes me by the ass and lifts me into his strong arms before striding to my room. I distantly hear the door slam and realize we must have left it open. Either that or Bri has stolen my pizza and made a run for it. Actually, on second thought, there's no way I'm leaving this room to find even a slice of pizza left.

Thoughts of pizza disappear from my mind the moment I'm thrown across the room and slam down in the center of my bed. A sharp gasp tears from me, but then he's right there, coming down on top of me. Hunger flashes in his eyes, and I know without a doubt that this is about to be a wild ride.

My thumbs dig into the waistband of my pants and I struggle to pull them down while he tries to rip my shirt over my head. I get my pants to my knees before giving up and using my feet to kick them off. My pants have hardly hit the ground before my fingers are clutching his shirt, the desperation urging me on.

Jaxon's lips crash down on mine, and I have to pull away before I get lost in his kiss. "No," I pant. "I need you now."

He grins and pushes himself off the bed and hoooooly shit. The undone belt buckle and the low-riding jeans with no shirt shows off his perfectly sculpted body and has me panting for him. Fuck, I could come before he even touches me.

He smirks as he watches me check him out. "See something you like?" he teases as he kneels one knee at the end of the bed before reaching for me. He grips me under my knees and hauls me to the end of the bed so my legs are dangling off, and a loud gasp pulls from the back of my throat.

Jax takes my knees as I push up onto my elbows, needing to watch as he slowly separates them as if he's opening a long-awaited gift. I suck in a breath, watching how his eyes flame with hunger, and I can't hold back any longer. "You need to touch me now, Jax," I demand.

"With pleasure," he growls, taking my legs and throwing them over his shoulders.

Oh, God.

He dives in like a starved man, and I'm instantly seeing stars. He fucks me with his tongue, his fingers working their magic as he licks, nips, and sucks at my clit. He pushes my body right to the edge, only to tease me and take me further.

I come on his face, and just when I think it's all over, he stands up and looks at me with that same ferocious hunger. His pants drop to the ground, freeing that delicious, big cock, and not a second later, he's scooting me back up the bed, his cock impaled deep inside my cunt.

After coming four mind-blowing times, we collapse in an exhausted heap on my bed, gasping for air. We fucked at the top of the bed, the end of the bed, the floor, and on my fucking dresser. "Holy shit," I pant, my hand falling to his chest. "You can come over here and do that any time you want."

He lets out a laugh before pulling me into his chest, his hand coming down with a firm spank on my ass. "In that case, I better feed you so you have enough energy for tomorrow night."

"Is that a promise?" I ask, my stomach rumbling. Reluctance pounds through me, but I scramble off my bed and find my skimpiest lingerie to pull on just for him.

"Fuck," Jax says, sitting up and grabbing my waist, hauling me back into him. His lips trail over my stomach, his big hands roaming over my body. "It's a fucking guarantee if you're going to be wearing that."

"Well, if you give me a little warning next time, I bet I could find something a little more exciting than this," I grin, thinking of the whole Victoria's Secret collection in my top drawer, but I've definitely seen some things online that I think might just do the trick.

Jax groans with desire but eventually scrambles out of bed to pull on his jeans. With him no longer distracting me, my gaze shifts around my room and my brows furrow, finding my guitar laying haphazardly across my desk. Moving off the bed, I pick my guitar up off the desk and turn to Jax. "You didn't move this, did you?" I question, unable to resist strumming my fingers across the strings before placing it back on its stand.

"Babe, I just got here. I didn't have a spare second to touch anything but you," Jax says as he pulls his shirt back on, though his response isn't necessary. I know it was that little she-devil I live with. She can't help but snoop around my room, but I get it. It's a sister thing. It's no different to the way I can't help snooping through my brothers' shit every time I visit.

We head back out to the living room to find Bri asleep on the couch with the empty pizza box resting on her stomach. With a chuckle, Jax pulls out his phone and takes a quick picture before explaining himself. "It's Bri," he says with a shrug. "I'm bound to blackmail her one of these days, especially with you as her roommate now."

I roll my eyes and watch as he swiftly picks her up off the couch and pops her down in her bed, my heart warming at this spectacular man he's become. He returns a moment later and orders Chinese, remembering all my favorite dishes while I scan through Netflix. He pulls me in beside him, and I'm reminded of all the times we did this as kids.

I've barely finished my dinner before I start falling asleep on the couch, my body completely spent. He pulls me in tighter and the next thing I know, he's sliding me into my bed with a gentle kiss on my lips.

My alarm sounds through my room, and I groan as Bri comes bounding in at six in the morning. Why the hell did we make this stupid pact to run every damn morning? "Oh, thank God," she says in relief, noticing that Jax didn't stay the night. "I wasn't sure if I'd walk in on your morning screw or not."

"You could have knocked," I suggest.

"Oh, hell no," she laughs. "I mean, I don't want to see you getting it on, but I'm sure watching Jax in action would be a real treat."

I can't help but laugh. "It really is."

Getting out of bed, I pull on my training crop and running shorts, my only motivation being the possibility of seeing Jax out leading his team. I pull my hair up and follow Bri out the door, slamming it closed behind me with a nudge of my ass.

The chilly Denver morning has me desperately wanting to rush back inside to my warm bed, but I'm not that weak. I took on this stupid pact, and I will see it through. We start off with a slow jog to get our bodies warmed up before getting into a proper run when a shiver takes over my body. I glance around me, having the strangest feeling of being watched. I take a good look, but in the darkness, I find nothing. I'm probably just imagining things.

I turn back to face the path, only to have my strange feelings and thoughts interrupted by Chatty Cathy next to me. "So, what's the story with Jax?" Bri asks. "Last I heard, you were heading to the wedding with a broken heart and now he's showing up at our door with dinner for me and three orgasms for you."

"Four actually, but thanks for keeping count," I laugh. "And for the record, that pizza was for me."

She shrugs her shoulders and grins. "You were letting it go cold. What was I supposed to do?"

I roll my eyes and get on with the story. "My stupid brother invited him to be one of his groomsmen, and none of the pricks thought it was a good idea to tell me," I explain. "I didn't know until I was halfway down the aisle and almost face-planted in shock."

"Yeah, I kind of figured he was there," she muses. "But it doesn't explain how things changed."

"Well, if you'd quit interrupting me, I'd be able to tell you," I say as I give her a pointed look. She holds her hands up in surrender then makes a show of zipping her lips and throwing away the key.

I roll my eyes but can't help cracking a smile. "Well, it was up to the speeches part of the night and Logan and Carter mentioned our parents, and I got a little emotional and started crying, so I ducked outside and Jax followed. He made me feel better before he tore into me with an interrogation, and I guess he finally got the answers he was after because he seemed . . . I don't know, at ease maybe."

"Wow," she says. "So, what does this mean? Are you guys back together?"

"Honestly, I have no idea," I tell her with a sigh, starting to get puffed out from our run. "He hasn't really told me where we stand, so I'm taking what I can get at the moment. I think he still needs a bit of time to figure out what he wants."

She seems deep in thought for a moment before cringing and turning to me. "And if he's still screwing around and giving the rest of the girls on campus anything they can get?"

"Then you may as well shoot me now," I tell her. She gives me a look to suggest I'm being dramatic, and while I might have taken that a little too far, the sentiment stands. "Look," I say, explaining myself. "You and I know two very different versions of Jaxon. You know him as the trophy-winning manwhore on campus, whereas I know him as the man who loved and protected me since I was a kid. He has strong values and is a respectable man, no matter who he portrays himself to be now. I guess I just have faith that while he's trying to sort out this thing with me, he won't consider sleeping with someone else."

She watches me for a moment, and she must decide she likes what she sees before letting it go. "Okay," she says with a nod, "Out of everyone on campus, you're the only one who knows the real Jaxon, so I'm going to take your word for it."

"Thank you," I smile as we head around a corner.

"So, what do you think is holding him back?"

"My guess is that it's because I left him before. I mean, he's a man. He isn't going to admit that he's scared of getting hurt, but I think that's what it is. I hurt him really bad when I left, and I don't think he trusts me anymore."

"Well, that's a simple fix. You need something to prove to him that you're in it for the long haul," she says.

"And what would that be?"

"I'm not sure you're going to like the idea, but I'm just going to put it out there. It's totally artificial, but I think it just might work," she says, before becoming mute and concentrating on her run. Great. I guess I'll just have to wait and see what the little she-devil has in mind.

We turn another corner and a grin tears across my face as we see the hockey team heading our way on the opposite side of the road. But today, we'll play it smart. I'm not getting thrown over any shoulders this morning. The boys get closer, and I can't help but grin at Jax.

I have absolutely no plan in mind, but I give him an evil smirk and cross the road to run directly in front of him, the same way he had done to me. His eyes narrow with suspicion and my smirk only gets bigger, but he doesn't move.

Damn it, the asshole is calling my bluff.

He jogs closer, and I do the only thing I can possibly think of. "Get ready to bolt," I murmur to Bri as I reach behind her and pluck the little water bottle out of the special waistband of her shorts.

I pop the lid as quickly as possible and drench Jax just as fast. His mouth pops open as he registers what's going on, and I see the look in his eyes before he even moves. I scream for mercy and take off like a bat out of hell, dragging Brianna behind me.

He's much faster than me. He always has been, but he allows us to get away, and once we turn the corner, we have to stop to catch our breath, slowing to a dawdle. "He's going to get you back for that," she warns me.

"I know," I grin, absolutely loving these little games with Jax. "I can't wait."

We get back into our jog when another runner passes us and does a double take. "Oh, hey," he says, backing up and jogging backward in front of us so that we don't have to stop. Something pulls at a memory as I take in the guy's face, but I can't for the life of me remember what it is.

"Um, hello," I say as Bri gives him a slightly awkward wave.

"You're Cass, right?" he asks with an odd look in his dark eyes, a look that tells me he doesn't actually need my clarification. I can't explain it, but something is putting me on edge with this guy. I give a hesitant nod before he continues. "I'm Matt. I'm kind of that dickhead who groped you at Micky's the other week."

"What?" I ask in shock as I stumble over my own feet.

Holy shit. This is the guy who practically attacked me at Micky's. Had Jax not been there, I probably would have ended up bruised and bloodied in the back alley behind the bar. Actually, what am I saying? He did leave me bruised.

"Yeah," he cringes. "I, ahh, just wanted to apologize about that."

"Oh, um," I say, a little uncomfortable, desperately needing to get away from this guy. "Yeah, it's fine," I say hoping that's enough to send him on his way.

"What?" Brianna barks out in horror with wide eyes, startling us both. "It's absolutely not *fine*," she demands, then gets right into the guy's face as rage flares in her eyes. "You touched her when she said no. You ground your dirty, sweaty body into her when she said no. You kissed her neck after she said no. You wanted more when she struggled against you," she continues as her face starts turning red. "You bruised her skin and tried to force your hand down her pants. None of that is *fine*. She was lucky that Jax was there to knock your sorry-ass out or she probably would have ended up in the hospital completing a rape kit."

Woah. Go, girl.

Matt's eyes grow dark and angry, and he leans over Bri, getting back in her face. "I'm not a rapist," he spits at her. I notice his hands beginning to clench into fists at his side, and it looks like he's physically trying to hold himself back from hitting her.

Where the hell is that bunch of hockey boys when you need them?

"Could have fooled me," Brianna grunts, then takes a calming breath. "Look, I don't know you. I doubt it, but you might even be a nice guy when you're not drunk. But the way you acted at Micky's was unacceptable and quite honestly, it freaked out every woman in that bar. You need to get yourself help or you're going to end up behind bars."

He scowls at her before glancing back at me with narrowed eyes and taking off. "Holy shit," I say to Bri. "You really put the fucker in his place."

"Yeah, I did," she grins then admits, "I've actually been thinking about that a lot. I've had the whole speech planned out for weeks now."

"I can imagine," I laugh, as we pick up where we left off.

"I can't believe you were going to let him off the hook."

I shake my head. "It's not like I wanted to, but the guy gives me the creeps. I just wanted him gone."

"Yeah, I get it," she says. "But I think guys like that who think it's okay to act that way toward women need to be put in their place."

"Agreed," I sigh. "Let's just hope we never have to see the bastard again."

We cut our run short and head home before getting on with our day. I finish classes just after lunch and am about to head home when I get a call from Bri. "Hey, where are you?" she asks.

"On my way home. Why?"

"Oh good," she says, a little too giddy, which puts me on edge. "You know how we were talking about doing something to prove to Jax that you're committed?"

"Yes," I say slowly, a strange anxiety pulsing through my veins.

"Awesome," she sings through the phone. "I'll meet you in ten."

Damn her. That's the second time she's left me hanging. If only I could read her mind.

Bri gets home a few minutes after me and grabs my car keys before physically putting me in my passenger's seat and driving off. "Where are you taking me?" I ask, warily.

"Can't tell you. You'll think about it too much and chicken out."

I groan but don't bother pushing her on it. I know it's no use, she'll never crack.

"Hey," I ask as she hums away to herself while navigating the afternoon traffic. "Did you steal my favorite black lace panties?"

"Eh?" she grunts, looking at me like I've lost my mind. "I don't want your dirty-ass underwear. Who knows where that shit's been?"

I roll my eyes. "So . . . that's a no?"

"Hell yes, it's a no," she laughs, focusing on the road while trying to glance at me at the same time. "Did you check the laundry? Sometimes the machine eats my socks or maybe it got stuck behind the vanity in the bathroom," she suggests with a secretive grin. "I've lost a few things behind there."

I ignore her later comments. "I've checked everywhere, even the washing machine, and they're not there. I've pretty much turned the whole house upside down."

She cracks a grin, and I know exactly what she's going to say before the words come tumbling out of her mouth. "Maybe Jax stole them. He might have become sentimental about his conquests over the past three years. He probably has a drawer full of used panties with a polaroid picture of each girl attached."

I can't help but laugh as I swat at her shoulder, imagining it so clearly, but she couldn't be more wrong. "Jax isn't a creepy fetish guy."

She shrugs her shoulders. "Just saying. How well can anyone truly know another person?"

The conversation is cut short when she starts reverse parking my car like a pro, and I gape at her efforts, more than impressed. We hop out of the car and she loops her arm through mine while leading me through a maze of stores. She stops by a liquor store and grabs a bottle of vodka before silently continuing her journey.

My nerves start to spike. Where the hell is she taking me?

"Better start drinking," she says, handing me the bottle. I reluctantly take it and crack the seal before taking a burning sip.

Bri takes a turn into an open store, and I have to backtrack to get a good look at the sign above, unveiling her plans to me. "What?" I shriek. "You want me to get a tattoo?"

"No, I want you to get your nipples pierced," she says with as much sarcasm as she can possibly muster up before breaking out into a wide grin. "Yes, dumbass. You're getting a tattoo," she continues, "And you better make it something good. Something symbolic between you and Jax."

"Oh my God, Bri. This is insane," I tell her.

"No, sweet cheeks. It's fantastic."

I have to admit, her plan does have a little merit. If Jax can see that I'm dedicated enough to get something permanently put on my skin to symbolize how much I love him, then surely he can see that I'm here for good, right?

I lift the bottle of vodka to my lips and take a deep pull before turning to the man behind the counter. "Let's do this shit."

CHAPTER 16

JAXON

I walk up the driveway I have recently become very familiar with, and raise my hand to knock on the door when I see two faces peering out the curtains, watching me. One filled with lust and the other with absolute devastation.

Rather than knock, I push through the door and stand in the hallway. I narrow my gaze at them as I try to figure out what the hell they're up to. Cassie and Brianna kneel under the window with their heads turned in my direction, and I raise a questioning brow and watch as they fall into uncontrollable fits of laughter.

Glancing around the room, I find an almost finished bottle of vodka and it clicks. These chicks are wasted. As they roll around on the floor trying to contain themselves, I scoop up the bottle and head into the kitchen to put it on the highest shelf of the cupboard, knowing it would be too much effort for these idiots to bother getting it back down.

I smirk to myself before heading back into the living room, finding the girls have finally recovered and are now scowling at me with their hands on their hips. "Excuse you, Mr. Big Shot Hockey Guy," Cass starts off, pointing her finger at me. "Where the hell do you get off waltzing in here, disturbing our afternoon, and taking our alcohol away?"

"And where the hell is my pizza?" Brianna asks as her eyes narrow in on me. Well, at least that explains her look of devastation when I arrived.

"I assume you're here to try and get me on my back?" Cass continues with attitude before wagging her finger in my face. "But don't even think about it, Mister. I'm not one of your little hussies who's going to open my legs at your say so."

"That's right, sister." Bri adds, "You tell him." They give each other a sideways glance before lifting their hands in a very sloppy high-five.

Jesus Christ. Save me.

I focus all my attention on my girl. "Cassandra Waters, shut the fuck up," I demand, waiting for her attention to fall back to me. "First of all, I'm here to ask if you wanted to go to dinner with me, but apparently you're a little too tanked, and secondly," I say, annoyed that I'm having to even say this. "If you happen to end up on your back at the end of the night then that's a win for both of us. And for your information, I damn well know you're not some cheap hussy. I would never treat you that way. I haven't been with anyone else since the day I saw you in that damn class. You're in my head, Cass. The same way you used to be."

She gives me a dreamy smile with glassy eyes and starts to say something when Brianna cuts her off. "Aww," she says, looking just as dreamy as Cass does. "He loves you."

I roll my eyes, ignoring Brianna, because let's face it, both Cass and I know I never stopped loving her. Admitting it out loud is the problem. I turn back to Cass who takes a step in my direction. "You want to take me to dinner?" she questions, excitement shining in those beautiful brown eyes.

"Can you sober up enough to remember it tomorrow?"

"I think I can manage that," she tells me.

I give her a grin. "Can I treat you like a filthy little whore after?"

She bites her bottom lip as her eyes fill with lust. "Only if it's hard and fast and ends with me screaming your name."

And that right there is why this woman drives me insane. I stare right back at her while my mind fills with all the things I want to do to her, but Bri's whining pulls me away. "Oh my God, would you two stop? I mean, unless you're planning on including me, then this is just mean."

My eyes flick to Brianna because well, I'm a man, and she mentioned a threesome. I raise my brow in question. I mean, only if Cass was down for it. But then, I'm not sure I like the idea of sharing my girl.

"Ugh," Cass complains. I'm pretty sure she even stomps her foot.

"I know you two are sort of the king and queen of threesomes around here. But I don't share."

I walk right up into her personal space and whisper in her ear. "You will never have to share me."

Her eyes immediately whip up to meet mine, and I see a million questions behind those beautiful eyes, but I don't give her a chance to voice them. "Go get dressed," I tell her, sending her on her way with a firm spank to that perfectly plump ass before dropping into the couch and flicking on ESPN.

She lets out a frustrated groan, knowing I'm holding something back, but she does what she's told. Bri sits and watches for a while before a gleam appears in her eyes and she disappears from the room.

I don't have time to dwell on it before Cass comes down the hallway looking like an absolute snack in a black dress that clings to her body and dips low between her tits. She matches it with strappy black high heels and my mouth starts to water.

"Fuck me," I whisper as she struts past.

"I'm not a little girl anymore, Jax," she says, like the little seductress she is.

"No, you most certainly are not," I agree. I follow her to the door and reach around her to open it like any well-behaved gentleman should. As we reach my truck, I offer my arm and help her up, because let's face it, her father would come back from the grave and bust my balls if I didn't.

"Where are we going?" she asks as I climb into my truck and start the engine. I give her a pointed stare before turning back to the road.

"Right, okay. I get it," she scoffs, once again annoyed to be held back from her answers.

Her eyes light up when I pull into the parking lot of her favorite Italian restaurant. She looks over at me and gives me a knowing smile before grabbing her purse and hopping out. I meet her at the front of my truck and silently lace my fingers through hers.

Leading her through the door and to our table, she gapes at me with wide eyes. "You booked?" she gasps.

A grin plasters across my face. "Yes," I say, knowing exactly where she's going with this.

"You've never booked a restaurant in your life."

I pull out her chair and help her in before heading around and sitting before her. I order her a glass of wine and get myself a beer so the waiter can scamper off.

"What's all this about?" she asks.

"Can't we just enjoy dinner together?"

"No," she scoffs. "You have an ulterior motive or . . . I don't know."

"I haven't seen you in three years," I remind her. "Is it too much for me to want to spend time with you?"

She considers it for a moment but gives up her line of questing with a slight nod.

The waiter comes around with our drinks and takes our orders as my gaze rests on her, blown away by her dazzling beauty. "Tell me about New York?" I ask as we wait for our dinner.

Her brows furrow as her gaze lifts back to mine, hesitance in her eyes. "You really want to know about that?" she asks, nervously.

"Yeah, I do," I admit with a small nod. "We used to be together every day. Not a thing happened in your life that I didn't know about. Even though it sucked that you weren't around, I still feel like I need to know every detail about your life."

"Okay," she says, a soft smile spreading across her face. Then with that, she launches into her spiel about her life over the past three years. She tells me about her dorm mate for the first year and the apartment she moved into after that. The friends she made and the ones she regrets.

We sit at the table for hours filling each other in on all the details of our lives before the restaurant staff starts giving us dirty looks and subtle hints to vacate the table.

"Come on," I say, walking around and helping her from her chair. I settle the bill and lead her outside where we walk past my truck and to a little park.

A tiny little smirk plays over her lips, and I grow suspicious. "What?"

She grins up at me. "I was just remembering that time I was in my first bikini and you were gawking at me from your bedroom window like a dirty little perv. You were probably jacking off so hard you would've been tearing the skin right off your dick."

"Ha. Babe, it wasn't the bikini that had me gawking," I explain. "It was the first time I noticed you had tits." She rolls her eyes, but I continue. "I swear, it went from like nothing to something overnight."

"Shut up," she says, nailing me in the ribs.

"That's not even the worst I did," I admit.

Her eyes narrow on me. "Spill it, Payne. Get it all out in the open."

I grin as I recap the story. "We were maybe sixteen or seventeen, and I'd gotten home from hockey camp early, so I snuck over to surprise you, but you were in the shower with the door cracked." She narrows her eyes in suspicion, clearly wondering where the hell this is going. After all, we used to shower together all the time. "You were rubbing that sweet little clit and moaning."

"What? Noooo," she shrieks, her hands flying to cover her face, completely embarrassed. "Tell me you're lying?"

"Hell no," I scoff. "I pushed the door open real slow so you wouldn't notice, dropped my pants, and came right along with you."

"Jax," she whines. "You didn't."

"Babe, I would never lie about you touching yourself. It was pure heaven. It was the best welcome home present you could have gotten me." She ducks her head under my arm and refuses to meet my eyes. "Don't be embarrassed," I tell her. "You used to perform for me all the time. I loved it."

She groans out my name once again, and I can't help but laugh, which she apparently doesn't appreciate. I curl her more firmly under my arm as we find a bench that looks out over a small pond and take a seat.

Pulling Cassie into my lap, she leans into me, right where she belongs. "Thanks for dinner," she murmurs as she turns her head into my neck and kisses me softly. That's not enough for me, though. I reach up and take her face in my hands and gently raise her chin until we're eye to eye. I pull her into me and kiss her, letting my feelings shine through.

"I'm sorry," I whisper as she pulls back. "I should have done this weeks ago."

She closes her eyes for a brief moment, taking relief in my words. She drops her forehead to mine. "It's okay. You needed time. I hurt you. I get it."

"I missed you, Cass," I whisper, brushing my fingers down the side of her face. "I've known since I was a kid that I can't live without you, and I don't know why I believed I could do it now. I was stupid and stubborn, I should have gone after you and brought you home."

"No," she demands. "I didn't deserve that. I left. I was the one who made the mistake and let my pride get the best of me. I hate myself for putting you through that, but I promise, Jax, I'll never hurt you like that again."

A tear falls down her cheek and I pull her into me again. "I know," I say, realizing for the first time that I truly believe it. The Cass that I grew up with and fell for has come back to me. She has managed to somehow look past my reputation to see that the old me is still in here, dying for her to find. Now, as I watch her pouring her heart out, I know I don't have to wait for her to earn my trust. She already has it.

"I love you, Jax," she murmurs into me. "I've never stopped."

I hold onto her just that bit tighter as her words wrap around me, not realizing until this moment just how desperate I've been to hear those words on her lips. "I know. I love you, too."

She pulls back slightly, tears of happiness falling from her eyes. She wipes her cheeks with the back of her arm, once again telling me how sorry she is, and I hold her until the tears have run their course.

"You really haven't been with anyone else since that day in class?" she asks a little sheepishly.

"No, babe," I tell her, then let her in on the truth, not really knowing how she might take it. "The reason why there were so many girls was because when I was with them, it gave me a break from thinking about you. The triplets disappeared right after you did, and it was like I was abandoned by my family. I had this massive void and no idea how to fix it. I sulked around for ages until I realized that I could dull the pain with alcohol and sex. It never lasted long, but it helped. It was never the same though. There was never a connection, not like there is with us."

She sits in silence, taking it all in before looking back up at me with a frown. "I guess it's just weird knowing that most of the girls on campus have been with you."

I can't help but grin. "You're not jealous, are you?"

She rolls her eyes but a grin takes over. "Shut up," she laughs as she tries to swat me away. And just like that, the final piece of the puzzle falls right into place.

"Come on, babe. Let me take you home," I say, trying to get up only to be stopped by a very stubborn Cass.

"Wait," she says, looking around the park before continuing. "I sort of did something today," she tells me.

I watch her through narrowed eyes. "What?" I ask suspiciously.

Cassie looks around again, probably making sure we're alone before adjusting herself on my lap until she's straddled over me. She comes up on her knees and swiftly hoists up her dress before lowering her ass back to my lap. She gives an embarrassed cringe before lifting her dress up a little higher and pulling down the edge of her underwear, revealing a bandage just inside her lower hip.

Oh, geez. This is not what I think it is.

"Hold my dress," she requests. I do as I'm told, and she reaches for the bandage to slowly peel it back, and a grin crosses my face before she has even finished. A tattoo reading *Jax* in cursive writing rests on her inner hip, in a place where only I would ever see. "Do you like it?" she asks, nervously.

"Fuck, babe. I love it," I laugh. "I mean, I'm kind of stunned but . . . fuck."

"It's super cheesy, but I wanted to do something to prove to you that you're my forever."

With those words, I crush my lips to hers, letting go of her dress. She gasps as she hastily tries to stick the bandage back on while keeping up with my lips. With her dress still sitting around her hips, I do the one thing any man would do in my position.

My hand comes down between us and instantly slips into her underwear while her hands work to undo my belt buckle. Within moments, her fingers are curling around my cock and working up and down. Needing to be inside her and feel her heat all over me, I wrap my arm around her waist and pull her in closer.

Cassie rises up and guides herself on top of me before dropping down and giving us both the relief that we're so desperately craving.

She rides me like a seasoned pro, gripping onto my shoulders and in no time at all, she's exploding around me, her pussy clenching and claiming me as her own. She doesn't stop moving as her high rocks through her, and with that, I find my release with a low groan, shooting hot spurts of cum deep inside her pussy.

Her head drops to my shoulder, and my hand roams up and down her back. "Holy shit, Cass. You're amazing," I whisper.

"Mmhmm," she whimpers in agreement.

"Alright, babe," I say after a few minutes. "Let me take you home so we can do that all over again."

"Okay, yeah. I need new panties," she explains, then after seeing my blank stare, she continues. "No condom."

"Right," I say as understanding dawns. I scoop her up in my arms and walk her back to my truck, and can't help but laugh as I put her in and she cringes as she sits down. Despite taking wicked pleasure in her discomfort, I make my way to my side and get in to drive her home.

"Speaking of panties," she says as I reverse out of the parking spot. "You haven't got a trophy drawer full of girls' panties, do you? I'm missing my favorite black lace ones."

I stop my truck in the middle of the quiet road and gape at her. "Babe, the rush is seeing you in them and then watching them slide down those legs of yours. I'm sorry to tell you, but I don't get off by pocketing them afterward."

"Damn. I kind of hoped you did. At least then I'd know where they are," she sighs.

"You better not have lost those ones," I tell her, hitting the gas again. "They're my favorite, too."

"Sorry," she shrugs apologetically. "They're definitely gone. I've looked everywhere."

I promise to buy her some new ones, and it's not long before we're pulling onto her street and she recognizes the black truck in her driveway. "Shit," she groans with a heavy sigh. "Tell me that's not Carter's truck?"

"Maybe he got lost on his way to Sluts'R'Us?" I suggest.

Cassie throws me a sideways glance, her lips twisting into a wicked grin. "He could have always called you for directions," she throws back at me with a sexy-as-hell sparkle in her eye.

"Touché," I laugh as I pull up beside Carter's truck.

"Let's just hope he's here to see me and not Bri," she murmurs as she jumps out of my truck.

I scoff, bringing my truck to a stop. "Doubt it. It's after eleven at night."

Cassie harrumphs and marches down the path to the front door before twisting the handle and shoving her shoulder into it. "Carter Thomas Waters, get your bitch-ass out here right now, and you better make damn sure it's clothed," she calls through the house.

I hear laughter coming from the hallway and have to stifle my own.

Carter comes into view with a half-naked Bri behind him. He works on the button of his jeans, and it's damn obvious what's just gone down. Unsurprisingly, Cass immediately lays into him. "What the hell do you think you're doing here? I told you, none of my girlfriends."

Carter just laughs, more than pleased with himself. Though, I'm sure it'll be a different story once Bobby finds out about this. Either way, this is about to get good. So I do what anyone else in my position would do and take a seat on the couch, kick up my feet, and get comfortable for the show.

CHAPTER 17

CASSIE

Carter Waters is the biggest manwhore I've ever met. I'm beyond furious with him. I can't believe these two, and now he has the nerve to look at me with a stupid grin. "What'd you expect?" he says with a shrug.

I see fucking red.

"Are you fucking serious, you . . . you manwhore! I hope you thoroughly enjoyed yourself because it won't be happening again."

"Well, yeah actually, I did enjoy myself. Thanks for asking," he says, proudly. "I'm extremely satisfied. Why didn't you tell me she was such a little firecracker? I would have been here weeks ago."

"WHAT?" I yell at him, momentarily stumped as my jaw falls open. The audacity of this moron. "What?"

He gives me a lazy shrug before heading to the kitchen and coming out with a beer for himself and Jax, as though the moment calls for a celebratory drink. If only he knew his drinking buddy just railed me in a public park.

Turning my attention to Bri, I give her the look of death. "You. I should have known better," I accuse as I storm right up to the little minx. "What do you have to say for yourself, you skank whore?"

"Hey," she laughs. "This is all your fault."

Jaxon's laughter in the background has me slipping closer to the edge. "How the hell does this STD fest have anything to do with me?"

"You left your phone here. He called. I answered. It's simple really," she explains, falling on the couch beside Carter.

"Oh my God. You two have some serious making-up to do," I demand.

"Righteo," Carter scoffs.

"Argh," I groan with frustration as I flop into a chair that's well away from everyone, cross my arms over my chest and sulk, happily picturing how good it would feel to nut punch Carter. Something fluffy rubs against my legs, and I stand back up to find my dressing gown draped over the couch.

"Oh my God, Carter Waters, if you were wearing my dressing gown after your sweaty sexcapades, you can bet your life there'll be an ass-kicking in your near future." I shiver, picking the gown up by as little material as possible and throwing it in the laundry. That thing is going to receive the most thorough laundering of its life before it ever touches my body again.

They ignore me as they question Jax about what the hell is going on between us, and I snatch the beer out of Carter's hand on my way back to the couch. He doesn't deserve one tonight.

"Oh, hey," I hear Jax pipe up a few minutes later, glancing at my brother. "While you're here, can you give me a hand with something?"

Carter mumbles a quick yeah and they get up and head out to Jax's truck. My eyes narrow on their retreating bodies, having absolutely no idea what Jax could be up to. I'm not left wondering for long though as they march back in a moment later, their arms piled high with all my recording stuff, keyboard and everything.

Panic tears at my chest as I stare at the boys. "Um, what do you think you're doing?" I question as Bri's face scrunches in confusion.

"I'm setting this shit up," Jax responds. "Where do you want it?"

"I don't want it," I snap.

He ignores me and makes the executive decision to take it through to the dining room.

Bri comes up beside me and looks at me with narrowed, curious eyes. "Why the hell is Jax setting up a recording studio in our dining room?"

With a sigh, I leave her gaping at the boys and grab my laptop. I take a seat at the table and invite her to sit next to me while the boys continue their work. I power up my laptop and jump straight to YouTube, typing in my name and finding the page I haven't visited for three long years.

Turning it toward her, I watch as she gapes at the screen, taking in the countless videos and the three hundred thousand followers.

"Explain," she demands as she begins to scroll.

Sighing, I let it all out. "I'm a bit of a singer. Or at least, I used to be," I tell her, getting a well-deserved scoff from each of the boys. I ignore them and continue with my explanation. "Growing up, I was always singing, so Mom threw me headfirst into music lessons. I loved it, it's one of my few passions. So, when I was about fourteen, I started recording—"

"Fuck," she screeches, cutting me off. "You have half a million followers."

"Really? Last I checked there was only half that."

She lets out an impressive scoff, and I get back to my explanation. "As I was saying, I started recording some covers and Jax created a YouTube page and started posting them, even though I had absolutely no idea."

"Ha," she laughs. "Typical man."

I grin but continue on with my story. "I sang for me because it made me happy, but the boys were always pushing me to make a career out of it. By the time I came across the page, I already had thousands of followers, and the boys gave me no choice but to go along with it. So, every few days, I'd record another cover and Jax would post it."

She nods her head, a little in shock, and hits play on a cover of *Irreplaceable* by Beyonce. "Holy shit, Cass. You're fucking good."

Once again, the boys scoff at the remark. "She's a bit better than good, don't you think?" Jax suggests.

"Uh, yeah," she breathes. "Why'd you stop?"

My eyes flick to Jax, who I notice already has his heavy stare on me. I let out a sad sigh. "I couldn't sing when I left for New York," I say, leaving it at that. But just as I knew she would, she understands me perfectly. With a small smile and a quick nod, she pulls up the next video.

"Hey, this one's recent," she muses as she hits play.

"What the hell?" I ask as the song I sang at the wedding plays through the small speakers of my laptop. I snatch it from her and stare at the screen, knowing from the angle the video was taken this would have been shot by either Carter or Logan. I stare at the screen completely dumbfounded, until I notice the caption—*Ladies and gentlemen, she's back!*

"Fucking Logan," I mutter under my breath, remembering those exact words he said to me at the wedding after I sang. Though at the time, I was too focused on Jax to have really paid attention to anyone else.

"Bloody hell," Brianna says, watching the screen over my shoulder. "You should have a recording deal by now."

I press my lips together and cringe, really wishing she hadn't bought this up. "What?" Jax asks, noticing my hesitation.

I look up from the screen and give him a nervous look. "I sort of had two labels seek me out when I was in New York."

"WHAT?" Brianna screeches as Carter straightens himself, paying a little more attention to the conversation.

"Calm down. I didn't accept it."

"What?" This time it's Carter questioning me. "Are you fucking kidding me? I love you, kid, but sometimes you do the most idiotic things."

"What's the big deal? I don't want to be some big celebrity singer with no life. I want to be a physiotherapist. You all know this. I sing for me because it makes me happy, not for some fat, balding dude in a suit who will make all the decisions and butcher my songs."

Jax's gaze narrows on me, and I realize he's trying to figure me out. "You sure?" he asks.

I think it over and realize that I honestly don't know. I want to sing, but I also want to be a physiotherapist. The thought of becoming some big-time celebrity scares the shit out of me. I shrug my shoulders and Jax steps forward, taking my shoulders in his big hands. "What's the matter?"

"I don't know. I guess I want to sing, but I want it to be for me. I don't want some big record label having a say in what I can and can't do."

He nods his understanding. "What if we just go back to what we were doing before? Maybe you could record some of your own songs and post them, too?"

At that, my chin lifts, and I look up at him. "I like that idea," I say, wrapping my arms around his waist.

"I thought you might," he says with a wink before leaning down and pressing his lips to mine.

"Ugh, if you two are going to start that again, I'm out," Bri declares as she takes my laptop off the counter and disappears into the living room.

With a laugh, Jax gets back to helping Carter set up my recording stuff, and I leave to shower. Within minutes, the door opens, and Jax strips before sliding into the shower with me. "Thank you," I murmur into his chest as he wraps his arms around me. I don't have to explain what the thank you is for. He just knows what I'm referring to. He knows me. "Is Carter gone?"

His eyes become hooded as his hands begin to roam. "You think I'd be in here with you if he was still under this roof?"

"Good point."

I pick up my bottle of bodywash, frowning as I struggle to shake the last few drops out of the bottle. "How many showers have you been having here?" I question, forgetting just how regularly he has to shower when taking into account his multiple training sessions. "I've never gone through a bottle this quickly before."

"I'll buy you some more," Jax whispers in my ear, bodywash the furthest thing from his mind. "As long as this never has to stop."

With that, we quickly finish showering before Jax turns off the taps, wraps me in a towel, and leads me to my bed.

When six in the morning rolls around, our alarms go off at the same time, and I groan as I try to get out of bed. "Stay," Jax mumbles as he puts his arm around my waist and pulls me against him until I can feel his erection poking me in my ass.

"Mmm," I moan, rubbing against him and closing my eyes.

Jax's hand snakes down my body and slips inside my sleep shorts right as a loud knock rattles the doorframe. "Get your ass out here, Cassandra Waters. We made a pact," Bri yells as lively as ever. "Jax will have to deal with little Jax himself."

"Will she eventually go away?" Jax asks, pushing his fingers deep inside me.

"No way in hell," I laugh as I turn to face him with a grin, his fingers sliding out of me. "Raincheck? Besides, the boys will bust your ass if you're late."

He ignores me as he begins to nuzzle my neck, but when the door flies open and a determined Brianna comes storming in, she yanks the blankets off us and grabs my ankle. She gives a massive tug and pulls me straight off the edge of the bed.

"Oomph," I grunt as my ass connects with the hard wooden floors.

"Oh, great," Bri exclaims, clapping her hands together with fake enthusiasm. "You're up."

"Damn it," I mutter, getting up off the floor and starting to look for my workout clothes. Jax reluctantly does the same, searching for his things. He bends to grab his shirt, and his muscles roll then flex as he pulls the shirt over his head to cover that glorious, sculptured body.

"Wow," Bri mutters next to me, both of us gaping at the sight.

"Yeah," I whisper back to her. "You sure we have to run? I could get a better workout right here."

Jax stiffens and turns to see what's caught our attention, giving us both a view of the front as his shirt falls into place. He smirks, immediately knowing what's up. With a wink, he grabs his keys off the bedside table, kisses my cheek, and struts out of my room. But his ego isn't the only thing inflated.

Bri and I cool off and eventually manage to make our way out the door for our morning run, and as much as I hate it, my persistence is starting to show. My legs feel stronger, and my fitness levels are better than they've ever been.

We return an hour later and get ourselves breakfast. Brianna starts to play with my recording stuff after we've finished stuffing our faces, so I show her how some of it works since neither of us needs to be in class until after lunch.

It doesn't take long for Bri to convince me to record a cover, so I grab my laptop and search the music for Taylor Swift's *Red* and immediately get in the zone. Bri sets up the camera, and I move in front of my microphone to get started.

"Hi, guys," I say into the camera. "Sorry for disappearing on you. I was taking a little break, but as my asshole brothers and friends have given me no choice, I'm back. Hope you like it."

I turn back to the microphone and hit play on the music.

Fifteen minutes later, I'm showing Bri all the ins and outs of how to edit and post the video to my YouTube page. Another ten minutes later, the notifications start rolling in.

"Holy shit. People really love you," Brianna grins as she scrolls through the comments. "Why don't you post an original song?"

My stomach drops, and my eyes widen. "Umm, nah," I say with a shake of my head. "Too soon. Besides, all my latest stuff is kind of depressing."

"Well, are you happy now?" she asks.

"Yes . . ." I grin, knowing where she's going with this.

"Good, so we throw out your old stuff and get started on the new."

"What? Throw it out?" I shriek, horrified by the suggestion. "What kind of monster are you? I couldn't part with it. I mean, it's still good stuff, just not the kind of stuff I want to sing about or record."

"Righteo," she chuckles. "Then why don't you add that last notebook to the pile you probably have collecting dust under your bed and start a fresh one?"

I roll my eyes. "It's in my closet actually."

A text comes through to my phone, and I recognize the old number like the back of my hand. It's probably time to program him back into my contact list.

Jax - Nice song selection.

A chuckle rips through me, and I roll my eyes as I hit reply.

Cass - Yeah, just something that came to me. I didn't really put too much thought into it.

He and I both know I'm lying. Every song I have ever posted has had some sort of meaning to me, whether it's the way the song makes me feel or that the lyrics say something about what's happening in my life. *Red* by Taylor Swift is just that. The lyrics perfectly sum up how I feel about Jax.

Jax - Liar.

"How long would it take you to write a song?" Brianna asks, stealing my attention away from my phone.

"Honestly, with everything that's been going on with Jax, I'm pretty sure I've already got one completed. I've just got to get it written down and work out a melody," I explain. " I'm probably a bit rusty though."

"Shit. Well I know what we're doing today," she says, dragging me out the door.

We walk a few minutes down to the store and load up on notebooks, music books, pencils, sharpeners, and erasers. I spend my morning excited about recording something original for the first time, while Brianna searches for articles on how to become a top-earning manager.

After lunch, we both sulk as we have to stop what we're doing and get ready for classes, but the moment we're home again, it's right back to work.

By dinner time, I've recorded the music and am getting started on the vocals. I nervously hit record as I turn toward the camera and introduce my new song. "Hey guys, me again," I start, my hands shaking beneath the table. "I know I rarely post twice in one day, but here we are. This is my first original song, so forgive my nerves. I only started working on this piece this morning, so it's a little rough, but I couldn't wait to share it with you." I let out a shaky breath before giving the camera a wide smile. "This song is dedicated to the love of my life." And with that, my fingers curl around the base of the microphone, and I hit play on the music, preparing to pour my heart out.

A tear slips out the corner of my eye, but I focus on the lyrics, making sure the one person this song is for can truly understand the message I'm trying to convey.

Precisely four and a half minutes later, Brianna squeals in delight as she hits post.

After pouring a glass of wine, I sit back on the couch, a sense of accomplishment coming over me. I could really get used to this feeling, and I have Jax to thank for it.

My phone chimes, indicating I have a new text, and I grab my phone to find a group message from my brothers.

L, C, S - Mom and Dad would be proud of you, dork.

CHAPTER 18

JAXON

I step off the ice after a late training session, utterly exhausted, and the boys and I head to the locker room with only a few quiet conversations between us. Whipping off my training gear and skates, I consider just grabbing my shit and leaving so I can shower at home.

"Fuck," I groan, knowing myself too well. I'll end up crashing and going to bed stinking of sweat. I grab a towel and rush through a quick shower before packing up my shit. Before leaving, I reach into my locker and grab my wallet, phone, and keys.

I unlock my phone to find a missed call from Dad, which is promptly ignored, a message from Cass, and a YouTube notification telling me Cass has posted another song. My brows fly up. Two in one day! Cass is really getting back into it. I've never been so proud of her.

Opening her text, I realize it's from over two hours ago.

Cass - Night. Xx.

Not wanting to wake her, I don't reply. Instead, I open my YouTube app and find the notification for Cassie's song. I hit play on the video, and my eyes immediately land on her beautiful face, framed by her long, chestnut hair.

She turns toward the camera and introduces the song the same way she's been doing for years, only this time, it's different. I turn up the volume just to make sure I can hear her properly. I mean, it's pretty damn late, and I'm fucking exhausted.

She didn't just say this was an original song, did she?

I hit pause and grab my hockey bag off the ground before ducking past Bobby. I fly through the door, desperate to be in the peaceful silence of my truck where I can concentrate on her song without distractions.

Slamming the door behind me, I quickly turn on the ignition, only to have to wait the agonizing few moments for my phone to connect to my truck. As soon as it's finally connected, I hit play on the video.

It starts with Cass playing the keys. Even though it doesn't show that, I just know she would have composed the music herself and pre-recorded it so she could sing to her own music. The melody takes me away before she even sings a word.

The moment she opens her mouth, I'm completely blown away,

and I know without a doubt this song is for me.

The beautiful notes and melodies come from the heart as she sings about forgiveness and regrets, how she tore up a love and devastated her own heart. She looks deep into the camera with tears pooling in her eyes as she tells the world that she will fight for me until her dying breath and won't stop until she's finally earned forgiveness for her mistakes.

But what she mustn't realize is that she has already been granted that forgiveness. I will never let her slip through my fingers again. She's my world. Always has been, and always will be.

She belts out her song, giving it every ounce of passion and dedication she possesses. There's no doubt in my mind that she could sell out stadiums night after night if she wanted to, she's just that good. But I stand by her decision. Her voice is hers and hers alone to do with it as she pleases, and I swear, after seeing this video, her decision has never made me so damn proud. This is Cass, the real Cass, finally sharing herself and her gifts to the world in her own way, on her own terms.

I listen to her song twice more before peeling out of the arena parking lot and driving straight to her place.

Finding the spare key hidden below a rock in the garden, I let myself in, making sure to lock the door behind me. I make my way to her room and watch her sleeping peacefully for a moment before stripping down to my underwear.

I gently lift the covers, not wanting to wake her as I slide in and wrap my arms around her. I pull her close, the way my body has craved for the past three years.

"Hmmm, what are you doing here?" she murmurs in her sleepy haze.

"I need to hold you," I tell her as I nuzzle into the soft skin of her neck and close my eyes. "I saw your song. It's beautiful."

A yawn takes over her. "It was for you."

"I know," I murmur. "I love you, Cass. You hold my heart in the palm of your hand, and I promise you, I will never let you go."

"I'm not going anywhere," she says, turning in my arms and placing a feather-soft kiss on my lips. "You're stuck with me forever."

"There's no one else I'd rather be stuck with," I say, smiling against her lips.

"I love you," she whispers, catching my lips with hers once again.

"I love you, too," I murmur as I play with her hair, knowing it helps her sleep. "Good night, Cass."

"Night," she says as she falls back into a peaceful sleep, staying there all night wrapped in my arms.

It's been a few weeks since Cass and I sorted our shit out, and to say the time has flown by is an understatement. She's slotted back into my life like she was never gone. Like her being by my side every day is as natural as the sun rising in the morning.

I know the girl like the back of my hand, yet every day we're discovering the kind of people we've become over the last three years.

I consider myself one hell of a lucky bastard to be able to experience all these things with her for a second time. And at the risk of sounding like a fucking pussy, I've never been happier.

Pushing across the ice, my blades cut in as I shoot myself forward with only ten seconds on the clock. Coach Harris screams, his face turning red as he makes us fight until the very last moment. We already know we've won, the score six to four, but I refuse to give in just yet. Playing it safe is how you lose.

The crowd roars throughout the arena, chanting and cheering, already celebrating for their favorite team. I know without a doubt that Cass is one of those people, most likely already on her feet, probably jumping up and down with my number on her back. The thought pushes me faster.

I watch as our opponent corners Bobby, and I open myself up for him to shoot the puck. My stick scoops up the speeding puck with practiced ease as he fires it toward me. Xander and Shorty cover my flanks and protect me from the opposition's defense as I sprint forward.

With two seconds on the clock, I see my opening. I shoot the puck, and the little bastard flies past the goalie's pads, straight into the back of the net right as the buzzer sounds.

The crowd roars as my team tackles me. We're halfway through the season and still undefeated. Not a single team has managed to bring us down. The boys climb off me and I get to my feet, only to be assaulted by the guys once again, with excited high-fives and claps on the back.

I can hardly hear their excitement over the roar of the crowd, but

I see it plain as day on their faces. I look up into the crowd to find my girl, only to find she isn't there. Brianna stands in Cassie's vacated spot. She gives me a grin, and points toward the aisle of the grandstand.

My eyes swivel in that direction to find Cass rushing down the stairs, elbowing past the spectators trying to exit the grandstand. She pushes past one last guy and makes her way to the ground level, but she doesn't stop there. She pushes forward with her eyes locked on me.

I pull off my helmet as I skate to the edge with a grin. I jump the barrier and the sexiest little minx I've ever met flies through the sky and catapults herself into my arms.

Her lips crash down on mine, and I'm distantly aware of the camera crew to my left. I pray this moment doesn't end up on ESPN, but even if it does, it's not going to stop me from kissing my girl.

"You were awesome," she says before diving back in with another kiss. "I'm so hot for you right now."

I kiss her until Coach is yelling at me to *'Put the girl down and get your ass in the locker room.'* I feel her grin against my lips. "Got to go, babe."

"Okay," she says as I put her on her feet. "I'll see you after."

With that, I head back to the locker room, but Bobby and I are bombarded with cameras and end up giving interviews before we finally make it back.

Coach gives us a brief chat and congratulates us, before yelling to make sure we're on time and pushing ourselves harder for the rest of the season. We're finally dismissed to shower and get ready for our traditional night out at Micky's.

Half an hour later we pull up at the bar, and the boys pile in to find our usual table reserved. The waiters come around and drop drinks into our hands before we've even asked for them, taking any food orders as they go. After the game we just played, each and every one of us order a main meal. I even make sure Cass and Bri get a side of fries, because I know the boys will still be hungry.

Our night goes just as any other post-game night goes. We drink, we eat, we party, and we pick up. Or, at least the other guys do. But with the label of being the undefeated Dragons and Kings of Denver, it's really not hard for these guys to find a willing chick around here.

Cassie and Brianna disappear onto the dance floor, and I give her the *be careful* speech. I know it's not needed anymore, as she hates drinking too much when we come here now, but you can never be too careful.

A text draws my attention and I pull my phone from my pocket.

Miller - Fucking awesome game, man.

I hit reply.

Jaxon - Pretty sure I broke a few of your records during that one.
Miller - Don't count on it, bro.

Grinning, I slip my phone back into my pocket and relax as I watch my girl dance. That is, until Xander gets up from the table, acting suspiciously once again. I watch as he weaves through the crowd, past the dancers, and takes a seat at the bar, far away from any of the guys.

If he wanted another beer, all he had to do was wave over a waitress and he would have had one within seconds. There's no need for him to have gotten up like that.

I watch with a narrowed stare as the new chick behind the bar approaches him and places a glass down in front of him with a knowing, flirty smile. They talk for a while before I realize it's comfortable. Too comfortable. It's like they know each other somehow.

"Hey," Bobby says as a french fry bounces off the side of my face.

I zone in on Bobby with a scowl. "What?"

"What's up with you? You're looking at the bar like you're fucking lost or something."

"Nah, man," I say, shaking my head as my eyes return to Xander. I nod toward him with a lift of my chin and watch as Bobby's eyes follow my gaze. "Something's going on with him. He was covered in bruises the other week but denied anything happened."

"Seriously?" he asks. "Is he in some kind of trouble?"

I shrug my shoulders. "I don't know, man, but I know he sure as fuck doesn't want to talk about it."

I see scenarios ticking over in Bobby's mind, and I'm sure it's probably all the same stuff I've already considered. His gaze flicks back toward Xander, the same way mine has for the past ten minutes, but I've decided I've had enough.

Grabbing my beer off the table, I weave my way through the crowd and take a seat on the empty stool beside him. "Hey, man. What are you doing all the way over here? There's a party going on, and we're the guests of honor."

He gives me a regretful smile as he continues to nurse the glass on the table. "Just chilling out with Charli here," he motions toward the chick behind the bar, who lifts her chin in acknowledgment before getting back to work.

Xander looks down at his watch before grabbing the glass on the bar and throwing back what's left. "Let me guess," I say. "You've got somewhere to be?"

"Yeah. Sorry, man," he cringes.

"Is there something you need to talk about?" I ask. "You're not in any kind of trouble, are you? I can't have shit coming down on the team, especially now we're getting closer to the finals."

He shakes his head. "Nah, no trouble. Just got stuff going on," he says, before his eyes quickly flick to Charli's.

"Alright, man." I get up off my stool and give him some space. "You know where to find me if you need anything."

He gives a tight nod before getting up off his own stool. "Thanks," he says before turning away.

"Hey," I call after him. "Don't show up for training covered in bruises. I need your head in the game if we're going to take out the championship again."

"Sure thing, man," he says with a grin before turning away and ducking out the side door of Micky's. I look back to the bar to acknowledge Charli before leaving for my table, but I notice Xander's left his wallet on the bar.

I duck through the crowd after him and slip through the side exit. I look up and down the side alley, but don't see him anywhere. I pull my phone out and quickly send a text.

Jaxon - Dude, left your wallet on the bar.

His response comes almost instantly.

Xander - Shit. Be there in a sec.

Pocketing my phone, I wait in the side alley, guessing he will return to this spot.

A guy in a dark hood comes up from the bottom of the alley, and I mind my own business, figuring he will walk on by. That was my mistake.

My eyes are trained down when the guy grabs me and slams me up against the brick wall. My head rebounds off the brick, but I've had worse hits in hockey to be affected by it. Especially with the burst of adrenaline suddenly surging through my veins.

I push the guy back and the move has his hood falling off, revealing his face. It's dark in the alley, but there's enough light to recognize the sick fucker. It's the guy who tried to grope Cass.

"What the fuck?" I growl as I push off the wall to get in his face. I notice his hand buried deep in his pocket, shaped in a fist, as if he is holding something there.

"Karma's a fucking bitch," he snarls moments before his fist comes hurtling toward my face. I try to duck, but the amount of alcohol in my system has my reflexes on fucking vacation. The guy nails me in the jaw and my body falls back against the wall.

My head starts to spin, and the world goes blurry before quickly righting itself again. Shit, had this guy knocked me out or damaged my vision, I would have been fucked for the rest of the season. He could have potentially ruined my career.

By the time my vision clears, the asshole is coming for me again, so I push myself up from the wall. There's no chance in hell this guy is getting a second go at me.

I bend at the waist and charge at him. His body lifts off the ground, and I slam him into the opposite wall. The move forces his fisted hand out of his pocket, and I notice a pair of black lace panties that I would recognize anywhere.

He rubs the lace between his fingers as his eyes light up in a sick excitement before bringing them up to his face.

That motherfucker.

I see nothing but red.

There's no doubt in my mind they're Cassie's missing underwear. The tiny pink bow at the top is a dead giveaway, and I'm sure if I got them off him, I'd even see the tear in the lace from where Cass stopped me from ripping them off her body.

My fist goes flying before I even realize what I'm doing. I nail him in his eye socket, enjoying the sound of his head bouncing off the brick wall behind him, but I don't stop there. I slam him with an uppercut that has him folding over and gasping for breath.

"Stay the fuck away from her," I warn the sorry bastard as I steal the panties from his clenched hand.

He growls in frustration, and it's then I realize that he's here to have another crack at Cass. The thought alone has my knee coming up and nailing him in the guts once again.

"She's fucking mine," he spits as he straightens himself out and tries to come at me again, but the guy is too winded. I catch him by the neck of his shirt and pull him up to my height.

"I've fucking warned you once already," I snarl. "Don't make me do it again."

The asshole scoffs at my warning, and I let go of his shirt. He drops to his feet as my fist hurtles toward his temple. When it slams against his head, he drops to the ground like a sack of shit.

Anger pulses through my veins with a desperate need to get Cass back in my arms where I know she'll be safe, but as I go to turn back to Micky's, I hear someone behind me.

"Dude," a voice sounds through the alley, "I didn't realize you had it in you." I turn to find Xander behind me, looking over the guy and taking in his injuries. "Everything good here?"

"Yeah, man," I say, stepping away from the guy. "Just had a little misunderstanding is all."

He lets out a small scoff. "Right," he says before searching the alley and finding his wallet laying on the ground. "Thanks for this," he says, holding up the wallet and disappearing at a jog.

The side door flies open and Shorty barges out with a chick in his arms. He looks at me with a grin before noticing the unconscious guy on the ground. "The fuck happened here?" he questions.

"The same dickhead I knocked out last time came back for round two."

"Shit," he grunts before turning his attention to the chick who's trying to slide her thong down her legs. He looks back to me. "You done with the alley, man?"

"You know, it's a lot more hygienic in a bed," I remind him.

He shrugs once again. "Nah, this'll be too quick to worry about finding a bed."

I roll my eyes and glance back at the guy, making sure he's well and truly out before I leave. I head on through the side door, and my eyes immediately search out Cass. She's still on the dance floor, and relief pulses through me as I come up behind her and wrap my arms around her body. "Are you ready to go, babe?"

She turns in my arms and her eyes widen in shock. "What happened?" she gasps, gaining Brianna's attention and a few of the guys. Cassie's hand lifts to my face, and I try my hardest not to shrink away from her touch because, let's be honest, it fucking hurts.

"Nothing," I tell her. "Just some dickhead wanting to settle an old score."

She presses her lips together, and I see the look in her eyes. I know she's not convinced by my casual attitude, but there's no way in hell I'm telling her who the guy was. It would freak her out knowing he was here, though I'm pretty sure my warning was enough this time. There's no way this dickhead would try for a third round. Not if he values his life.

"Seriously, Cass. It's okay," I tell her.

She pulls me into her arms and holds me tight. "Are you okay?"

she murmurs just for me to hear.

I look into her eyes and see nothing but concern. "Yeah, babe. I'm fine."

She presses her lips together once more as she considers my answer, then she takes my hand and leads me to the bar. She orders a bottle of water and waves goodbye to Brianna, who confirms Bobby will take her home.

We get out into the street and she hands me the water. "Umm, thanks?" I say as my eyes discreetly move up and down the road and alleys.

She rolls her eyes but grins at me anyway. "It's not for you to drink, you moron. It's cold. It's to soothe your face and stop the swelling. And besides, you wouldn't want everyone thinking your girlfriend beat you up. I think that would damage your street cred."

I scoff, but can't help smirking at the little she-devil. "First of all, I highly doubt anyone would think someone as . . . petite as you would be capable of beating on me. And secondly, if anyone asks, I'd just say it happened in bed. They'll assume we play rough, and I'll still come out the hero. Winners all around."

"I hardly see how I come out a winner in that situation."

"Babe," I grin. "I'm a fucking beast in bed, everybody knows it. I have a whole reputation built around it. So basically, as long as everyone knows you're the one I'm fucking, then they all know you're getting your world thoroughly rocked each and every night, which you are," I explain with a wink. "Therefore, you're a winner."

"Ugh, shut up," she laughs as she rolls her eyes. "I was nervous your ego might have deflated with that punch, but it seems it's intact. In fact, it might have even grown," she smirks as we turn onto her street. "Be careful, you might not fit through the door anymore."

I grab her around the waist and pull her back into my chest. "My ego isn't the only thing that's fucking big," I murmur into her hair as I nuzzle in to find her neck.

As she feels my cock grinding against her, she rolls her tongue over her bottom lip, hunger in her eyes. "And hard . . ."

I grin. "And ready . . ."

I feel her thighs clench together as her bottom lip slips between her teeth. "Hmm, I don't know," she teases as she pretends not to be taken by my wicked charm. "I've had better . . . and bigger."

"Liar," I murmur as I scoop her up in my arms and rush her down her driveway. My lips crush against hers, and she's stripped naked before we even make it to her bedroom.

CHAPTER 19

CASSIE

I'm trying to get my ass out the door, and Brianna is being a little bitch, apparently too sick to come with me to the boys' game tonight. "Please," I beg for the twentieth time to a girl who has been vomiting non-stop for the past twenty-four hours.

"You've got to be kidding, right?" she groans at having to engage in any type of communication. "You know I'd love to go. I hate missing games. I don't think I've missed one of Bobby's games since we were kids."

"I know," I mumble, as I sulk on the couch.

"And?" she prompts.

"And I'll text you updates as it goes."

"And?"

"And I'll video all the important parts," I say, mimicking her voice as I roll my eyes at her. "Though, I'm pretty sure you can watch it live somewhere."

"Ugh," she groans. "I don't have the energy for that shit. Just send me the good stuff."

"Fine," I grumble, sinking back onto the couch again.

"Oh, and you better take your car. I think the boys would flip if they knew you walked all that way by yourself," she tells me.

"Yes, *Mother*," I smirk as she quickly sits up and holds her stomach.

I watch with bated breath as we wait to see what little game her stomach is going to play when she lets out a breath. "False alarm," she says, relieved, before laying back down and pulling the blanket back over her shivering body.

I check the time on my phone, and I know it's either leave now or miss the opening. And I have to admit, watching Jax leading his team out and taking the ice like an absolute God—so proud and full of confidence—it kind of gets me hot, and I don't want to miss that.

I stand up and pull Jaxon's jersey over my head, and a thrill runs through me knowing that I'm the woman who wears his name and number on my back. It makes me proud to be his girl. "Alright," I tell Bri as I grab my keys. "I better go. Do you need anything?"

She looks up at me with big puppy dog eyes. "Could you grab my soup first?"

"Really?" I grin. "Maybe you should get your boyfriend to come and take care of you."

"Shut up," she says with a grin that she couldn't possibly avoid as her mind goes straight to the guy who swore he would never be a one-woman kind of man. But I guess miracles do happen. "Carter doesn't do sick, and besides, I don't want him to see me like this. His idea of looking after me is sexual favors, and as much as I want that, I'd probably blow chunks all over him and ruin any chance of him returning."

I try my best to shake the image out of my head as I stride to the kitchen to fetch the woman her soup. "You'd be surprised by the kind of stuff Carter would put up with for the woman he loves."

She looks doubtful, but eventually allows me to leave.

A moment later, I'm piled into my car and backing out of the driveway. I turn up the volume on my playlist and belt out a little Celine Dion as I trek over to the ice rink, watching the clock as I get stuck in the roadwork on the main street.

A chuckle rips from my chest as I remember Jax and Bobby getting stuck at this exact same place only a few short months ago, stumbling across me and Brianna in our pole dancing class.

The clock continues to tick, and I get a sinking feeling that I'm going to miss the opening that I love so much. I fidget and tap my nails on the steering wheel as I anxiously wait for the traffic to move along. After another few minutes of not going anywhere, I pull out my phone and send a quick text to Jax.

Cassie - I'm running late. Don't let that game start without me. Love you.

Jax - And deprive you of that tingly feeling you get when you watch me skate? Wouldn't dream of it. Drive safe.

Another ten minutes later, it finally starts to move, and I gun it. I get to the ice rink with a few minutes to spare, and without a single parking space available, I pull into the athletes' lot and park across the back of Jax's truck. It's not like he'll be leaving before I do.

I quickly check the time as I put my Beetle in park and turn off the ignition. Relief washes through me. If I run, I might just make it. I notice a few other people also rushing to make the start of the game, and I pull out my phone once again as I rush forward.

Cassie - Just running in now. Kick ass tonight.

Jax doesn't reply, but I don't expect him to. Coach Harris is probably giving the players their pep talk before sending them out on the ice.

I slip my phone into my pocket and push forward, trying not to physically run to avoid looking like a desperate fool, but honestly, I'm walking pretty damn fast. The doors to the stadium come into view, and I grin knowing exactly where my seat is, unlike the idiots around me who are all going to have to search through the crowd for their spots.

As I finally reach the building, something grips me from behind and yanks me back, dragging me around the side of the stadium. I let out a squeal as I'm pulled completely off balance, and I have to scramble to try to catch my footing. A dark shadow crosses my vision, but I ignore it, desperately trying to save myself from falling flat on my face.

My ass hits the ground, and I know without a doubt that there's going to be a bruise. I hardly have a moment to dwell on it before the dark shadow appears directly in front of me, a sick, twisted grin on the fucker's face.

My eyes widen, recognizing the asshole from Micky's, and I try to scream. I desperately look around for a shred of help, but in the rush to get inside, it's left the parking lot a fucking ghost town. The asshole slaps his hand over my mouth, and I flinch at the pain. Or maybe it's the feel of his skin on mine once again.

Fear blasts through my chest as I try to crawl away, calling for help again, but it's useless. He's too strong. His eyes sparkle, enjoying my fear, and I know without a doubt that I have to get out of here.

"I've been waiting for you," he tells me as his eyes flash with something dark, and I realize just how much trouble I'm in. He grabs me by my hair and yanks me up, and my feet scramble beneath me, trying to catch myself to relieve some of the pain. My hands fly to my hair as I try my hardest to claw his hand away.

My heart beats rapidly in my chest, and I promptly recognise the signs of my freak out. My gaze flicks left to right, desperately searching for a way out of this. What the hell am I going to do? How am I going to get out of here?

Kicking my legs out, I attempt to hit him, but he jumps back out of the way. "Mmm, feisty," he mutters, getting a better hold on me and starting to drag me away.

I continue to claw at his hand in my hair, trying to free myself. I know I must be cutting him, as I feel the wetness beneath my fingers, but all it does is spur him on. He adjusts his hold in my hair and uses the hand over my mouth to slap me, hard. I whimper in pain as the hand returns to my mouth. "You're going to regret that," he tells me, and using his hold on my hair, he leads me back toward the parking lot.

No. No, no, no, no. This can't be happening.

I try everything I can to get free. I kick my legs out and drop all my body weight to the point he has to drag me, but nothing works. I just need something to use as a weapon—or at least something to cut my hair from my skull to be freed.

We reach a dark car and I continue fighting, trying my hardest to get free from the bastard. Fear of being shoved into his car consumes me. I can't allow that to happen. I don't know shit about this guy, where he plans on taking me . . . what he will do to me. The thought alone is terrifying and has me begging for freedom.

Needing to open his car, his hand falls free from my mouth, and I instantly scream out, which only makes him smirk a little more. Tears of pain stream down my face, but I don't get a chance to look around to see if anyone's coming before he puts his other hand on the back of my head and slams it down into the metal frame of his car.

My head spins, and despite struggling to stay awake, darkness forces its way around me.

CHAPTER 20

JAXON

Coach Harris stands in the center of the room, giving us his usual pre-game pep talk. His words have the boys riled up and ready to go, but for the first time, the effect isn't the same on me. Something feels . . . off.

I can't put my finger on it. But whatever it is, I don't like it.

I try to tune the feeling out and concentrate on Coach Harris. After all, we're more than halfway through the season and we're in the top position to take this thing out. Semi-finals and finals are quickly approaching, and I need to have my head in the game—now more than ever.

Some lady with a clipboard knocks on the locker room door, letting us know the start of the game has been delayed by ten minutes due to the ice rinks Zamboni breaking down. I can't help but think this is a sign that something bad is going to happen, and my guess is that it's this game. Bad things always happen in threes. First, Cass is running late, though she should be here by now. Second, the Zamboni breaks down, so what's going to be third?

Maybe I'll miss a shot or fuck something up. There are most likely scouts in the audience who are watching me, waiting to see if I'm the kind who will crack under pressure. I don't know what it is, but my gut tells me something's up.

It could be nerves, but I haven't been nervous before a game since I was a kid. This shit is as natural to me as breathing. It has to be something else, but what?

Coach knocks over the trash can at the end of the room and tips out a bucket of pucks at the other, instructing us to take some practice shots to help keep us warm while we wait for the ice.

Our helmets come off, and I stand in line to take a few shots. My aim is perfect as usual, and I take a backseat from shooting to help the guys with their aim, but that sinking feeling continues to grow until I can hardly concentrate.

Not long after, the lady comes back to tell us it's go time, and I quickly race to my locker and grab my helmet. I rip off my gloves and check my phone. There's a text from Cass telling me she's here, sent at least twenty minutes ago. But that one text from her eases me just a bit. I can handle fucking up one game as long as Cass is there afterward.

I jam my phone back in my locker, pull my gloves and my helmet on, and take my position at the door to lead the boys out. They all fall in line behind me, but my head is out of it. My eyes stray to the ground as I go over all the possibilities.

"Jax," Coach hollers, a clear annoyance in his tone. My head snaps up to him, and I notice everyone is waiting on me. "Where's your head, Payne?"

"Sorry, Coach," I mutter as my eyes revert back to the ground.

Bobby slaps me upside the back of my head, and I turn around with a scowl. "Dude," he hisses as he gives me a wicked nudge to get out the door. "Pull it together."

I reluctantly lead the boys out of the locker room and my stomach sinks further as I come out of the hallway and enter the stadium. The noise from the crowd is deafening, but I push on. As soon as we turn the corner, my eyes flick up to Cass in the crowd, but I don't find her there.

My brows furrow. She hasn't missed a game all season, and she sent a text saying she was here. I look over to the food lines, even though she has never eaten stadium food in her life. Just as expected, she isn't there. Could Brianna have gotten worse and she had to go? If that were the case, she would have texted me again.

I turn back to Bobby. "Have you heard from Bri? Is Cass with her?"

He gives me a strange look, probably wondering why the hell I'm thinking about his twin sister at a time like this, but I know he sees something off in my eyes as he answers, "She's fine, just got some bug. Last I heard, she was starting to feel a bit better. Cass was coming by herself. She should be here," he says, casting his eyes up at the grandstand. "Where is she?"

"Don't know, man," I tell him as I continue looking around the stadium. "She texted twenty minutes ago saying she was here. She should be in her seat. It's not like her to miss a game without telling someone where she is."

The thought hits me like a freight train.

The sinking feeling.

It's Cass. Something's happened to Cass.

I take off like a bat out of hell, Bobby hissing my name behind me. "Where the hell do you think you're going?" Coach demands, catching me at the end of the line.

"It's Cassie. Something's wrong," I tell him. "Please, I just need to check if she's okay. I won't be able to concentrate until I know."

Anger flashes behind his eyes, but he gives in and lets me go. "You have thirty seconds," he says under his breath, clearly very pissed off, "then your ass better be on that ice."

I take off again with no time for a thank you.

I burst through to the locker room and the metal door crashes against the back wall before slamming closed once again. I tear off my helmet and gloves before I've even made it to my locker, and I pull my phone straight out.

I call Cass and wait the agonizing moments for her to answer, but she doesn't. The call rings out and goes to her voicemail. I try a second time and a third before I find Brianna's number.

She answers immediately. "Aren't you supposed to be on the ice?"

"Is Cass with you?" I rush out.

"No, why? She left ages ago."

"She texted twenty minutes ago saying she was here, but her seat is empty," I tell her. "She didn't go home?"

"No, she's not here," Brianna says, slightly alarmed. "She would never miss your game."

"Fuck," I curse as I hang up the phone. I try Cassie's number again and get nothing.

Where the hell is she? I tear off my skates before I can even figure out a plan, and within seconds, I grab my keys and am halfway to the door when Coach barges in.

"What the fuck is going on, Payne?" he demands as he blocks my exit.

I'm frantic and hardly have a moment to spare for him, but it's out of sheer respect that I don't push him aside. "Something's wrong. I have to go."

"Like hell you do," he bellows. "Start talking."

With an agitated groan, I let it out. "Cass isn't here, she would never miss a game. I feel it in my gut. Something's happened. *Something's wrong.*"

He hangs his head as he thinks it over. He and I both know that if she were in danger and he didn't let me go, he would never forgive himself. "Fine," he grunts. "But you get your ass back here as quickly as possible."

I'm flying out the door before he has even finished his sentence.

I run through the doors of the arena and fly down the stairs, only to stop at the bottom, thankful that she has a bright yellow fucking

Beetle that I could spot anywhere. My eyes scan the whole parking lot and come up with nothing, before I remember she thought she was late. I rush around the side of the building to the athletes' parking and find her Beetle parked behind my truck.

Relief surges through me. Maybe she was here all along, and I'm just overreacting, but that feeling still remains in the pit of my stomach. I take off toward her car, tripping over a black pile of something on the sidewalk as I go.

I reach down and pick it up to find a handbag, and I peek in the top to recognize one of Cassie's notebooks.

Shit.

I look around and see spots of blood on the ground, and I know without a doubt my gut feeling was right. Something has happened.

I follow the trail of blood, which leads me to an empty car space, and I immediately think the worst.

I pull out my phone and hit call on Logan's number as I sprint off toward her car just to double-check that she isn't there. "Yo, fucker, what do you want?" he says into the phone. "Wait, don't you have a game?"

I ignore his questions. "Have you heard from Cass? I think she's been taken from the stadium. I found her bag on the sidewalk and a trail of blood that leads to an empty parking spot."

"Fuck," he curses. "Taken? Who the fuck by?" My mind goes to one person, and if I'm right, the bastard is going to be sorry. "Fuck, fuck, fuck," Logan roars before going quiet for a moment. "Umm . . . Okay. We put a GPS tracker on her phone when she moved," he tells me. "Does she have her phone on her? Is it in her bag?"

I rush over to my truck and empty out the bag's contents into the back. "No, I rush out. No phone."

"Good, she might have it on her," he says, sounding as though he's put me on speakerphone, and I'm sure he must be looking up the GPS. "It's searching," he tells me, and I hear the frustration in his voice, wishing it would go faster. "Come on," he grunts, running out of patience.

I get in my truck and turn on the ignition, waiting for his go-ahead. "Shit, here we go," he rushes out. "I'm texting you the address. It's about a five-minute drive."

The text comes through not a second later. "Got it."

With Cassie's car blocking me in, I floor it up and over the parking island and over the sidewalk, knocking down a few light reflectors on my way. "We're on our way," Logan says before hanging up.

I fly up past the side of the stadium and past the drops of blood where I'd found her bag. My fear settles just a bit knowing that the triplets are on their way, but I will beat them there by miles.

My truck screeches onto the road, and I barge in front of oncoming traffic only to be honked at by pissed-off drivers, but I honestly don't give a shit right now. All that matters is getting to her.

Speeding down the road, I honk and weave through the traffic, daring these fuckers to get in my way. The thought crosses my mind that maybe she's fine. Maybe she met a friend and took off, but I know that isn't true. Cassie is in trouble, and there's nothing I wouldn't do to find her.

Looking down at my phone, I double-check the address and push my foot harder to the ground. My engine roars as I push it faster, power surging me forward.

Hold on, baby. I'm coming for you.

CHAPTER 21

CASSIE

My head pounds and my nose is assaulted by an awful stench as I struggle to open my eyes on this cheap, uncomfortable bed. My body shivers, and I pull my hands up to rub my face, but something is holding them down.

Wait, bed?

What the fuck?

My eyes fly open, remembering the asshole from Micky's and the way he slammed my head down against the frame of his car. I attempt to sit up, but I'm stopped by the binds around my wrists and ankles that are tied to the corners of the bed. I search frantically around the room as memories of being assaulted and knocked out come rushing back.

I choke on my fear, a loud sob tearing from the back of my throat. Where the hell am I?

My breath comes too fast as I search the room, only finding darkness, and I wonder if my vision is fucked after getting my head knocked into the side of a car. Maybe I'm in some place that has the windows boarded up, but I know it's worse than that—I'm locked in a basement, tied to a bed, just waiting for this asshole to come down and assault me again.

A shiver takes over me, and I look down, horrified to find I'm in nothing but a bra and panties. Tears stream down my face. How the hell did I get myself into this situation?

My eyes begin to adjust to the dark room, and I take in my surroundings. It's a small brick room with one tiny window above a washing machine, but the window has been meticulously boarded up, not letting in a single thread of light.

Old wooden stairs lead up toward the main house, and my gaze locks on the door. Even though I know that's my only way out, I keep searching anyway, needing to know exactly what I'm dealing with here. I need to keep looking, keep searching for something . . . *anything* that I could use to help me.

Bri is sick at home, and as far as she's aware, I'm at the game. The triplets would have no idea what's going on, and why should they? But Jax … He's my only hope, and he's in the middle of a massive game. He may notice I'm not in my spot in the grandstand, but he would just assume I'm sitting somewhere else.

I'm on my own. I have no hope, and by the time any of them

realize I'm gone . . . fuck. Who knows what could have happened to me.

After I finish scanning the room, I realize just how fucked I am. There's nothing sharp left in the room, not that I would be able to reach anything with my hands and feet bound anyway. I locate all my clothes on the ground and realize they're torn to shreds, and my hope starts to plummet.

My brain goes into survival mode, and I reach down to feel along the small parts of the bed frame within my reach. Hope begins to surge within me as I feel a screw under my finger, and I jam my nail into it, trying my hardest to turn it. That hope quickly fades as my nail splits and bleeds, shooting agony through my finger. I curse, but try to keep quiet. The last thing I want is to draw attention to myself and let the fucker know I'm awake.

I keep working on the screw, but only end up with each of my fingers bleeding.

What am I going to do?

I hear creaking coming from above, and realize the guy is moving around the house. I pray he isn't coming this way anytime soon. Why rush? Not a soul knows I'm down here. I'm all his for the taking.

Fear laces every thought in my mind, and I hate that I'm not stronger and wasn't able to fight him off, just like in Micky's. Without Jaxon, he would have taken me that night, and there's not a damn thing I could have done about it. For fuck's sake, I grew up with three big brothers. I should know how to get out of shit like this, but they treated me like a princess.

I try to work faster at the screw, but it isn't budging, and as I realize I've been wasting my time, I start searching for an alternative.

Trying to pull at the bounds on my wrists, I desperately try to break them, but once again, all I end up doing is hurting myself further.

The door at the top of the stairs creaks open, and my gaze snaps up, terror pounding through my veins. My heart races as a sliver of light shoots through the room, but it is quickly blocked by the silhouette of a man.

He slowly makes his way down the stairs, leaving the door open behind him, probably so he can see whatever it is he's going to do to me. As he reaches the bottom step, I can make out the features of his face, and I want nothing more than to tear him to shreds. He strides toward me, the devil in his eyes, looking me up and down while licking his lips in hunger.

Bile rises in my stomach, but I hold it down. The mere thought of this creep touching me makes me sick.

"Hello, Cassandra," he purrs, watching me with interest.

My eyes are wide and fearful, but there's not a chance in hell that I will look away. I can't risk it. I know what he wants, and I realize he won't stop until he gets it. That knowledge has me in an absolute panic, but what I fear more is the unknown.

How far will this monster go? Will he have his way with me and dump me somewhere, or will it be worse? Will I remain down here for weeks until someone finds me, or will he kill me to cover his tracks?

My sharp stare tracks his movements as he comes closer and runs his fingers up the length of my body. I try to move away, but my bound arms and legs make it nearly impossible. His eyes heat at the touch, and I choke back vomit. "So beautiful," he says, his eyes on my chest. "I've been waiting a long time to have you, but that damn hockey player just kept getting in the way."

My mind spins back to the night at Micky's when Jax was punched, and I can't help but wonder if Jax was protecting me from this guy, once again. And if it was, I pray that Jax fucking annihilated him.

His eyes continue to sail over me with a sick excitement, and it has me wondering if this has happened to some poor girl before me.

He sits down on the bed beside me, leaving his fingertips trailing over my stomach while his eyes remain locked on mine. "I've been watching you," he tells me. "Day in and day out for months now. I think I might even know your schedule better than you do, and I must say, you're quite a predictable little thing." Understanding dawns through me at his words, and that sick feeling of dread has the bile rising up again. It was him in my room, rummaging through my clothes and wearing my dressing gown. Paging through my notebooks and getting off on the scent of my bodywash. It wouldn't surprise me if my black lace panties were in his pocket as we speak.

"Your schedule never changes," he continues, "but I like that in a woman. No surprises." His eyes roam my body in hunger, as his fingers move lower on my stomach, exploring my body in the most violating way.

No, no, no. Please don't. I'm not ready for this. Not ready to lose myself.

I know it's ridiculous to prepare for a moment like this, but if I could mentally check out, it might make the abuse a bit easier. The only man I have ever been with is Jax, and I know he will still love me afterward, but I can't stand the thought of my body being ruined for him . . . ruined for me. How could he love me wholeheartedly when I'll never be able to love myself again?

His fingers linger on the inside of my hip, right where my tattoo sits. "But you know what really surprised me, and quite frankly, what severely pissed me off?" he growls. I refuse to answer, and my silence spurs him on. "I was there you know, the day your skank friend convinced you to mark your beautiful skin with this filth," he spits, pulling down the edge of my underwear to reveal Jax's name. "It was the same day I stopped you on your run. Do you remember? I introduced myself, but I bet you're too shallow to remember my name, aren't you?"

He's right. I can't remember his name. Maybe I am shallow, but I honestly don't give a fuck right now.

"That little bitch deserves to be shot for the way she talked to me," he says. "I knew I should have just taken you then. I should have knocked the bitch out and had my way with you right there, but there were too many people, too many witnesses. They wouldn't understand what we have."

I scowl up at him. How could someone be so fucking deranged? I can't hold my tongue any longer. "You're fucking scum," I spit at him. "Just you wait until my brothers and Jax catch up with you. You're going to regret the day you ever saw me."

He smiles down at me, the same way a parent would smile at a misbehaving child. "Darling, that isn't going to happen," he says, so sure of himself. Though I know the truth. My brothers would never let this guy get away with it, and who knows what lengths Jax would go to.

The guy takes a breath and looks around his sickening little basement. "This is special, isn't it?" he muses as his eyes come back down to me adoringly. "Just you and me, with all the time in the world."

"You're fucking delusional."

He shrugs his shoulders before pushing off the bed and getting back to his feet. He reaches into the back pocket of his jeans and pulls out a pocketknife that makes my mouth go dry. My eyes widen as I feel the blood drain from my face.

I watch as he looks down at his knife and then flicks open the switchblade. His eyes light up with excitement, and then he looks back down at me. "I think it's time we get this show on the road."

My breathing becomes labored as his knife lowers to my body. I didn't expect this. I know he's going to hurt me in the most volatile way, but the scenario where he pulls a knife on me never entered my mind, and I feel I need a few moments to mentally prepare myself. But it's too late, I've run out of time.

The knife comes toward me, and I watch it with wide eyes. I try my best to squirm away, but the bounds on my hands and feet are keeping me in place, like his perfect little canvas. Tears flow down my face as I realize this could be the beginning of the end. "Hold still, baby," he murmurs wickedly, as the blade comes in contact with my hip.

Instead of the knife plunging down into my flesh, it slips under the side of my underwear until the material is held up off my skin by nothing but the blade. Then with a quick flick of his wrist, the material slices in two and the fabric falls away, revealing my tattoo.

His deathly gaze focuses on the ink as darkness and anger cloud his features. I sense him move before he does it. "No!" I scream out as his blade comes down on me, slashing deeply through my tattoo.

I scream out in agony, instantly feeling the sharp sting as the warm blood oozes down my hip and between my legs. Sobs rip from my chest as the stinging intensifies, but he doesn't stop there. His blade comes down again in the opposite direction, slicing through the tattoo once again to make an X.

I scream and cry out, not just in agony, but for the symbolism behind the tattoo in which he's just taken away and destroyed.

His hand connects with my face in a harsh slap as he tries to get me to shut up, but it's no use. I can't stop, and I won't. "You better shut the fuck up before I show you what else my knife can do."

Yep, that shut me up.

I try my hardest to swallow my sobs, and I close my eyes, not wanting to see anymore. "Open your eyes," he spits, slapping me again. "I've waited too long for you to not watch every fucking second of this."

I reluctantly open my eyes to find him sitting back down on the bed, looking over my body, his gaze lingering on the bloodied tattoo. "Much better," he muses before lifting the knife again, this time slicing the other side of my underwear, and up through the center of my bra.

I lay before him, naked and vulnerable, tears in my eyes, wishing it was already over. A small amount of relief pulses through me as he folds the blade back into the hilt and tucks the damn thing in his back pocket.

His hand comes up to my chest and he takes my breast in his palm, giving it a painful squeeze before rubbing my nipple between his fingers. His touch makes me choke on my own vomit. His other hand skims down my stomach and over my bloodied tattoo. Pain rips through me, but it's quickly forgotten as he continues on down past my hips and between my legs.

No, no, no.

His hand becomes wet with my blood, but the feeling only spurs him on as he cups my pussy, grinding down against my clit with the heel of his palm. "You like that, don't you?" he grins at me as he forces his fingers between my folds and presses down, pinching my clit with all he's got. "Fuck, yeah," he groans, continuing to rub my nipple as he painfully explores my clit. "I'm so fucking hard."

He suddenly lets go and stands beside me, his hands going to his jeans as he makes quick work of removing his clothes.

He palms his pathetic excuse of a dick, rubbing the blood from my wound into his skin, and I realize the sick fuck is using my blood as lube. His hand comes down between my legs again, though this time he bypasses my clit and heads straight for my cunt.

His fingers dive in painfully, and I cry out. "Yeah, I knew you'd like that, you fucking slut," he says as he continues to palm his dick and thrust his dirty fingers into me. He smirks as he steps further up the bed, and I know without a doubt that he's about to force his cock into my mouth.

A loud banging comes from the house above and has the creep freezing before ripping his fingers from my cunt. "Fuck," he spits, pulling his jeans on. "Don't say a fucking word."

My heart pounds, watching as he races up the stairs two at a time before closing the door behind him. There's a distinct lock before I hear him rushing through the house.

The banging on the front door intensifies, and I realize it sounds more like someone trying to break the door down.

I fucking hope so.

I listen out desperately, trying to hear voices or some kind of evidence that someone is here to get me, when I hear the familiar sound of wood splintering and feet rushing across the floor. There's another loud bang—different from the earlier one—before I hear his angelic growl. "Where the fuck is she?" Jax roars.

Hope blooms in my chest, and I scream out over and over again. "HELP! JAX! I'm here," I cry, the desperation crippling me. "In the basement. Please."

The sound of something—or someone—dropping to the ground rattles the wooden beams overhead, and a moment later, the basement door is kicked in.

Light shines into the darkness, and I have to squint my eyes as the figure stands at the top of the stairs. My eyes quickly adjust, and I crumble.

Tears spring from my eyes.

My badass hero.

CHAPTER 22

JAXON

Kicking in the basement door, I peer into the darkness, and it takes all of two seconds for my eyes to adjust and find my girl. My blood boils from the sight. Her naked, limp body is tied down to a bed, and she's covered in blood from the waist down.

She whimpers when she sees me at the top of the stairs, and it quickly turns into full-blown sobbing. I rush toward her, but I'm afraid to touch her. My heart shatters at the sight, but I know she's hurting so much more.

I drop to my knees beside her, reaching for her wrists. "Are you okay?" I rush out, trying to soothe her, while also trying not to break. My gaze sails over her body, trying to find where the blood is coming from, and I find the deep gashes across her tattoo.

The blood has been smeared across her body and down between her legs. Rage burns through me, and I'm barely able to keep myself beside her as the need to race back up those stairs and kill the motherfucker rages through me. The only thing keeping me here is the knowledge of just how badly she needs me.

I force my eyes to continue their inspection. Her right breast is red and raw, her face appears to be hit, and there's a massive lump on her temple. My teeth grind in fury.

How the fuck dare he?

Gently running my hand over her hair, I furiously look around the room for something to free her binds. "He touched you?" I ask, even though I already know the answer.

Her eyes squeeze closed, and big fat tears escape between those beautiful lids. "Please, Jax," she whimpers. "Just get me out of here. Please."

Shit. I latch onto her bindings, but pulling on them only makes it worse. It's then I notice her bloodied fingers and cracked nails, and I realize she was trying to get herself free.

"He has a knife in his pocket," she tells me with absolutely no emotion in her tired voice.

I press my lips together, hating the idea of leaving her right now, but I have to. I have to do this for her. Dashing up the stairs, I find the guy I left knocked out cold on the hallway floor and quickly search his pockets to find the knife. I give him a swift kick to the ribs before I flick it open and see Cassie's blood still staining the blade.

I fly down the stairs two at a time, desperate to get back to Cass, and I do my best to put her injuries out of my mind so I can focus on getting her out of her bonds and to the hospital. I slip the blade as gently as I can under the fabric and free her wrists before moving to her ankles. All four binds leave deep bruising on her skin, and I can't help but wonder if they're this bad because Cass had been fighting against them, or if they were that tight in the first place.

She tries to sit up but cringes in pain, and I gently push her back down. "Don't move," I tell her. "Let me find your clothes and then I'll help you."

"They're destroyed," she whispers with a broken sob before nodding toward a raggedy pile near the bottom of the stairs. Realizing they aren't worth saving, I still race over to them and grab a slip of fabric before handing it to her with instructions to hold it against her wounds to try and stop the bleeding, but all that does is make her hiss in pain.

Slipping my jersey over my head, I help her to sit up before pulling it back down over hers. The jersey comes down over her body and bunches at her waist so it will at least come down past her thighs when she stands. Hopefully that will offer her some kind of comfort, but I doubt she will feel any until she's out of this place and in the safety of her own home.

"Come on, babe. Let's go," I tell her softly, bending down and gently scooping my hand under her knees. She automatically wraps her arms around my neck and allows me to lift her.

The movement jostles her, and she cringes in pain, most likely from the cut through her tattoo. I make my way up the stairs, being careful with my movements, and turn my back as I walk past the fucker who did this so she doesn't have to see him.

As I walk through the house, the front door is flung open and Cassie's brothers pile through, looking as imposing as ever. They take in the scene before them and relief washes over their faces until they have the chance to look her over properly. I see the moment their eyes take in the bruises and the blood covering her legs. Instant rage takes over them with Logan and Carter disappearing first.

"He touched her?" Sean demands.

"Not sure how badly," I explain as she cries silently in my arms.

His gaze finds Cassie's, and she looks away, too ashamed to meet his stare. Sean's heartbreak is obvious as he takes a breath. "Get her to the hospital."

With a nod, he follows after his brothers, but I call out after him. "I'll give you ten minutes before I call the police. I want that fucker behind bars."

He doesn't acknowledge me, but I know he heard me. Confident he has this under control, I make my way out to my truck knowing that Sean is the brains behind this operation. He'll be able to rein in his brothers before the cops arrive and leave without anyone the wiser.

The cops will storm the place and find enough evidence to put him away for a long fucking time, and if they somehow fail and that bastard gets free . . . Well, he'll have me and the boys to deal with then, and I can guarantee he won't get away with his life.

I gently slide Cassie into my truck and make sure she's comfortable before heading around to my side. My engine still rumbles from when

I bailed out of it, barely remembering to put the truck in park, and before she has to look at this place for one more second, I take off to the hospital.

We're a few minutes in and the silence is killing me. "Do you want to talk about it?" I ask, hesitantly.

She shakes her head ever so slightly as a few stray tears stream down her cheeks, "No," she whispers, her hands shaking against her thighs.

"Okay," I murmur before glancing across at her. "I'm going to call the police the moment we get to the hospital. They're going to ask you some questions."

She closes her eyes but nods her head. "How'd you find me?"

I give her a tight smile knowing that any other day, what I'm about to tell her would infuriate her. Today is different. She'll be thankful for her brothers' overprotective qualities. "Uhh, your brothers put a GPS tracker on your phone after you went to New York," I explain. "I called Logan, and he was able to tell me where to find you."

She gives me a half smile as she lets out a breath. "I should have known."

I look her over, and she seems to be doing a little better. There's a little more color in her face and relief in her eyes. She still has a million miles to go before she's her normal self, but at least it's a start.

"You're really okay?" I ask.

She looks up and reaches across the console to lace her fingers through mine, and I grip onto her like she's my only lifeline. "I will be," she tells me, barely able to meet my eyes. "Thank you for coming for me."

Lifting her hand to my lips, I press a soft kiss against her skin. "Always."

We pull up to the hospital, and I quickly park and get out before rushing around to Cassie's side and helping her out. I take her inside and explain exactly what's happened, and Cass is immediately taken into a room and told to wait while they call a doctor to come and examine her. They warn Cass that they're required to call the police, and I let them know not to bother as I already have the phone ringing against my ear.

Stepping out into the hallway, I stay where Cass can see me and speak to the cops, even though I'm positive the nurse is doing the same thing. I let them know the address of where I found her and I'm told they will send a few officers out there to investigate, while some will be sent to meet with Cass and take our statements.

As soon as I end the call, I find Sean's number and give him the heads up that the cops are on their way. Hearing my call, Cass yells out to me, and I stride back into the room when she indicates to pass the phone.

After handing the phone over, she wastes no time. "That . . . that asshole has my phone with all my music on it," she says. Sean must reply as she continues. "Good, now get your asses out of there. I'm not leaving here only to have to stop by the station to bail you fuckers out."

I hear strained laughter coming through the phone, and I know Sean is putting it on just to reassure Cass, but who gives a fuck?

Whatever Cass needs right now, she's going to get it. She ends the call and hands me the phone as I take a seat beside her bed.

We sit in silence, waiting for the doctor when she sucks in a breath and looks at me. "Your game," she says, horrified.

Shit. I'd completely forgotten about that.

"Don't worry about it," I tell her. "Coach was fine. He allowed me to go. I would've come anyway. Nothing would have stopped me. I should probably call him to let him know what's going on."

She nods, and I get up once again, hating the idea of being apart from her. As I go to walk away, she grabs hold of my hand, pulling me back. "Don't . . . don't give him too many details," she whispers.

"Of course," I say with a nod, holding her broken stare. After a short pause, she lets me go, and I head back into the hallway, already dialing Coach Harris' number. He rarely has his phone on during a game, but I know he would have it on today, waiting to hear from me.

"You far off? The boys need you," Coach questions as he answers the phone, the noise of the game in the background making it nearly impossible to hear.

"Sorry, Coach," I say with heavy regret, hating the idea of letting my team down. "I won't be making it tonight."

"Your woman okay?"

There's a short pause as I try to calm myself. "She will be. We're at the hospital now, just waiting on the cops."

"Shit," he curses. "Is it that bad?"

"Yeah, Coach," I tell him, giving it to him straight. "It's worse."

"Alright, son. Good call. Go be with your girl," he says as the crowd goes nuts and drowns him out. He hangs up quickly, and I hope that was for a good reason and not a bad one. The thought is gone from my mind as soon as I see the nurse from earlier escorting two chick cops down the hallway, and I'm thankful they're women. I have no idea how Cass is going to handle strange men right now.

I duck in before them and warn her they're here, and they gently rap on the door as they enter. The cops glance at me before turning their attention to Cass. The one on the left starts. "Hi Cassandra. I'm Officer Samuels, and this is Officer McNaught. We've come to talk to you about the ordeal you've been through today. Would now be a good time to ask you a few questions?"

"I guess," Cass shrugs.

Officer McNaught takes a slight step forward. "Now, I know this can be uncomfortable and awful to talk about," she says, her eyes flicking toward me. "Would you prefer we do this in private?"

Cassie's hand flies out and takes hold of mine, squeezing it until her knuckles turn white. "No. Jaxon stays," she demands, her eyes widening in panic at the thought of being separated.

"You're sure?" Samuels asks.

"I better be," she says, pulling our joined hands into her lap. "After all, I'm going to marry him one day."

My head whips in her direction, catching her stare, and I raise a questioning brow, watching as she gives me the smallest nod in return.

"Alright, Cassandra," Samuels says as she pulls out a recording device and places it on the end of the bed, while NcNaught pulls out a notepad and pen. "Why don't you start from the beginning."

Cass does just that, and my anger flares the further she gets through the story. She gets to the part about the knife and how he cut her, and I physically have to hold myself in my chair to keep from going after the bastard once again.

She comes to the end and tells them how I cut her loose with the same knife, and I pipe in to let them know I still have it on me. Samuels pulls out an evidence bag, and without hesitation, I pull it out and drop it into the bag.

Cass finishes her story, and after asking a few questions, the cops turn to me, asking how I was able to get from the door to the basement. I tell them what they need to know while reminding them how he held a knife, lining it up as the perfect self-defense claim. I only fail to mention that I didn't know he had a knife until after the fact.

The cops move on and start taking pictures of her injuries as the doctor comes in, and they quickly finish up, allowing the doctor to take over. The cops leave but return a few minutes later to let Cassie know the bastard is in custody.

Cass sighs into the pillow and closes her eyes, trying not to look as the doctor stitches her wound. "It's over, babe. You'll never have to see him again."

She keeps her eyes closed, her hand still clutching mine, and I feel as her whole body relaxes.

Once she's finished being checked over, the doctor tells her she's allowed to shower but that she'll be here overnight for observation as well. With that, the doctor excuses herself and shuffles out the door.

I help Cass shower, and by the time she's dressed and stepping out of the bathroom, her brothers are in her room waiting, her phone clutched between Sean's fingers. They fill us in on everything that went down in that house after we left, leaving out particularly gruesome details that would make Cassie's skin crawl. Though I have no doubt they'll share those details with me the moment they can.

After the hospital staff brings Cass a sketchy dinner, the boys order UberEats, and as soon as we've annihilated our meals, I check in with Bobby to find out the score of tonight's game. I'm not surprised to find they won. I must say, I'm proud of my boys for pulling it together without me and still managing the win. They're just that good.

After refusing to leave her side, a nurse wheels in a bed and allows me to stay the night with her. The extra bed isn't necessary though, seeing as Cassie pulls me in beside her.

Before I know it, the morning sun is streaming through Cassie's hospital room, and the doctor is clearing her with instructions to keep the wound clean. When she's discharged, I hold her hand and lead her out to my truck to drive her home.

Once we've arrived, I help Cass down from the passenger seat, but she insists on walking herself to the front door, even though her hisses of pain silently kill me. Hell, just getting her to take pain meds is a mission on its own. She's so fucking stubborn, just like her brothers.

Cassie's fingers curl around the door handle, and a smile begins pulling at the corner of my lips. She pushes the door wide to reveal her living room filled to the brim with her friends and family. Hell, even the whole hockey team is here, Coach Harris included.

I briefly wonder where their cars are parked, but the thought is gone the second Brianna rushes forward and wraps Cass in her arms. "I'm so sorry," Bri cries. "It's all my fault. If I'd been there, it never would have happened."

"Shh," Cass soothes, holding her tight. "It had nothing to do with you. He was a ticking time bomb, and he took his opportunity. Had it not been yesterday, it would have been today or the next day. We couldn't have known."

Brianna nods as Bobby steps into their sides, wrapping his arms around both the girls and giving them a gentle squeeze. "I'm glad you're okay," he murmurs to Cass, who gives him a fond smile.

One by one, everybody checks on her until exhaustion takes over her face, and her brothers start kicking them out until it's just our close circle. I take a seat on the couch, and Cass falls into my arms. When Brianna does the same with Carter, Bobby scowls at them from across the room, which has Cass grinning into my side.

The boys pass around some beers and Bri cranks the music, and that's how we stay, chatting and drinking until the late hours of the night. "Are you ready for bed?" I ask Cass after her fifth yawn in a row.

"Yeah," she says, getting up from the couch and saying goodnight to everyone.

I follow behind her and help her into her pajamas before she climbs into bed, and I follow suit, sliding in beside her, my arms curling around her and pulling her in tight. "I'm so sorry this happened to you," I tell her as she settles onto my chest, her hand dropping to my stomach.

"I know," she murmurs. "You saved me, Jax. If it weren't for you

. . .”

She trails off, and knowing just how hard it is for her to find the words, I press my lips to hers and kiss her with every ounce of passion I possess, letting her know just how grateful I am to have her in my arms.

Cassie kisses me back, and as I feel tears on her cheeks, I gently pull back, hoping to God I haven't pushed her too far. "Is this too much?" I ask, looking deep into those eyes that I have loved for nearly a decade.

She shakes her head, the tears still coming. "It's exactly what I need."

She presses her forehead to mine, and I hold her tighter. "I love you, Cass, so fucking much," I whisper into the night, "and no matter what, I will always be there to catch you. I'll never let you fall."

"You're my whole world, Jax. In that basement . . . I thought I was never going to see you again."

Reaching up, I push her hair behind her ear and press a feather-soft kiss to her lips, those tears killing me. "I'll never let that happen, Cass. We're gonna grow old together. You're going to have my ring on your finger and our baby in your gut."

A smile pulls at the corner of her lips, and she does everything she can to try and smother it. "Ugh, Jax," she groans, looking at me as though I hold her whole world in the palm of my hand. "Do you have to put it that way?"

I smirk as I roll us over so I hover above her, being careful not to disrupt any of her injuries. "What better way to put it?" I murmur.

"Whether you like it or not, you'll be my wife, and we're going to have a tribe of kids. We'll have a beautiful home in the hills so we can be near your parents, and you'll have that stupid Great Dane you've always wanted."

She grins up at me. "I want to call him Diesel, and he'll probably chew all your hockey gear."

"He better not," I warn her.

Her eyes sparkle as she looks up at me then opens her legs before hooking them around my waist. "Oh yeah?" she questions, that confidence marred with a slight hesitation that she tries to hide.

I grin down at her, my cock straining to be freed as those beautiful eyes sparkle with mirth, daring me to meet her challenge, but I see it for what it is. She needs to know that no matter what happened to her in that basement, no matter who or what touched her, she will always have my whole heart. That she will always be the only woman I desire. I hate that what he did to her has formed a cloud of doubt in her mind, but goddamn, I will do anything to ensure she knows just how much she means to me.

With that, she frees my cock as I slide her pajama bottoms and panties down her legs, and I slowly push deep inside her, watching the way her eyes flutter with satisfaction. Silent tears well in her eyes as she wraps her arms around my neck and pulls me into her. "Don't you worry about it, baby," I growl in her ear. "I've got you."

EPILOGUE

CASSIE

We're at the Frozen Four in New York as the final buzzer sounds, and I'm already on my feet, screaming his name and cheering for the boys. Pride bursts through my chest, unable to tear my gaze away from my man, who's just led his team to become the two-time, undefeated, National Champions.

The mighty Dragons skate around the ice like a bunch of animals, and it's not long before each and every one of them has lost their sticks and helmets and pile on top of each other to celebrate.

Bobby breaks free from the pile and is at the barrier in the blink of an eye, and Brianna cracks up beside me as she watches her twin brother grab their coach, mid-interview, and throw him over his shoulder. He takes Coach toward the pile of champions and launches the old man on top, probably fracturing a few bones in the process, but Coach Harris doesn't seem to mind. Hell, he celebrates right along with them.

Jax somehow gets free from the bottom of the pile and races toward the edge, looking up at the crowd to find me, and the second his gaze locks on mine, a wide grin rips across both our faces. I circle my hands around my mouth and scream out, "I love you!"

He presses his fingers to his lips and raises his hand back to me. "Love you," he mouths before a mischievous sparkle hits his blue eyes. He moves into the center of the ice and turns to face the audience directly before holding both his hands up to the sky. The crowd roars for him as he takes his final bow for the season.

"God, that kid is a show-off," Carter says from the seat behind me as Sean scoffs in agreement.

"Where do you think he gets it?" I ask, turning around to give Carter a pointed stare.

"Whatever," Carter scoffs as he grabs Brianna from the row in front and drags her up over her seat and into his lap, making sure to jostle and kick me as much as humanly possible in the process.

I turn my attention back to Jax and watch as a reporter with ESPN waves him down, and he skates over to give the after-game interview.

"Come on," Logan says. "He's going to be a while. We'll meet him back at the hotel."

I go along with the boys, only because Jax had said exactly the same thing before the game and insisted that I don't wait around. I know for a fact he'll call me from the locker room, which makes it a little easier to leave.

Two hours later I stand in the hotel bathroom, putting on mascara and contemplating how strange it feels to be back in New York. Without warning, Jax flies through the door looking as sexy as ever in his official team suit. He bypasses the bathroom as he looks for me, then backtracks to find me in a slim black dress and the highest black strappy heels I could find.

Jax stands silently at the door of the bathroom, mentally undressing me. "Don't even think about it," I warn. "It took way too long to get ready."

Ignoring me, he licks his lips and slides his suit jacket down his arms, letting it fall in a heap at his feet. My gaze follows the movements as his hand reaches for his tie, giving it a tug before raising it over his head.

His eyes flame with hunger as he unbuttons his shirt, and I press my thighs together, trying to relieve the throbbing ache between my legs. He steps toward me, and my bottom lip disappears between my teeth as a shiver sails over my skin.

Jax's hand moves to his belt, and with a quick flick, it's discarded on the floor as I start to pant like a needy whore, desperate for his touch.

He takes one more step, and he's finally here, reaching for the hem of my dress and bunching it between his skilled fingers. He lifts it up over my head, leaving me in nothing but my black heels and lace lingerie, just the way he likes it.

His gaze travels over my body, groaning with need, which only makes me crave him that much more. Seeing the hunger in my eyes, Jax's fingers curl around the lace of my black thong, ripping it off my body as I gasp, so ready for him.

He unzips his pants and pulls himself free before grabbing my ass and lifting me. My legs twine around his waist as he slams my back into the glass wall of the shower, and before I even get a chance to scream his name, his thick cock is buried deep inside me.

"Fuck," I moan, the undeniable pleasure rocking through me as he stretches me wide.

He fucks me hard and fast, the two of us barely able to catch our breath. It's animalistic, filled with intense need, and as he rubs my clit I come hard on his cock, my pussy shattering around him. He comes with me, his fingers digging into my hips, and goddamn, they're going to leave a bruise. But I wouldn't have it any other way.

As we come down from our climax, we collapse to the bathroom floor with me straddled on his lap and his cock still buried deep inside me. "You're so fucking beautiful," he pants, trying to catch his breath as he drops his forehead to mine.

"You're not so bad yourself, Captain," I tell him. He smirks at my attitude and crushes his lips to mine, hard and passionate at first, before changing to something deeper and filled with raw emotion.

Jax pulls back and looks me in the eye, his fingers brushing the hair back off my face. "I love you, Cass," he murmurs. "I was going to wait, but this right here, just you and me. This is where it's real."

My brows furrow, watching as he reaches back across the bathroom floor and drags his pants across the tiles toward us. He searches through the pocket before pulling out that familiar little black box, and I gasp, understanding what he's doing.

Jax meets my eyes as he opens the box to reveal the beautiful ring within, the very one he used when stating his intentions to my father nearly four long years ago.

My eyes fill with tears as I wait with bated breath, hanging on his every word. "I was going to take you to dinner with your family and Bri, but right now, just you and me, nothing gets better than this," he says, looking me right in the eye. "You've been my girl since I was twelve years old, and I don't know how, but I fall more deeply in love with you every fucking day. We've been through every up and down this world could possibly throw at us, and yet somehow we've come out stronger."

The tears fall down my cheeks, and he takes a breath, those eyes boring into mine and making sure I truly hear him. "Cassandra Waters. I love you, and I can't wait to make you my wife. Tell me, fuck. Please tell me that you'll be my wife."

Undeniable joy fills my veins, and I throw myself into him, crushing my lips to his. "Yes, Jax," I cry through our kiss. "Yes, I'll be your wife. Every day of the rest of our lives. Nothing would make me happier."

Jax smiles against my lips, and I feel as though he's just handed me the whole world. My every dream and fantasy since I was twelve years old unfurling right here between us. Our worlds have collided once again, and this time, I'll never let him go.

Jax picks us up off the floor and takes us to the bed where he proceeds to make the sweetest love to me until Logan comes banging at the door.

We make it down to dinner and are in the middle of eating when Jax announces that he has asked me to marry him. Bri's scream is loud enough to almost get us kicked out of the restaurant, and she launches herself across the table, throwing her arms around me as my brothers go nuts, ordering every bottle of wine the restaurant holds.

The majority of his teammates are in the same restaurant, and I can't help but laugh as Aaron and Shorty physically pick up their tables and come to celebrate with us, clapping Jax on the back and giving me congratulatory hugs.

Within seconds, the restaurant turns into the best party New York has ever seen, and as I get up and stride around, I let out a shriek when Jax grabs me around the waist and pulls me down onto his lap. My arm falls behind his neck as he holds me tight, pressing a kiss to the sensitive skin below my ear. "I signed with the pros," he tells me.

My head whips in his direction. "What?" I screech, my eyes bugging out of my head as my heart races with happiness. "Holy shit, Jax. Are you serious?"

He smirks up at me. "You heard me, babe," he says. "Bobby, too."

I grab hold of his face and crush my lips against his, getting a roaring approval from our friends and family. "Which team?" I ask, grinning against his warm lips, trying to remind myself to come back to the whole Bobby thing later.

His smile turns from a smirk into an adoring grin. "You know that big house in the hills we talked about?"

"Yeah?" I prompt, knowing he's about to tell me all my dreams are coming true.

"It's all yours, baby."

"What?" I practically sing. "Colorado? You signed with the Colorado team?"

He smirks, but a voice from across the table steals our attention. "Ahh, get fucked," Logan curses, shaking his head. "You're not on my team, are you?"

Jax grins right back at him, a devilish sparkle hitting his eyes. "You better watch your back, Logan," Jax tells him, his hand gripping my thigh. "Colorado has a new star player now."

In your PUCKING DREAMS

THANKS FOR READING

If you enjoyed reading this book as much as I enjoyed writing it, please consider leaving an Amazon review to let me know. https://www.amazon.com/dp/B0BSDHV1QS

For more information on the Kings of Denver, find me on Facebook –

www.facebook.com/sheridansbookishbabes

STALK ME!

Join me online with the rest of the stalkers!!
I swear, I don't bite. Not unless you say please!

Facebook Reader Group
www.facebook.com/SheridansBookishBabes

Facebook Page
www.facebook.com/sheridan.anne.author1

Instagram
www.instagram.com/Sheridan.Anne.Author

TikTok
www.tiktok.com/@Sheridan.Anne.Author

Subscribe to my Newsletter
https://landing.mailerlite.com/webforms/landing/a8q0y0

MORE BY SHERIDAN ANNE

www.amazon.com/Sheridan-Anne/e/B079TLXN6K

DARK CONTEMPORARY ROMANCE - M/F

Broken Hill High | Haven Falls | Broken Hill Boys | Aston Creek High | Rejects Paradise | Bradford Bastard

DARK CONTEMPORARY ROMANCE - REVERSE HAREM

Boys of Winter | Depraved Sinners | Empire

NEW ADULT SPORTS ROMANCE

Kings of Denver | Denver Royalty | Rebels Advocate

CONTEMPORARY ROMANCE (standalones)

Play With Fire | Until Autumn (Happily Eva Alpha World)

PARANORMAL ROMANCE

Slayer Academy [Pen name - Cassidy Summers]